New Blood

Melrose Part One

A novel by Paul Dorset

Copyright 2011 Paul Dorset
Paperback Edition

License Notes

This book is licensed for your personal enjoyment only. This book may not be re-sold or given away to other people. If you would like to share this book with another person, please purchase an additional copy for each recipient. If you're reading this book and did not purchase it, or it was not purchased for your use only, then please return to the provider and purchase your own copy. Thank you for respecting the hard work of this author.

ISBN-13: 978-1466330429
ISBN-10: 1466330422

For Debra -

I never was a husband that, who comfortably fed,
Could sit around, do nothing, or simply stay in bed.
So I've followed all my passions and begun the author life,
Chased along at every chapter by my loving, caring wife.

For My Readers –

There are places to come visit in Melrose.

1

Beau rolled over onto his back and stared up at the bedroom ceiling. He tried to watch the flickering shadows as he waited for the giddiness to subside a little. As he fought back the feeling of nausea that was trying to overwhelm him, he took in a deep breath. It had been another long night and one that still wasn't over.

He carefully pulled himself up to a sitting position, looked around the room and shook his head. Pink! He hated pink. There were fluffy cushions scattered everywhere with teddy bears lining the top of the dresser. They looked almost lifelike in the dim moonlit bedroom. Beau turned away from them, closed his eyes and breathed deeply once more.

In the distance he could hear the clatter of someone noisily coming home. He waited until the sounds had died away before opening his eyes again. His head still felt hot and he knew it would be several more minutes before he could think straight. It was no use rushing. It was always like this. He had made that mistake before; to try and leave only to collapse onto the floor. Tonight he had the time. He was in no hurry and it would only take a few minutes to walk back to his apartment. His apartment. Yes, he was looking forward to getting back into his own bed. He glanced around the room again. How could other people live in such a mess? There was no space for anything. And the bed was soft. Like it had been used by generations of people before the current owner. The ex-current owner. Beau smiled as he looked down at the body lying next to him.

She had been nice enough. Young and perky and new to the area. Just how he liked them. No one would likely miss her for a while. Besides, by the time she was found, there would be very little of her left to examine. Beau smiled again and pulled the bed covers up a little to cover the woman's naked body. Her skin was already drying quickly and the telltale odor that always accompanied death lingered in the air. He reached down and ran his fingers through her long blonde hair and twisted it slightly as his strength slowly returned to him. Then he let her hair go and closed her eyes. A small shiver worked its way down his spine. It always unnerved him to see them staring back up at him.

Beau swung his legs over the side of the bed and pulled up the sheet to completely cover the woman. He didn't need to watch the process; he had seen it before and it was not pleasant. He was still amazed at how the human body could do such things. Or rather how he could make the human body do such things. It was a gift and a curse at the same time. But he must not complain, it was something that was getting him places; just as he had been informed all those years ago. And now taking someone else's life seemed almost acceptable. Almost normal. Of course it wasn't and deep down he knew that, but there were motives why he continued. Good motives. And besides, as long as he continued to be careful, there was no reason why he would ever be discovered.

Beau stood up and took a couple of steps towards the bottom of the bed. His legs were still weak and he needed to place a hand on the bed to steady himself. A wave of giddiness rushed through his body once more and he was forced to close his eyes and take another deep breath. He hated this part. And each time it seemed to take a little longer than the time before to fully recover. This was something he was going to have to ask the Anons about when he next got to speak to one of them. Still, there was no time to worry about that now. It was time to get home. He opened his eyes again and tried to refocus. The bedside clock showed two-fifty. Fifteen minutes tops and he could be back in his own apartment. He gathered up his clothes that were strewn about the floor and made his way to the living room. It was completely dark in there except for the glow from a small nightlight on the far wall. A noise behind him made him twist his head. It was only a cat. These girls always seemed to have cats. Something he never understood. He made his way to the couch, sat down and sorted through his clothes. Then he dressed as quickly as possible and walked across the room, back towards the door. With a final glance behind him he quietly opened the door. He waited for the cat to wander outside before slipping through it himself, pulling it shut behind him. Two flights of stairs later and he was on the pathway, keeping to the shadows and walking away from the apartment complex. He pulled his hood up over his head and put his hands in his pockets.

The cold March air bit at his face and a few drops of rain fell on him as he walked. There were still a few cars on the road, but no one was paying attention to him as he wandered the streets past the edges of the town center, across the old railway tracks and on towards his apartment. On nights like this he often wished he drove but that was one thing he had learned early on. Leaving as few clues as possible was the most important thing. By not driving and staying local he was almost hidden in plain sight. He didn't look out of place and no one would think anything of him if they saw him. Unfamiliar cars were something much more noticeable and besides the Melrose police often pulled people over late at night. He could never risk that. Beau walked past the bus terminal and along the street to his apartment complex. A few minutes later he was in his living room, sat exhausted in a chair.

The clock on the DVR showed three-eighteen. Three more hours until he had to get ready for work. It was going to be a tough day ahead of him. He was too tired to make his way to the bedroom and so he just slumped in his chair and closed his eyes. Sleep wasn't going to come easily though. It never did. And when it did come he knew it would be filled with nightmares. Those nightmares that always accompanied death. How many was it now? Eight, eleven? Somewhere around that number. He couldn't exactly remember. It wasn't important. And then there were the countless other experiences. Those times in the early days when he had just left them half-dead, not knowing just what he had been capable of. Those girls had surely recovered, but what had become of them he hadn't known. And now as he advanced in the ranks of his office, the need had become greater. And it was getting more difficult to find new women. Maybe he would have to move soon. Move away from Melrose to another city. But that in itself might be something that would point back to him. No, he was going to have to stay in Melrose. Perhaps the need to kill would go away at some point. Maybe when he was the head of the company. Yes, maybe then. Beau finally drifted off to his dreams.

"You new in town?"

The young woman smiled back at Beau and twirled the ends of her hair. "How do you know that?"

"You just have that look about you. Where you from?"

"Germany."

"Germany? I've never been there. Is it nice?"

"Is that your best chat up line?"

"I wasn't aware I was chatting you up."

"You aren't? Oh well, that's a shame." The woman handed Beau an empty glass. "Maybe you'll get me a drink though?"

Beau laughed as he wandered over to the bar to get the woman a drink. Perhaps tonight was going to turn out well after all. He ordered the drink and checked his pockets. Yes, the mushrooms were still there from the week before. Excellent. That would make it easier and so much better. He paid the barman and took the woman her drink. "Here you go."

They had chatted for a while before she had suggested he come back to her apartment for a nightcap and within minutes he had known that the night was his.

Beau muttered in his sleep as the dream continued.

The suggestion of the mushrooms had gone as expected and soon he was able to focus her mind as he wandered through it, searching for those pieces he could use for himself. This woman was surprisingly open and he took his time taking those parts he wanted, taking care to cover his tracks as he moved through her head. Finally when it was done and it was time to leave, he slowly withdrew, lingering on the edges, enjoying the vision of her seeing him. She had no idea that within moments he would be gone and so too would her life. He let her enjoy the last few moments then suddenly felt the remnants he had left behind approaching him fast. He only had a few more seconds. He needed to disengage before those memories overtook him and crossed over as well. She smiled and whispered his name as he tied the last knot inside her mind and withdrew back into his own body. Then he closed his eyes as she opened her mouth and silently screamed. No noise came out. He had taken that as well, but if she had been able to he knew it would have been blood-curdling. Her eyes were wide open, vacant and staring straight through him. He could sense that too. It was a vision that would stay with him forever. Her eyes stared straight through him. How could you? That's what they were saying. How could you do this to me? Who are you? What gives you the right? Why? They all silently asked the same questions and he had no answers for any of them. It was what he did. His special power. How he got through life. And every time he killed another the visions burned in his mind. Beau shifted in his chair and muttered again. His eyes jolted open and he sat upright. He put a hand to his burning forehead and wiped off the sweat. Six-twenty. It was time to get ready for another day at the office.

2

Lucy pushed her fingers hard against her temples to try and relieve the pain a little but it wasn't working. The throbbing continued to pound her head. She squeezed her eyes shut and let out another silent scream. Then she pressed her fingers harder against her head, but it was no good. The pain was just too strong. In the dark she fumbled around and found the bedside light. She grimaced even more as the room lit up.

Four-forty. She had felt it building during the night but now it was completely unbearable. There was no alternative and she was going to have to get up and see what she could do about her migraine. Lucy pulled back the covers, took her dressing gown from the chair beside her bed and slipped it on. Then she gingerly made her way to the kitchen, hoping she wouldn't wake Sabrina who was asleep in the other bedroom.

In the kitchen she poured herself a large glass of water, drank it down and then poured another. She turned off the kitchen light and returned to her bedroom with the glass. She clumsily retrieved a couple of Excedrin from the bottle in her bathroom cupboard and swallowed them down in between large gulps of water. Then she put the glass on the side of the counter top and got back into bed and turned the light off. The pain continued to shoot through her.

It seemed these migraine headaches were getting more frequent and she wished she knew what was causing them.

After all they had only started during the last year or so. In fact as far as she could remember, she had only been getting them since she arrived in Melrose. Certainly all through her school days in England and her college days in Georgia she didn't remember a single migraine. Maybe it was something to do with the wonderful pacific north-western weather she had heard so much about. But that seemed crazy to her. How could the weather cause her to get migraines? She pushed her fingers to her temples again as another wave of pain burst through her.

Lucy crossed over to the window and opened the blinds a little to look outside. It was tough to tell in the dark of the pre-dawn morning but it looked like it was raining again. Another wonderful day of weather to look forward to. This was her first winter in Melrose and she was currently undecided whether it would be her last. The fall had been superb, a big change from the humidity and unbearable heat of Georgia. But the winter? That had been another matter. She had come to America from England to get away from the miserable winters and here she was, stuck in the middle of a very miserable American winter. She let the blinds go and sat on the edge of her bed and closed her eyes. The Excedrin still hadn't kicked in.

Four-fifty. At least another hour before she was due to get up. Now it was a question of whether the migraine would subside enough in that time to allow her to function properly. She had already taken several days of sick leave from her job at Nyble Storage and she knew that sooner or later someone would say something to her. Several colleagues had already made side jokes about her part-time status. She took a deep breath and opened her eyes again. It wasn't shifting. Jarring stabs of pain continued to course through her head. The very thought of getting showered and dressed sent another wave of pain through her.

Lucy reached down and switched the radio on. At least a little morning music and frivolity might help take the edge off things. Lucy leaned her head back against her propped up pillows and closed her eyes again. She tried to tune out the pain in her head as she listened to the morning traffic reports and weather. Yes, it was going to be another rainy day with a chance of some snow flurries later. Great. She half-smiled as that thought passed through her head. She had actually taken the job in Melrose because of the proximity to the mountains. She had meant to go skiing in the winter, or at least take a hiking trip, but she hadn't gotten around to it so far. Her flat-mate, Sabrina, hadn't seemed so keen on all that. She was more of a party animal. *There'll be plenty of time for that next winter*, she had said to her several times. Lucy supposed she was right. After all, at twenty-two years old they were both supposed to be out having fun all the time. Fun. Having a migraine certainly wasn't fun and nor was it fun listening to and watching the rain beat down.

Lucy squeezed her eyes shut tight again as another wave of pain hit her. The Excedrins were doing nothing today. And it would be a few more hours before she could take any more. Another round of weather reports started up on the radio and Lucy took some deep breaths to help her relax a little.

The sound of Sabrina's shower awoke Lucy from her doze. Five-fifty. She raised a hand to her head. It was still pounding. It didn't look like she was going to be able to go into work again today. Another great start to the week. Maybe she should go and see the doctor once more. Last time the doctor hadn't been able to help much. They had sent her for several tests, but nothing had shown up. All the doctor could suggest was to take Excedrin Migraine tablets as necessary. Hundreds of dollars spent on healthcare and all she was getting was over the counter tablets. Some things about America just didn't make sense to her sometimes. She heard the shower turn off and music click on. It would be another hour before Sabrina ventured out of her bedroom.

Lucy continued to lie in her bed and listen to the radio as the rain beat against her window. There had already been an accident on I-405 and traffic was backing up everywhere. This was the daily life in the metropolis of Seattle. Weather and traffic. Everything was weather and traffic. If you had a job in one of those careers you were set for life. Lucy half-smiled. Or technology of course. This was a huge area for technology companies and that was what had brought Lucy to Melrose after all. She was a software engineer for a company that wrote cloud backup services, something that was apparently big business in the computing world. In all honesty she wasn't really that fascinated in technology but the job was interesting. They had told her at school that she had a gift for problem solving and getting a job in software engineering had seemed the logical fit. Nyble Storage had recruited her straight from college and offered her a great benefits package. And actually she had mostly enjoyed the last seven months. Everything was now vested and she was an employee with full benefits. In another couple of years she should be able to pay off the last of her loans and she was looking forward to having her mum and sister come out and visit in the summer. As long as the weather improved.

"You okay, Lucy?" Sabrina asked a little while later, poking her head into Lucy's bedroom. "I noticed your light wasn't on and it was all quiet in here."

"Migraine."

"Sorry. Is there anything I can get you?"

"No, I'll be fine. I'm going to have to spend another morning in bed. I'll call my office a little later."

"Are you sure?"

"Yeah, I'm fine, really. I've taken some Excedrin and I'll take a couple more later."

"Okay, take it easy. Get some rest. I'll see you later, bye." Sabrina pulled the door closed behind her.

Lucy had only gotten to know Sabrina after her arrival in Melrose. She had answered an ad for a room-mate and the two of them hit it off immediately. Several people had commented they looked a little like sisters, even twins. They were both tall and blonde, Sabrina was a little shorter than Lucy, and they were both twenty-two. Sabrina had grown up locally and several of her family lived nearby. Lucy had even met a few of her relatives. They both worked in different companies though. Sabrina worked for Zygote Technologies, which wasn't actually in Melrose at all, and exactly what they did she wasn't quite sure. Sabrina seemed very vague about it whenever Lucy asked. Still, they had become sort of best friends now and did most things together, especially at weekends.

The pain in Lucy's head had subsided a little and the Excedrins were at least taking the edge off. Lucy sat up in her bed and contemplated getting up to go to work but decided it was not a good idea. She had done that before, only to be sent home again. In fact she had had to be driven home by one of her colleagues and that had proved to be an embarrassing experience. No, she wasn't really well enough to go to work today. Maybe after lunch if the migraine wore off. The worse thing about these pains was the feeling of uselessness. No bright lights, no reading, no watching TV. She just had to wait it out. And she usually couldn't sleep either. She usually ended up listening to the radio for hours at a time.

The sound of the apartment door slamming woke Lucy from her doze. Seven-thirty-five. It was starting to get light outside. The rain was still beating on the window though. The traffic on I-405 was now even worse and the man on the radio was advising people to take I-520, I-90 and I-5 and avoid the eastside altogether. Maybe it was just as well she was staying home.

Lucy pulled on her dressing gown again and wandered into the living room. She pulled her laptop from her bag and booted it up. She soon had her corporate email account open and she composed an email to her boss and copied her co-workers to explain she had a migraine. She said she hoped to be in after lunch. Then as soon as she was done, she closed the lid of her laptop to shut off the light. She put it back in her bag and walked over to the kitchen, took a banana from the bowl on the counter and sat down to eat it. It was going to be another long day.

3

Beau pulled into the parking lot at Zygote Technologies and found his usual space. He parked the blue Mercedes and pulled out his things from the back seat before locking the car and walking into the building. He nodded at the receptionist and made his way down the corridor towards his office.

"Hey Beau, how's it going?" asked a tall and skinny guy standing in the entrance to the kitchen.

"Good Sam, very good." Beau squeezed past his friend and poured himself a coffee. "Do anything over the weekend?"

"Went up to the mountains and did a little snowboarding. You should come along next time."

"Maybe I will," Beau replied, picking up his coffee and squeezing past Sam again. "Maybe next weekend."

"I'll hold you to it."

Beau wandered down the corridor a little further and pushed open a door to let himself inside. He put his coffee down on his desk and let his bag fall from his shoulder onto the floor nearby. "Great," he muttered to himself as he noticed the yellow sticky note on the monitor of his PC. "What does he want now?" Beau picked up a notepad from his desk and left his office without even turning on his PC and made his way further along the corridor to the corner office where the Senior Vice-President of Marketing, Peter Ramsey, sat. He knocked and went in. "You needed to see me?"

"Yeah. Hi, Beau. Take a seat will you? And close the door." Peter shuffled a couple of papers and waited until Beau was sat down in front of him. "Yeah. There's been a few changes at corporate. I just thought you ought to know. I was going to call you, but I only found out the final details this morning when I got in."

Beau swallowed. He didn't like changes. Everything had been going really well recently. And usually, well usually after an experience like he had had the night before, things went really well. This was already worrying him. "What's up?"

"Gavin's out. They've cut the whole department."

Beau shuffled uneasily in his chair. Gavin was his boss and if they had cut the whole department then surely he was going to be cut too. "Oh."

Peter smiled. "No, you're okay. Actually you were specifically mentioned by corporate."

"I was?"

"Yeah. Seems like they have plans for you. We're putting you in charge of Outside Sales. You're being made a Director."

Beau slumped back in his chair. "Director? Outside Sales? Wow! Thanks."

"Don't thank me. Like I said, it came from corporate. Not that I disagree of course. You've done a great job since you've been here, Beau." Peter got to his feet and extended a hand to Beau. "Congratulations."

Beau got to his feet as well. "Thanks Peter. I don't know what to say."

"It'll take a while to sink in. We're moving you to Gavin's old office too. That'll be tomorrow though, once they've sorted it all out. Also corporate are coming here on Thursday. They'll want to meet with you, I'm sure."

Beau let Peter's hand go and sagged back down in the chair. "For a moment I thought you were going to fire me."

"Between you and me, I thought they might be firing all of us. I don't think sales are going as well as corporate expects them to be. I guess it'll be all up to you now!"

"Thanks. Anything else?" Beau got to his feet as Peter shook his head. "Okay, what should I tell everyone?"

"Better keep your head down this morning. There's a lot of things to get through. I'll announce it later this afternoon when I've got through everyone. In the meantime please don't say anything."

"Sure. Business as usual. I'll see you later." Beau turned and walked back towards the door. A minute later he was seated in his old office in a fog of disbelief. "Director of Outside Sales. Not bad for a twenty-three year-old nobody!"

"You coming to the pub?" Sam asked, putting his head around Beau's door later that afternoon.

"I'll be there in a few. You all go on ahead. There's just a couple of emails I have to send out. Paddy's?"

"Of course. Is there anywhere else?"

Beau smiled. "I guess not. I'll be right behind you." He watched as Sam made his way back up the corridor before he slumped back in his chair. It had been a tough day. Everyone had wanted to know what was going on and had come to ask Beau. It had soon become obvious that Beau wasn't being let go along with the rest of his department and people wanted to know why. All in all, twelve people had lost their jobs that day. It was the biggest set of redundancies he had seen at Zygote. Maybe business wasn't so good after all. But he still had his job and that was all that currently mattered. And a promotion too. He took a final look at the list of people who would now report to him and made a mental note of things he was going to have to say to people. None of them knew any of this yet. Tomorrow. It would wait until tomorrow. He turned his attention back to his PC and typed the final couple of sentences of the email he was going to send first thing in the morning. That should do it. Then he closed down his PC and picked up his bag from the floor next to his desk where he had left it in the morning. He hadn't even eaten his sandwich for lunch. Oh well. He turned off the office light and made his way back down the corridor towards the exit. Everyone else had already left for the day.

Twenty-five minutes later and he was parked in the lot outside Paddy's. He had considered dropping his car home first and walking over but that might encourage him to drink too much. No, it was better to drive and limit his celebration. There would be other times to go crazy. He locked up his car and walked the few yards to the pub. As soon as he entered a loud cheer went up and he saw his colleagues sat around a large table against the opposite wall.

"You took your time," Sam said, pushing a Guinness over towards him.

"Cheers," Beau said, taking a sip and putting the glass back down. "I told you I had a couple of things to do. And then I hit the traffic. No one in this city knows how to drive once it starts raining."

"Tell me about it."

"So Beau, who's going to be in your team?"

Beau looked up to see Tim anxiously looking his way. "Tomorrow, Tim. I'll be sorting this all out tomorrow. Tonight we are celebrating."

"To Beau," Sam shouted above the conversation. "May he prosper and not suffer the same fate as his predecessor."

"To Beau," everyone replied.

"Thanks," said Beau. "That's very reassuring."

"You'll be fine. You always seem to land on your feet," Sam said. "I don't know how you do it. I wish I had a tenth of your luck."

"Luck, eh? You think it's luck. More like hard work."

"Sure Beau. Hard work. Cheers!"

Beau and Sam clanked glasses and drank from their beers. Beau put his glass down and took a look around the table to see who had come. What were the politics tonight? Sam, Tim, Peter, Sabrina, Wendy and some woman that was seated next to Sabrina. "Who's that sat next to Sabrina?" Beau whispered, turning to Sam. "Is she new? What department is she in?"

"She's just a friend of Sabrina's I think. She doesn't work at Zygote."

Beau nodded at Sam as his eyes wandered over the woman's face. She looked very pretty. He snapped his gaze back to Sam. "Did you order food already?"

"We've got some wings and onion rings coming. I think Peter ordered some nachos too."

"Good, I'm starving. I didn't even eat lunch today."

"You need to take better care of yourself, Beau. You're always doing that. You need a woman to look after you."

Beau smiled, staring again down the table. "Yeah, I do."

Sam laughed. "I'll find out from Sabrina, okay?"

Beau picked his glass up again. "I'll hold you to that."

Just then the food arrived and conversation died down as people started eating. Sam got up and moved along the table a couple of seats to sit next to Tim. "Who's that girl with Sabrina?" he whispered.

"That's her room-mate. I think her name's Lucy. I've met her once or twice before. She seems pretty nice. Why, you interested?"

Sam laughed. "No, not me. Beau. He was the one asking."

"Typical. He's always chasing after someone."

"Tell me about it. We need to get him hooked up. Maybe it will get him out of our hair for a while."

Tim laughed. "Well said." The two of them took a drink and nodded at each other. "Do you know who's going to be in Beau's team?"

"Haven't a clue and Peter's not saying anything. Actually I think this all came as a bit of a shock to him. Corporate obviously thinks Beau's the future face of the company. Peter's probably worried he might be on his way out."

"You think so?"

"I'm just speculating, but you've got to be worried if you're in his position. I mean, Peter's been here eight years and Beau less than two and Beau is already a Director. Someone in corporate obviously likes him."

"I guess we'll all find out tomorrow."

"Yes. There are probably going to be some big changes over the next few weeks. We'd better keep our heads down and let it all blow over."

"I'll pass the message on to everyone. We're all in this together."

"I'd better get back to Beau. He's looking a little lost at having to speak with Peter. Catch you later, Tim."

"Later Sam."

Sam got up and wandered back up the table and took his seat next to Beau once more.

"Well?"

"Lucy. We think her name is Lucy. Tim says she is Sabrina's room-mate."

"Thanks." Beau allowed himself a smile. Lucy. She definitely looked like someone he needed to get to know. "To Zygote Technologies." Beau drained his glass and let his eyes wander along the table to rest on the tall, slim figure of Sabrina's friend, Lucy. Oh yes, he was definitely going to get to know that woman.

4

The rain was beating down hard on the windscreen of Beau's Mercedes as he pulled into the parking lot of the Seven-Eleven, close by to his apartment, on his way to work. Seven-ten. He smiled. Ironic really. He could see there were one or two customers in the shop but the beat up silver Honda Civic he was looking for hadn't yet arrived. He turned his engine off and let the wipers stop half-way through their cycle.

A couple of minutes later the Honda Civic arrived and pulled into the space next to Beau's. Beau opened his door, ducked his head out into the rain and got out. Then he pulled open the passenger door to the Civic and climbed in alongside the driver. "Alright?"

The man nodded and sniffed as if he was fighting back a cold. "Alright."

"You got them?"

The man nodded again and reached into a pocket in his coat. "Two hundred and fifty."

Beau's hand stopped on its way to his jacket. "How much?"

"Two hundred and fifty. They were harder to get this time than I thought."

"Maybe I should go elsewhere."

"If you like. Makes no difference to me." The man let his hand drop to his lap.

"Alright, two hundred and fifty. But they had better be good. And next time I'm not paying any more than this. Do you understand?"

"I just make the deliveries. I don't set the prices." The man reached back into his coat and pulled out a small plastic bag. "The money?"

Beau pulled out a small wad of notes and counted out two hundred and fifty dollars. He handed it over to the man and took a hold of the bag. Then he opened it up and smelled the contents. "Good." He picked out a small piece from inside and rubbed it slightly between his fingers. "Looks good." Beau closed up the bag again and slipped it into his pocket. "I'll call you when I need some more."

Beau opened up the car door, got out and closed it behind him. Before he had even got back into his car, the Civic had gone. Beau stood briefly in the rain, watching it drive away, before getting back into his Mercedes. He brushed away the rain from his coat and sat quietly in his car for a few minutes, watching the windscreen steam up as he sat there. Then he turned on the power, opened the window a little and clicked on the radio. He had better get to work. It was going to be a busy day. Everyone would be expecting his announcements and his plans and he couldn't disappoint them. Still, at least he had some more mushrooms now. His hand involuntarily touched his coat pocket and he smiled. Who knew when he would have the next opportunity? Maybe this week, maybe next month. Things were going better than he had ever hoped.

Beau started his car and let the wipers do their work for a few seconds before he reversed back and turned the car around. Within a minute he was back on the road towards his office. He closed the window and smiled as he heard the weatherman say it would rain all day. Hopefully it would be a long winter this year and summer would take its time to arrive. He liked the cold and the rain. It allowed him to stay in the shadows whenever he needed to. And recently he had needed to do that a lot.

Eight-five. Beau pulled his Mercedes into the office parking lot and pulled his things together before he got out of the car and rushed towards the office. He nodded at the receptionist and made his way to his office. His first job of the day was going to be getting the email out. "Morning Sam," he shouted out as he passed the kitchen. He would get a coffee later. He pushed the door to his office open, closed it behind him and walked over to his desk. No sticky notes this morning. At least the day was his for a change. He smiled as he sat down and turned on his PC.

"Was that Beau?" Tim asked, turning around after he had poured his coffee.

"Yeah. Didn't even stop to get a coffee this morning. Must be in a hurry," Sam replied.

"So, what do you make of it all then?"

"The re-org? Have to wait and see I guess. I don't think it will affect us. Do you?"

Tim added some creamer to his coffee and stirred it a little. "I guess not. Although people have been moved to Sales before. And they might be looking for some technical help with their proposals."

"Well I don't want to be in Sales. Not that I don't like Beau you understand, it's just that I like what I do."

Tim smiled. "We both like Beau, Sam. But I think it's fair to say neither of us wants to actually work for him."

Sam crossed over close to Tim and sat at one of the tables in the coffee room. "Sit down a sec." He waited while Tim sat down next to him. "There's something about him, isn't there?"

"What do you mean?"

Sam leaned in a little closer to Tim. "You know. A little odd. It's like he's possessed or something."

"You don't mean that, do you?"

"Well, you know what I mean. Not possessed, but different somehow. I can't put my finger on it but he's not like us."

Tim took another sip from his coffee. "You know him better than anybody, Sam. So what is it?"

"I don't know. I really don't. But it's like he's going places and we're just here to support him if necessary. And if we're not necessary then we'll be chewed up and spat out. No matter who we are."

"I know what you mean. He does seem to be untouchable. Whatever he does turns to gold and he gets everything he wants. Even Peter seems a little wary of him."

"You think he's after Peter's job?"

Tim shrugged his shoulders. "Sure. Why not? Wouldn't you be?"

"But I'm not Beau, am I? Why would I want Peter's job?"

Tim punched Sam on the arm. "You're right there. You'd be a hopeless boss."

"Hey, I'm serious, Tim. This isn't really a laughing matter. There's definitely something about him, isn't there?"

"Well what's he like at the weekends when you hang out with him? Is he intense, or more laid back?"

"He's pretty normal really. We do things like you and I would do. I'm trying to get him to come snowboarding with me."

"Yeah, that would be a first."

"Anyway, we just need to…"

"Morning boys."

Sam looked up from his conversation. "Morning Wendy. How are you today?"

"Like everyone else I guess. A little nervous." Wendy crossed over to the coffee machine to pour herself a coffee. "I know you're both watching me."

Tim laughed. "Always, Wendy. You know we love to watch you."

"Shut up! You're just playing with me. I know what you really think about me." Wendy took her coffee and turned to face the two young men. "So what's the topic of conversation today?"

Sam finished his coffee and got to his feet. "As much as we would like to discuss that with you Wendy, I'm afraid it's top secret. For the ears of us boys only." He threw his empty cup in the trash and crossed over to stand next to

Wendy. "Besides, I really do have to get back to work. Didn't you hear, there's a new Sheriff in town?"

Wendy laughed. "A new Sheriff. I like that one. See you later, boys." Wendy gave Tim and Sam a mock wave and turned and left the room.

"Conference room?" Sam asked Tim later in the afternoon.

"Yeah, just coming. Just want to send this email."

"So what do you think it's all going to be about?"

"Formalization of all the moves I guess." Tim closed the top to his laptop and stood up. "Let's do it."

Tim and Sam wandered down the corridor to the conference room and took seats at the far end of the large table. The room was already nearly full with everyone from the office. Peter and Beau were discussing something in hushed whispers in the corner of the room. Finally they broke away from each other and took seats at the head of the table.

"Good afternoon," Peter said, looking around the room and trying to make eye contact with everyone in turn. "This shouldn't take too long. I just wanted to talk briefly about the re-organization and give you all an opportunity to ask a few questions. Okay?" He waited while everyone nodded and then he opened up a small folder in front of him. "Beau?"

"Right." Beau stood up and turned on the projector that was connected to a laptop in front of him. Everyone turned to face the whiteboard as the projected picture snapped into focus.

"This is the new organization here at the Pacific branch of Zygote Technologies," Peter continued. "As you can see there have been some major shake-ups." He took a brief sip of his water and waited for everyone to read through the complete organization chart. "The biggest changes affect those of you that have been moved into the Sales organization, under Beau. As you can see, we've pulled three of you, Wendy, Paul and Gwen from Technical Support, and Josh from Marketing, into the new organization. Keith, who is currently at the corporate office, will also be transferring here to complete the team. Any questions?"

"What's the rationale behind moving some of Technical Support into Sales?" asked Paul.

Beau put up a hand and spoke before Peter could reply. "The nature of a lot of the deals we are now trying to close means that we need a new kind of salesperson. Someone who can talk to the customer in terms that they really understand. Talk technically about the product and…"

Wendy leaned over to Sam and whispered into his ear. "You're right, Sam. It seems there is a new Sheriff in town and now I have been seconded to his Posse. Wish me good luck!"

5

Beau put his beer back on the side table and leaned back in his chair. It had been another long day and the activities of the week were already catching up with him. He closed his eyes and let his mind wander a little. Three years. Yes it had been about that long now since his first meeting with the Anons. At the time it had come as a complete surprise to him. He had just finished using a girl on the campus. Of course in those days he didn't know he could kill people. In fact he knew very little about what he could actually do. How things had changed. Beau smiled and let his mind drift into sleep.

"Beau? Beau Tempest?"

Beau had stopped in his late night walk back to his dorm and turned to face the voice. "Who's asking?"

The man approached him, stuck in the shadows with a hood that mostly covered his face. "You are Beau Tempest?"

"I am."

The man extended a hand to Beau. "I'm a friend. I need to talk with you."

Beau took a step back. He smiled as he remembered that. The man had scared him a little. The first thought that had gone through his mind was that it was someone from the college that had discovered what he had been doing.

"Seriously, I'm a friend. I'm not from the college. But I do need to talk to you. It seriously is a matter that could affect your life." The man closed in some more and kept his hand extended.

Beau shook the man's hand and tried to peer into his face. He looked older, maybe thirty. That was about all he could tell. "Yeah, I'm Beau."

"Let's go somewhere where we can talk. There's a late night Denny's down the street. I won't keep you longer than I need. I'll even buy dinner!"

Beau followed the man as he led him down the street and they walked into Denny's and took a table near the door. The man pulled his hood back and Beau studied his face. "You can call me Ted."

"Who are you?"

"What do you want to eat? I'm sure you're hungry? Let's order." The two of them ordered their food as soon as the waitress arrived and sat back staring at each other for a few moments. "Like I said, you can call me Ted," the man continued. "We have been watching you. Not so much me as others in our group. You have a special gift." Beau looked at Ted and tried to decide whether he should speak or not. "We know all about the girls you have been seeing. Sit down." Ted got to his feet as Beau got up. "Seriously, I'm not from the college and I'm not anything to do with the girls. Sit down." He waited until Beau had sat back down before he did the same. "I represent a group. We are called the Anons. We look out for those that are gifted. Those that are like you. Those that can make a difference in this world."

"What do you mean?"

"You do things with those girls, don't you? Things that are not normal. You control them and they make you feel all powerful. Isn't that right?" Ted waited and watched as Beau just sat there. "There are others like you. I am one of them. You are not alone. But you do not understand the gift you possess."

"What do you mean?"

Ted smiled. "You are a para-psychic."

"A para-what?"

"Para-psychic. You can enter the minds of others and take control of them. You know that, don't you?"

"I guess." Beau shifted uneasily in his chair. The two of them stopped speaking and paused as the waitress arrived with their order.

Ted waited until she was gone before continuing. "But what you don't know is either the extent of your talent or the effect it has on the women concerned."

"Well, I..."

"Eat. Let me tell you a little about yourself." Ted took a large bite of his burger and chewed it up before swallowing. "It probably started when you were about thirteen or fourteen and at first you just though you could read the mind of some of the girls at school. Then, when you fully kissed one you suddenly got an amazing rush and it was if she was totally in your mind. You had to have more and so you constantly tried to kiss girls, to get that rush all over again. But after a while the girls at school didn't want to know you. They seemed distant and word got around and all the girls ignored you. So then you went further afield. You probably joined a few clubs and tried to meet girls that way. But that dried up too. And finally you came to college where there has been a whole new supply of women for you. You're now going through them in the same way as you did when you were at school." Ted stopped talking and waited for Beau to speak. "Well?"

Beau finished his bacon and eggs and licked his lips. "That's pretty close. How do you know?"

"Like I said. You are a para-psychic. You are not the first and you won't be the last."

"So why are you here?"

"I need to tell you a little about your gift before you make some serious mistakes and either end up dead or in jail."

"Jail?"

"Someday you will kill."

Beau laughed. "Yeah, right. I'm a killer."

Ted leaned forward across the table. "Beau, let's get one thing clear. You are a killer. It's not a matter of *if*, but a matter of *when*." He took another bite of his burger and watched as Beau took in the information. "I'm here to teach you what you need to do and how to do it successfully. You will have this gift all your life and as you get older so the numbers of people you will kill will rise. If you are to remain a free man then you need to listen to everything I am about to tell you."

"You're completely serious, aren't you?" Beau asked.

Ted nodded. "Yes. Completely. So listen."

Beau had spent the next ten minutes in total disbelief as Ted explained just what Beau could do and what it would do for him. He remembered sitting at the table afterwards. Ted had just put down some money and left. Beau stayed there in shock for quite a while. He wasn't sure how long. He didn't even remember getting back to his dorm.

A couple of nights later Beau decided to try out some of things Ted had suggested. He had wandered into the city center and just picked up a random girl and they had made out in an alleyway between two buildings. Beau remembered how he had wandered through that girl's mind. The experience of it. He remembered picking up useful pieces of knowledge and memories, and he remembered the look on the girl's face when he was done and crossed back over. He had held that first one in his hands for quite a while. It had been a long death. He had not used the mushrooms that time. He didn't know if it was painless or not and the girl did not speak. She just stared back at him with a look on her face that he would always remember. And her skin. It had literally dried to a leather in front of him. It was as if all moisture had been taken from it. In the end he had just dropped her and run. He never looked back. The news the next day talked about a body being found but they never did say whether it was a murder or not.

Beau muttered a little in his sleep and his eyes jolted open. He reached out for his beer and finished the bottle before clutching it close to him. Three years he had been killing women now and it wasn't getting any easier at all. The desire inside him grew stronger every week. The desire for the power that accompanied the killings. When would it stop? Would it ever stop? Perhaps when he was the boss of Zygote. Perhaps then it would stop. But what if it didn't? What if that only led him onto another company? Something bigger. He was going to have to make contact with the Anons once again and find out some more truths. But that scared him. That scared him more than even the killings. There were things that perhaps he should never know; that he was better off not knowing. The Anons knew too many things about life and death. And surely there were consequences for everything in life. The thought suddenly struck him. Perhaps there was something he was going to have to do in return for all of this at some point in his life. Perhaps this was just the beginning of a journey, a horrible journey, he was going to have to make. Perhaps, perhaps. Yes, he knew too little. He got up, put the empty bottle down in the kitchen and made his way to his bedroom. There would be a day of reckoning. There was always a day of reckoning. He took his clothes off, climbed into bed and tried to keep the nightmares from taking him as he fell asleep.

6

"So, what do you want to do today?" Sabrina asked Lucy as they sat and ate breakfast.

"Nothing planned," Lucy answered. "It looks like the weather might be pretty nice for a change though."

"How about a harbor cruise?"

"The ones you've been talking about?"

"Yeah. Why not? Unless there's something else you want to do today?"

"No. That sounds a good idea. What time?"

"I think they're about lunch time. We have plenty of time to get ready. We should take the bus though. Parking downtown is just such a nightmare."

Lucy put the banana skin down on the coffee table and pulled on her long hair, trying to draw a few of the knots out. "I think I'll wear it up today. No one will notice."

"We're not going on a date, Lucy. You need to chill a little."

Lucy laughed and let her hair drop. "Yeah, I know. I just miss having a boyfriend. You know. Ever since Russ."

"Look, make the most of being free. Seriously, I'm happy not to have a boyfriend."

"You're gay, Sabrina. You don't need a boyfriend!"

"You know what I mean."

"Either way, I like men. And I'm not going to spend the summer without one." Lucy picked up her banana skin and got to her feet. "Or pretend to be your girlfriend for that matter."

"You're not my type." Sabrina laughed and followed Lucy from the living room. "We should plan to leave around ten-thirty. Okay?"

Lucy nodded, poured herself a cup of tea and made her way back to her bedroom. She had mostly enjoyed the seven months she had spent so far in Melrose, but now she needed to get her life in order a little more. She had to make some decisions about what she wanted to do. Apart from Sabrina, there were only a few people that Lucy actually knew. And they were really more work colleagues. Maybe she should join a local group of something and make new friends that way. She had hoped to get to know people at church, but either people there were very reserved or she had found the wrong church. Something else she would have to reevaluate. She took a sip of her tea and put the cup down on her dresser. Then she turned on the radio and let her mind wander as the music filled her room. At least she didn't have a migraine today.

A little while later she was showered and sitting in her dressing gown, drying her hair and thinking about what she should wear. The weather man had said it was expected to be in the high fifties with the chance of a few gusts of wind that might make it feel a little cooler. It was definitely a two sweater day. Lucy finished drying her hair and started applying her make-up. Just a few touches. At least that was one thing she preferred about Melrose to Georgia. Everyone in Georgia seemed to put on so much make-up. As far as she could tell, here in Melrose, it was even acceptable to wear none at all. She smiled. Just like England. Unfortunately, so was the weather. The totally unpredictable northwest weather.

Lucy got up and wandered over to the closet, pulled out a pair of jeans, squeezed into them and then pulled open a drawer in her dresser. After rummaging through a number of sweaters she pulled out two, one thin and black and the other thicker and pink. A few minutes later she was dressed and ready to face the world.

Sabrina was already sat watching TV as Lucy entered the living room. "Good choice," she said, glancing up from her chair. "It'll probably be a little cold on the water."

"So, you've done this trip before?"

"Several times, but it doesn't get old. It's fun. There are normally a few interesting people on the boat too. Mostly tourists." Sabrina got to her feet. "You ready then?"

Lucy and Sabrina pulled on coats, left the apartment and started on their walk towards the bus stop. There was still a slight chill in the air, but the sky was mostly empty of clouds and after a brisk ten minute walk they were stood waiting for the bus.

Lucy had been to downtown Seattle on a few occasions in the time she had lived in Melrose but only to meet people or to visit a few of the department stores. She had also had the compulsory trip around Pike Place Market and watched the men throwing large salmon to each other. But that was about it. As she and Sabrina got off the bus and started their walk through downtown she watched as crowds of people milled around every street corner. Homeless people shuffled along on the sidewalks and a few hopeful street musicians played a tune or two, waiting for someone to give them a dollar. Lucy stayed close to Sabrina, a little unsure as to how safe it actually was for her.

"Did you want to grab a coffee or something first?" Sabrina asked.

"I'm okay. Maybe I'll have something after the harbor cruise." Lucy linked arms with Sabrina and they walked down one of the steep streets that led to the waterfront. "It's a lot colder than I thought it would be."

"It'll warm up soon. You'll see. Another hour and the sun will work its magic. Besides, we're near the waterfront here. The winds are coming off of the bay. When we get down to sea level you won't notice the winds at all."

The two women continued walking and after a few more minutes were on the waterfront and had crossed over to join the crowds that were out walking. "It's busy," said Lucy.

"You should see it in the summer. You can't even move here. And then there's the cruise ship traffic. It gets crazy here at weekends. Come on, we're nearly there. The pier is just down here."

A few minutes later and Sabrina had purchased the tickets for the harbor cruise. The two women sat on a wall and waited for the boat and watched the passersby.

"Do you ever imagine to yourself what these people do?" asked Lucy.

Sabrina laughed. "No, not really."

"I do," said Lucy. "That lady there for example. She's escaped from her husband for the day and is off to have a secret assignation with a man from the city. Look, she's wearing her best shoes, and on a day like today. There's definitely something odd about her. And that man over there, the one with the gray jacket on. He's here on business from another country and is lost. He doesn't know where he's going. Soon he will pull out a map and take a look at it."

"You're crazy Lucy, did you know that?"

Lucy nudged Sabrina. "Look, see I told you."

Sabrina laughed out loud as the man with the gray jacket pulled a map out from his pocket and unfolded it. "Come on, I think it's time to get on the boat."

The two women got to their feet and made their way back to the pier and down the ramp towards the boat. "There's only a few people waiting," said Lucy.

"Looks like it'll be a quiet trip today then. Still, at least we can get a warm drink on board and look at the sights."

"Smile!" the man who was taking photos of the passengers said to Lucy and Sabrina as they waited their turn to board the boat.

"Wow! The Seattle skyline is pretty impressive from here," Lucy said a while later as the boat made its way around the bay. "Stand over there. I want to take a picture of you with everything behind you."

Sabrina crossed over to the side of the boat and Lucy took a couple of pictures. Then one of the tourists on board volunteered to take a photo of them both and they let him, laughing as they squeezed together to make sure they were both in the center of the picture. A little while later and the boat pulled back alongside the pier and the two women got off.

"Don't forget to look at your photo," the captain said as they passed him.

At the top of the pier the photos of all the passengers were waiting. Sabrina and Lucy quickly found the one of the both of them. "What do you think?" asked Sabrina.

"Sure, why not? It's only fifteen dollars and it's a good souvenir." Lucy took some money from her purse and paid for the photo. "Where to now?"

"Do you want to get something to eat?"

"Definitely. I'm quite hungry after that trip."

"Seafood, burger, fish and chips? What do you want?"

"Fish and chips?"

"Of course, Seattle is known for its fish and chips on the waterfront."

"Let's do that then," said Lucy. "Do you want to split one?"

"Come on. I know just the place." The two women linked arms again as they happily headed back along the waterfront.

"You coming with me?" Sabrina asked Lucy later that evening as they sat in their living room idly watching TV.

"No, I'm going to stay in. I'm quite tired after our trip actually."

"That's the sea air. Are you sure? The gang won't mind you joining us."

"I'm fine, Sabrina. Really. Besides, I don't quite fit into your group of friends."

"We're not that bad…"

"That's not what I meant…"

"I know. Lighten up will you? Come on, you should just come out once with us. You may even enjoy it."

"No, I'm going to stay in and read a book. I think I'll have an early night too. That migraine from earlier in the week messed up my sleeping. I could do with an extra couple of hours."

"If you're sure?"

"I am. I'll see you in the morning. Okay?"

Sabrina pulled her coat from the hook and wrapped it around her. "I'll see you in the morning."

As soon as the door shut behind Sabrina, Lucy turned off the TV and reached over to the coffee table and picked up her book. A night in to do a little reading was a good idea. Maybe a mug of warm hot chocolate would be good too. She put the book down again and walked over to the kitchen to put the kettle on. As she reached up to get the hot chocolate from the cupboard she saw the afternoon's photo out of the corner of her eye still lying on the kitchen-top. Lucy pulled down the jar of hot chocolate and then picked up the photo. She smiled. She and Sabrina looked happy in the photo. Maybe she could get to like Melrose in time. There really were a lot of things to do. She just needed to make a few more friends. Preferably of the male variety! She allowed herself a quiet laugh. Yes, she didn't want to find herself hanging out with Sabrina's friends at the weekends. Just what her mother would say to that, she really could only imagine. She put the photo back down as the noise of the kettle boiling shocked her back into reality.

7

"You sure you don't want to come? You'd be more than welcome."

"I'm fine, Sabrina. There are plenty of things I want to do today."

"What, like laundry?"

"Yes laundry, okay?" Lucy replied. "Now get out of here. I'll be fine."

"Just make sure you eat something." Sabrina buttoned up her coat, pulled the door shut behind her and made her way to her car. Her cousin Tim lived about seven miles away and today she had been invited over for Sunday lunch with him and his parents. It was always nice to go to their house. Whenever she went there she got completely spoiled. Sabrina pulled out onto the main road and briefly turned on the wipers to clear away a few spots of rain that were settling on her windscreen. The weather was already changing again. They were forecasting some snow later in the week.

Ten minutes later and Sabrina was knocking at the door of Tim's parents.

"Hey Sabrina," Tim said, hugging his cousin. "Come on in. My parents have been asking about you already."

"They have?"

Tim took Sabrina's coat. "Apparently you are more popular than me."

"Thanks." Sabrina followed Tim into the living room of the house and Tim's parents got up to greet her. A few moments later and she was seated with a glass of white wine in her hand.

"So tell us what you've been up to, Sabrina?"

"Nothing much. I've been busy at work. I'm sure Tim has told you there's been a lot of changes?"

"Yes, he said that there was a major reorganization. Your job was safe though."

"Yes, my job was safe. Unless they shut down the whole company I think I'll be alright there." Sabrina took a sip of her wine.

"And your love life?"

Sabrina blushed. "Really Aunt May? You want to know about that?"

"Of course I do. It's the only way your mother ever finds out anything about you."

Sabrina smiled and took another sip of wine. "Well, she's not the most supportive person of the choices I make."

"She cares about you. She is just a little different, that's all."

Sabrina leaned back in her chair and put the glass down by her side. "You mean she won't accept the fact that I'm a lesbian?"

"Sabrina, I don't want to get into that again. Your mother loves you. She's just been brought up differently, that's all." Aunt May crossed over and sat down in the chair next to Sabrina. "So are you going to tell me, or what?"

"There's really not much to say. I hung around with a few of my friends last night, but I'm still not dating anyone."

"And what about your new room-mate?"

Sabrina laughed out loud and picked up her wine glass again. "Lucy? No, she's not gay. She wants to get a boyfriend. She even told me that."

"Beau fancies Lucy," Tim said, pouring himself some wine.

"He does?"

"That's what he told me the other night. Well, in his way of course."

"Beau, the new boss at work?" asked Aunt May.

"Yes, that's the one."

"And what is this Beau like?"

"He's okay," said Tim.

"Dangerous," said Sabrina.

"Which one is it?" asked Aunt May.

Tim and Sabrina both laughed. "I guess it depends on who you are," said Tim. "He's alright. He's a bit intimidating and certainly someone you wouldn't want to cross. Everything he touches seems to turn to gold though. He's certainly making his way up quickly through the management positions at the office."

"Like I told you, dangerous," said Sabrina. "I don't know if I would date him if I was straight."

"He's good looking, isn't he?"

"Yes," replied Sabrina. "But like I said, I don't know if I could trust him. There's just something about him." She took another sip of her wine. "You've known Beau a while, yes?"

Tim nodded. "A while."

"And what do you know of his past? Does he have a girlfriend? What does he do at weekends?"

Tim thought for a moment before answering. "I guess I don't know that much about him. Sam's his best friend really. He says he's pretty normal. I know he had a girlfriend some time ago. But she disappeared. I think she moved back east."

"And you think I should tell Lucy that he wants to date him?"

"I'm not saying that. I'm just passing on information."

"Sounds to me like there's some mystery here," said Aunt May, getting up and turning to go into the kitchen. "And you needn't think I've forgotten what I was asking you, Miss, either. I've got to go and sort out the vegetables but we will continue this soon."

"Do you really think Beau's a little odd?" Sabrina asked Tim in a hushed voice.

"I don't know. I guess I'm willing to give him the benefit of the doubt. He's certainly driven to be successful. And maybe that's all it is. Maybe he's just not that good in social situations. And anyway, I wasn't suggesting that Lucy should date Beau. I was just passing on information."

"Okay." Sabrina handed over her wine glass to Tim. "I'll have a refill, please."

"Sure." Tim got to his feet and walked over to get the bottle of wine from the chiller.

Sabrina, Tim, Aunt May and Uncle Joe chatted about everything and nothing during lunch and mostly the talk was around Aunt May trying to find out who Sabrina was going to date. Tim kept trying unsuccessfully to change the subject and eventually it was Uncle Joe that stopped the conversation by insisting that he was getting bored by it and they should talk about something else.

"What do you think the chances of us getting snow this week are, then?" Uncle Joe asked.

"We're due for some," replied Tim. "We haven't had any down here yet. Everything has been up in the mountains and we usually get snow at least once a year."

"Well let's hope it's not as bad as two years ago. The whole of the eastside shut down for a week."

"I don't think they'll let that happen again, Dad. I heard they will use salt on the roads this time."

"Let's hope so."

"Anyone for dessert?" asked Tim's mother. "It's strawberry cheesecake."

"Definitely," replied Sabrina.

"Me too," Tim's father added.

May served up the cheesecake and after they had finished she brought in a small box and handed it to Sabrina. "Take this home with you. I'm sure your room-mate will like a little cheesecake."

"Thanks, Aunt May. I'm sure she will. Although she doesn't eat a lot."

"Well next time make sure you bring her here. I'll fatten her up a little!"

"Yes, Aunt May." Sabrina took the box from her aunt and got to her feet. "I'd better get back. I don't like to leave Lucy on her own all day. I'm sure she'll want to have some company this evening."

Tim brought in Sabrina's coat and helped her put it on. Sabrina said her goodbyes and was soon back in her car driving home once again with the strawberry cheesecake in a box beside her on the passenger seat.

"Lucy?" Sabrina shouted out as she entered the apartment. There was no reply and Sabrina went into the kitchen and put the cheesecake into the fridge. "Lucy? You home?" She looked into Lucy's room but she wasn't there either. She took off her coat, hung it up and sat herself down in a chair in the living room. Within a few minutes she was asleep.

"Sabrina? Why are you sitting in the dark?" Lucy said, closing the apartment door behind her and flicking on the light.
"What?" Sabrina opened her eyes and winced at the light. "You're home."
"And you were sleeping."
"Yes. Too much food at my Aunt's. Where have you been?"
"I just went for a walk. I went to church this morning and then I did my laundry. After that I just needed some fresh air. I went for a walk along the trail and I suddenly realized it was getting dark and I had to hurry home. The days here are still so short."
"You were on the trail in the dark?"
"Well only for a little while. It's not dangerous is it?"
"I don't think so. I'm more worried that you couldn't see."
Lucy laughed. "Yes, it was getting a little difficult by the time I got back to Melrose." She hung up her coat and flopped down next to Sabrina. "So how was your day?"
"Good. There's some strawberry cheesecake in the fridge if you're interested."
Lucy got to her feet again and walked over to the fridge. She pulled out the box and opened it up. "Yummy. This is just what I need. There's a lot here. You want some?"
"No, I'm still full."

Lucy cut off a portion, put it on a plate and returned the box to the fridge. "Oh well." She took a seat at the dining table and took a bite of the cheesecake. "Lovely. This is real good. Did your Aunt make it?"

"I think so. She wants you to come over next time."

"I don't know. I don't really know them."

"They always ask about you. Actually my Aunt was secretly hoping we'd be dating."

"Sabrina!"

Sabrina laughed. "I know. I told her you were straight. But at least she can talk about it. Not like my Mom." Sabrina got up and took a seat next to Lucy at the table. "I did find out something interesting though."

"Yes, what's that?" Lucy asked between mouthfuls.

"This guy at the office, Beau, fancies you."

"What? Who? I don't know anyone from your office. Except Tim."

"Last Monday evening when we went out to Paddy's, remember? The day you had your migraine? Well Beau was there. He was sat at the far end of the table. He's the one that was newly promoted to Director. Anyway, Tim said he told him that he fancied you."

Lucy scraped the last of the cheesecake from her plate and licked the fork. "I don't remember him. What's he like? Good looking?"

Sabrina smiled. "Yes, good looking. But I'm not sure if he's right for you. He's a bit of a control freak and solely concentrated on his career. I've no idea how he would treat you as a girlfriend."

"Thanks for the vote of confidence."

"I'm just saying, that's all. I just think you should be cautious."

"And you're not saying this to keep me for yourself then?" Lucy picked up her plate and wandered over to the kitchen.

"Of course not, Lucy. Just saying you should be careful, that's all."

Lucy smiled to herself as she put her plate in the sink. A secret admirer. Maybe some of her prayers at church had been answered after all.

8

"Nine-thirty, okay?" asked Beau, leaning over Wendy at her desk. "And bring everything you have on Project One-Eighty-Five. I think this will be a good visit. At least it will be a chance for you to see what we do out there."

Wendy stopped typing and looked up at Beau. "Yes Beau. I'll be ready. Just the project files?"

"I have all the presentations. Just bring the technical details. I don't know what we'll need." Beau took a step back and turned towards his office. "Nine-thirty. In the parking lot."

Wendy watched Beau disappear up the corridor before finishing off the document she was typing. Project 185. She couldn't even remember what project that was. She opened up a file on her PC and scanned through it. Wow, no wonder. It wasn't even anything she had been involved in. This was going to be interesting. She just hoped she wasn't going to be expected to talk about it in detail. She clicked on the link in the file and opened up all the relevant documentation. Then she sent it all to her local printer and decided to get another cup of coffee while she waited for it to print.

"What do you know about Project One-Eighty-Five?" Wendy asked Tim, returning from the coffee room.

"Nope. Not familiar with that one. Did you ask Sam? He knows most of them."

Wendy wandered over to Sam's desk and asked the same question.

"Don't know it. Is it new?"

Wendy shook her head. "Not sure. I'm supposed to go out with Beau this morning and we're discussing this project."

"Sorry, Wendy. Can't help you with it."

Wendy touched a hand to Sam's shoulder and turned back towards her desk. She stopped off at the printer on the way and picked up the large stack of paper that was waiting for her. "Wow!" she said quietly, dropping the files on her desk. There was no way she was ever going to read through all this before her meeting. All she could do was skim through and hope it was enough. She sat down and took the first of the documents from the pile. "Project One-Eighty-Five," she read. "*Creating a Self-Replicating and Auto-Improving Software Environment.* This sounds boring."

"You have the files?" Beau asked, as he opened the door of his Mercedes for Wendy.

"Yes, although it's not a project I'm familiar with."

Beau stopped in his tracks and let go of the car door. "What?"

"Project One-Eighty-Five. Today is the first time I have ever seen it."

"You're not serious, are you? I'm relying on you to be able to tell the customer the details."

"Sorry Beau, but I've never even seen this project before. And no one else seemed to know anything about it either." Wendy finished getting into the car and looked up at Beau.

"I don't believe it." Beau slammed the door shut and walked around to his side of the car. "Just what do you people do all day?" he asked, getting in beside Wendy and fumbling with his keys.

"Look Beau, don't get mad with me. I just do what I'm asked and this is a project we have never been asked to look at before. Okay?"

"It's just not acceptable. It's no wonder that corporate is firing everyone's ass in this branch." Beau started up the car and screeched out of the parking lot, nearly hitting another car as he exited. "Just what do you know about this project?"

"Only what I've read in the last hour." Wendy shuffled with the folders on her lap as she spoke. "And I didn't really understand a lot of that to be honest. It seems this is a prototype project that isn't fully developed yet."

"Everything we do here is a prototype, Wendy. Just what do you think Zygote Technologies actually does? We are at the cutting edge of software and biometric meta-technologies. We do what we do with the brightest people there are, and then sell our ideas to companies that can take them and commercialize them. I know we're only a Sales and Support organization here in Seattle, but my god, you need to at least know what the hell we do."

"Don't get mad with me, Beau. I may not be mister hotshot, but if I am to work on your team then you need to at least respect me."

Beau pulled his Mercedes over to the side of the road with a squeal of tires and let his hands drop from the wheel. "Look Wendy, you have absolutely no idea just what pressure we are under at Zygote do you? We are one of three companies looking to break into a three hundred million dollar a year turnover in this emerging technology. And if we are not the first then we might as well all pack up our bags now and go home."

"I'm just saying that not all of us are familiar with all our projects. We only support those that we have actually sold. That's why I was in Support, Beau." Wendy wound down her window and took in a deep breath.

Some of the color drained from Beau's face and he gripped the steering wheel of the car once more. "Yes Wendy. I am aware you were originally from Support. But I was told some of our brightest and best people were in Support. I was told that if anyone knew anything about our projects then Support was the group. Are you telling me I was told wrong?"

"We only know about those projects we support. Zygote doesn't give us a list of the projects that are under development or are trying to sell. Only those projects that have actually been sold. Didn't you know this?"

"Shit!" Beau banged his head on the steering wheel and then sat back in his seat. "Should we cancel today's meeting then? Maybe we should cancel meetings all week until the team has caught up with some of the projects we are actually trying to sell. I knew this company was messed up, but my god, talk about the right hand not knowing what the left hand does."

"Sorry."

Beau took another deep breath. "No, I'm sorry, Wendy. I just assumed everyone knew about all the projects. My bad. Never mind, we'll manage. I know a fair bit about this project and you can cover any technical issues I don't quite understand. Just go back to basics. If we're a little off kilter the customer probably won't even notice." Beau started the car and they rejoined traffic once more. "Look Wendy, I'm sorry. I'm under a lot of pressure at the moment and I really didn't understand how messed up it all is. I'm going to have to speak to corporate."

"Will I lose my job?"

Beau turned to face Wendy. "No, of course not. But corporate needs to fix this. They can't expect us to sell these projects without bringing everyone up to speed."

Twenty-five minutes later Beau pulled his car into a parking lot on the edge of a small business park and found a visitor's spot. "Just leave it all to me unless I ask you a question, okay?"

Wendy nodded, undid her seat belt and opened her door to get out. She took a firm hold of the files she was carrying and waited for Beau to join her from the other side of the car. "Let's do it."

Wendy followed Beau into the office and the two of them waited while the prospective customer was informed of their arrival. A few minutes later and they were sat in a conference room. Several other people arrived and introductions were made.

"Thanks for inviting us," Beau said, getting to his feet. "You know a little about what we do at Zygote but today I wanted to talk specifically about one of our latest projects. It's something radical and cutting edge and we see a lot of potential uses for it in the upcoming consumer-driven marketplace." He turned to Wendy. "Wendy, can I have the files, please?" Wendy pushed the project files over to Beau and watched as he shuffled them into his own kind of order. "Creating a Self-Replicating and Auto-Improving Software Environment, or as we call it, Project One-Eighty-Five." He waited for a few chuckles from the room before he continued. "I have in my hands here the blueprints for how all software companies of the future will be. We can do away with traditional programmers and leave nothing to chance. What we are talking about here is the opportunity to…"

Wendy tuned out as Beau went into one of his well-practiced sales pitches. She had heard them before and they were nearly all the same. Just a few words of difference or inflection, but basically the same. He was good. He knew how to keep the attention of a room of people. She looked around. They were all listening to him; some of them were making notes and others were simply nodding from time to time. A shiver went down her spine as her mind wandered back to the car journey. She hadn't seen that side of Beau before. Angry. In control. Dominant. She smiled involuntarily. It was kind of nice actually. At least he had apologized to her. He was part-human after all. She smiled again and found herself watching his lips as he talked. She looked down at the table embarrassed. What was she thinking? She had never even had a serious boyfriend before. She wasn't anywhere near as pretty as the other girls in the office. What chance did she have? Oh well. At least she got to work with him. Maybe she would learn something and make something of herself. That wouldn't be so bad. In the meantime she could dream. She could at least dream of those lips of his on hers. She blushed.

"Wendy?"

Wendy snapped her neck upwards. The room was staring at her. "Sorry?"

"Wendy," Beau repeated. "Maybe you could tell everyone a little about how seriously we take support in our organization?"

"Support," Wendy began. She knew this talk by heart too. She had had to practice it a thousand times on the phone to customers when they called in to the office. "Zygote Technologies values its customers as if they were each the only customer we have. We provide twenty-four seven call center availability that is staffed by experts in the field of all software technologies…"

9

Two-forty. It was already turning into a long day at work. Lucy stared up at the clock on the wall and watched the second hand tick around. Two-forty-one. Hopefully she could get out by five. It had been a very boring and uneventful week. Still, today was Thursday and Sabrina had said that several people were going out in the evening and that she was invited. On a school-night too! That was something to look forward to. Two-forty-three. She had missed a minute somewhere! Lucy stared at her laptop screen again and started to complete her weekly status report. The same as last week. Nothing had really moved forward and nothing unexpected had come up. Three minutes later and it was done. She saved it and closed the spreadsheet.

Perhaps a cup of green tea would help see her through the afternoon. Lucy got to her feet and wandered down the corridor to the kitchen. Half the office seemed to be out this afternoon. They had the right idea. The TV had said there might be some snow today and several people had called in to say they were working at home. But it was now the middle of the afternoon and although it was overcast outside it didn't look like it was going to snow. Lucy poured herself some hot water and took a green tea teabag from the cupboard above the sink. She looked out of the window, down onto the street below. The streets seemed mostly deserted. A few people were out walking but they were all wrapped up and looking cold and miserable. Lucy squeezed out the teabag and put it in the trash. She turned her back to the window and leaned back against the wall and lifted the cup of tea to her nose.

"Alright Lucy?"

Lucy looked up to see her boss entering the kitchen. "Yeah fine, Colin. Just getting a cup of tea."

"It's cold out today. And I don't think they have the heating set properly in the office."

"It's not too bad. I just needed something warm to drink."

"How's the status report?"

"All done. Not much has changed this week."

"Yes. It's been a fairly quiet week. Seems the threat of snow has kept several people out of the office." Colin crossed over to the coffee machine and pressed several buttons.

Lucy watched as the coffee machine made a number of noises and eventually spewed black gunge into a waiting cup. Everyone here seemed to drink coffee. And lots of it too. Lucy was happy to stick with drinking tea. "Do you think it will snow?"

"Probably not. I've lived here nearly twenty years and we very rarely get any serious snow. People make too much of it in my opinion." Colin took the filled coffee cup out from the machine and added some half and half. "Oh well. Better get back to my desk. I need to prepare the weekly management reports." He smiled at Lucy as he walked by and disappeared back up the corridor. Lucy took a sip of her tea and then walked back to her desk.

Three-twelve and two new emails. At last the analyst had replied to a couple of questions she had asked him earlier in the morning. He was one of the people who were working from home today. Lucy smiled. He had probably only just turned on his laptop. It seemed like there were lots of lazy people who worked in Nyble Storage. And to think that several of them commented on the sick days that she had taken. Lucy opened up her source files and scrolled down to the sections she had been asking about. At least she could make a few changes. That ought to see her through the last couple of hours before she left for the day. "Yeah, okay. I thought so," she muttered to herself. "I wish he'd said something earlier."

"Come on, hurry up," Sabrina said, pulling on her coat and standing by the door. "We're going to be late."

"And that matters because?" Lucy replied, hastily applying a little lipstick.

"Why were you so late home anyway? You knew we were going out tonight."

Lucy laughed as she dropped her lipstick into her purse. "Actually I thought I'd be home early tonight. I just ended up getting caught in some code I was writing."

"Well, hurry up. Let's go."

"Okay, okay. I'm ready." Lucy pulled her coat from the hook and slipped it on. "Where are we going anyway? Paddy's?"

"No. Tonight we're all meeting at Dunkles. It's a new dance club that's opened up on Broadway."

"Sounds very New York."

Sabrina laughed. "I don't think so. Let's go. You're okay to drive, yes?"

"I told you I would," Lucy replied. "It's work again tomorrow. I'm not drinking tonight."

The two women left the apartment and walked over to the battered car parked outside. "You should think about replacing this sometime too," said Sabrina as they got inside.

"It works and it's all I need for now. Stop complaining." The two women laughed as Lucy drove off. Sabrina gave directions and a little while later they were parked outside the latest nightclub that the area had to offer. "Who's going to be here?"

"Everyone probably. That is, everyone from the office. It seems Beau landed a big contract this week and we are all celebrating."

"Beau will be here?"

Sabrina turned and smiled at Lucy. "Yes, Beau will be here. But like I said, take it easy. Just watch him for a while. See what you think."

"What if he comes on to me?"

"Then play it cool. You know."

Lucy and Sabrina both giggled and linked arms as Lucy locked up the car before they walked over to the dance club entrance. They were soon inside and pushing their way through the crowded hall. "It's very busy," said Lucy.

"Can you see them?"

"I can't see anyone," replied Lucy, struggling to keep a hold of Sabrina as they pushed their way through people.

Finally Sabrina spotted her group at a big table in the corner and they both headed over to join them. "Hi, sorry we're late."

Lucy and Sabrina found themselves seats when two of the men got up and made some room. Sabrina introduced Lucy to several of the people she hadn't met before.

"Hi Sabrina, I thought maybe you weren't coming."

Sabrina looked up to see a short dumpy woman in a badly fitting black dress standing over her. "Hey Wendy. How's it going?" She scooted over a little to let Wendy sit down. "Wendy, this is Lucy, my room-mate. Lucy, this is Wendy."

The two other women said hello to each other and then ordered drinks from the waitress who had just arrived at their table.

"So you don't work at Zygote?" asked Wendy.

"No. I work at Nyble Storage. It's a cloud storage company," Lucy added, noticing the look Wendy was giving her.

"Cloud storage. Interesting." Wendy fidgeted in her seat a little. "And how do you like Melrose?"

"It's okay. A little cold and wet in the winter for my liking though."

"You'll enjoy the summers. Just wait a couple of months."

"There he is," Sabrina interrupted, poking Lucy in the ribs. "Over there."

Lucy followed Sabrina's gaze and saw a medium height, dark-haired and muscular man dancing opposite a short blonde woman. "Who's that he's with?"

"No idea. She's not from our company. Probably someone he's picked up tonight."

"He's really handsome, isn't he?"

"He is," replied Wendy. "Very."

Sabrina looked over at Wendy. "I didn't know you had a thing for him, Wendy."

Wendy blushed. "I don't. Well that is, not really. He is handsome though, isn't he? And very dominating."

"Wendy!"

"I can see what she means," said Lucy. "He certainly seems in control."

"You're just jealous, Sabrina," said Wendy. "If he was a woman you'd be all over him."

"Oo. Stop it! Please, I don't even want to imagine. You're sending chills down my spine. And not good chills I might add."

The three women burst into laughter and continued to watch Beau dancing on the floor. "You want to dance?" Sabrina asked Lucy after a little while.

"Sure." The two women got up from the table, squeezed past Wendy and made their way onto the floor. Soon they were lost in the music and conversation about the ideal dating partner.

"You can come back to my place if you like," the short blonde woman said a little later as she danced with the handsome man on the dance floor.

"If you like," Beau replied, nibbling on the girl's neck. "As long as you don't mind driving me."

"I didn't invite you to stay the night," the girl giggled, nuzzling up close.

"Then I promise I won't stay the whole night. Where do you live?"

"Bellevue."

"I can get a cab later. It's fine."

"If you're sure? It's just that I do have to go to work tomorrow."

"So do I."

The blonde girl took a step back from Beau and took his hand. "Let's go then. It's very noisy in here."

Beau glanced over at his table of work colleagues but they were all busily engaged in conversation. Just as well. He squeezed the girl's hand and followed her outside. "What's your name?"

"Jessica," she replied. "And what's yours?"

Beau smiled. He already knew her name. He had gotten it on their first kiss. "I'm Beau. Beau Tempest."

Jessica giggled again. "It sounds like something out of a romance novel. Something my mother would read."

Beau pulled up short. "You don't live with your mother, do you?"

"Of course not. I have my own apartment. Do I look like someone who would invite someone back to where I lived with my mother?" Jessica reached up and kissed Beau's cheek.

"I was just asking. I'm really quite shy you know."

Jessica squeezed Beau's hand tighter and wrapped her other arm around his back. "Shy, eh? Well I'm sure we can cure that. Come on. My car's just over here."

Beau breathed in deep. He could already smell the aroma of the night's promised success. Tonight he would explore another woman. Someone fresh and new. More experiences to live and wander through. He put his hand inside his jacket. The bag of mushrooms was there. As they reached Jessica's car, Beau pulled her close to him and kissed her passionately. "My shyness is fading away already." He released her and studied her face. She was already temporarily lost in the euphoria that was running through her head. "Let's get you home to bed."

10

Lucy put a hand to her forehead and grimaced. Another migraine. Four-forty-six. Why was it always so early in the morning? She squeezed her eyes tighter shut and tried to will the pain away but it was no good. Her head was thumping.

After taking a couple of Excedrins she crawled back into bed and pulled the covers over her head. It was going to be another bad today. At least she had got everything done at work the afternoon before. And it wasn't the drinks; she had only drank diet coke the night before. Maybe there was something in that? But probably not; she had been drinking it for years. Food? Nothing unusual. Noise? She had been going to nightclubs for years without getting migraines. No, it seemed like it was definitely something specifically to do with Melrose. It had only been since her arrival here that she had been getting them. And they were getting worse. Today she was definitely going to have to go to the doctor's.

Lucy screamed under her covers and tried to rub her temples. Nothing seemed to help and she lay as quiet as she could in the dark and imagined the minutes ticking by. She couldn't even bear to see the faint glow of the clock radio on her bedside table.

"Lucy? You okay?" Sabrina asked, coming into Lucy's bedroom some time later.

Lucy wriggled her head out above the covers and tried to peek out at the shadow standing in the lit doorway. "Migraine."

"I'm sorry. Is there anything I can do?"

Lucy shook her head. "I'll go to the doctor's later."

Sabrina backed out of the door. "Okay. See you later, sweetie. Take care." She pulled it shut behind her and Lucy got back under the covers.

The piercing light of day eventually forced Lucy to give up on sleep and struggle from her bed. Nine-twenty-two. She pulled on her dressing gown and made her way downstairs to find her laptop. A few minutes later she closed it back up and found her cell phone. "Yes, bad migraine… Urgent, yes… Nothing earlier?... Please?... Thanks. I'll be there. Goodbye." She hung up the phone and slumped back down on the couch. Some more Excedrin. She just wished the pounding would stop for a few minutes. Hopefully the doctor could give her something. There had to be a logical reason for it all. She just hoped it wasn't a brain tumor. She had read somewhere that unexplained bad migraines can sometimes be caused by brain tumors. She was too young for all that. She got up and wandered over to the kitchen. She poured herself some water and took a couple more Excedrin. She had about twenty minutes to get ready. No time for a shower.

"Hi," Lucy said to the doctor when she finally arrived in the room where Lucy had been waiting for the past fifteen minutes.

"Hello Lucy. Sorry to have kept you waiting." The doctor took a brief glance at Lucy's file. "What seems to be the problem today?"

"Migraine. It's my second one in about a week and they're getting worse. The Excedrins don't seem to make a difference."

The doctor touched a couple of fingers to Lucy's forehead and placed her other hand on the side of her neck. "Hmm, you don't seem to have a fever. And your pulse seems normal. Let's take your blood pressure." Lucy rolled up her sleeve and waited while the doctor took her blood pressure. "Seems normal too." She put the equipment back. "Second one this week?"

Lucy nodded. "I don't understand it. There doesn't seem to be anything in particular that triggers them. But when I get them I just can't do anything at all. I haven't got a brain tumor have I?"

The doctor laughed. "No Lucy. We did full scans the last time around. I'm sure that's not your problem. But something is definitely triggering them. And the Excedrins don't seem to work?"

"No. I have had to take a couple of days off work recently. It takes hours for the pain to disappear enough to go back to work."

The doctor read through Lucy's notes. "And you're sure you never had migraines when you were in England or in college?"

"No."

"Hmm. Are you allergic to anything that you know of?"

"No."

"Are you planning on getting pregnant any time soon?"

Lucy blushed. "No."

The doctor smiled. "I just have to ask. I'm going to write you a prescription for Almotriptan. It's something a little stronger. But you can't take it if you're pregnant or suffer from certain allergies. I just want to make sure."

"I'm quite sure."

"Good." The doctor scribbled a note on a pad she took from her pocket and handed it to Lucy. "Take one of these every time you feel a migraine coming on. You can take a second one a few hours later if the pain hasn't gone. But don't take more than that. Also, if they don't seem to work, contact me immediately. And if you start to feel dizzy or lightheaded, call me too. Make sure you read all the notes when you pick them up."

Lucy took the prescription from the doctor. "Okay."

"And either way, I want you to come back here after your next migraine."

Lucy nodded and got to her feet. "Thanks."

"And get some rest today. Don't go into the office. Make it a long weekend."

"Sure." Lucy smiled and walked back towards reception, through the open door the doctor was holding open for her. That was it. Five minutes of the doctor's time. And a prescription. This was surely healthcare at its best. The system in England seemed a lot better. Oh well, at least she had got to see the doctor as soon as she had needed. Lucy shivered as soon as the cold outside air hit her and she walked quickly over to her car. A quick stop at the pharmacy and she could get back home to bed.

* * *

"Where did you disappear to last night?" Sabrina asked Wendy as they poured themselves a coffee in the office.

"I went home early. There really wasn't anything exciting going on. And once I saw Beau dancing with that blonde girl, I lost interest in the evening."

"So you do like him?" Sabrina nudged Wendy in the ribs nearly forcing her to spill her coffee.

"No. Not like that. But I was hoping to talk with him. He is my new boss and maybe he can help me become a better salesperson."

"He had already left by the time Lucy and I went home."

"With that girl?"

"Don't know," said Sabrina. "I didn't see him leave."

"I think he must have done. He seems in a really good mood today."

"Wendy! What are you saying?"

Wendy laughed. "Well, you know…"

"Yes, I do know what you're suggesting. Like I said before, I find that thought horrific. Let's change the subject."

Wendy took a sip from her coffee. "So, you and Lucy? I saw you dancing?"

"Oh no. Nothing like that. She's definitely into men. She made that very clear to me. We were just having fun last night, that's all. I heard Beau fancies her though. But I tried to warn her off him a little." Sabrina leaned in closer to Wendy. "Actually I think he would be too much for her to handle."

"Too much for anyone, probably."

"Hey Wendy, have you ever suffered from migraines?"

"No, why?"

"It's just Lucy. She's had a few recently. Bad ones I think and I'm just a little worried about her. I told her to go see the doctor today. It's starting to interfere with her work."

"Migraines? My Mom used to get them."

"What did she do?"

"There was nothing she could do." Wendy took another sip. "Back then all you could do was take an aspirin and go back to bed. But they did disappear eventually. I'll have to ask her what happened. I'd forgotten all about them actually."

"Do you know anyone else that gets migraines?"

"No, I don't think so. And if they do I don't think they talk about it."

Sabrina emptied the remainder of her coffee out into the sink. "Nor me. It seems like it's a little rare up here. That's why I'm worried about her. I hope it's nothing serious. Maybe I'll go home at lunch time and check in on her."

"I'll come with you if you like. We can get a sandwich while we're out."

"Sure." Sabrina threw the empty cup in the trash. "Oh well, I guess I'd better get back to my desk."

"Me too," said Wendy. "I don't want Beau shouting at me again."

"What?" But Wendy was already halfway down the corridor before Sabrina could find out the answer to her question.

"You okay?" Sabrina asked a little later as she let herself into her apartment.

Lucy opened her eyes and looked up from the couch. "Yes, feeling much better. I'm just catching up on my sleep a little."

"Hello Lucy," Wendy said, closing the door behind her.

"Oh, hello Wendy," said Lucy.

"We brought you a sandwich." Sabrina pulled out several sandwiches from the bag she was carrying and handed one to Lucy. "Tuna?"

Lucy smiled. "Thanks."

"So what did the doctor have to say?"

"She gave me some tablets. Almo something. It seems to have done the trick. At least I've not got a brain tumor or anything."

"Of course you haven't," said Sabrina.

"Like in Sesame Street?" asked Wendy. The two women looked at Wendy. "Elmo?"

"Al-mo," replied Lucy. "But they did work like magic."

Sabrina pushed Lucy's legs from the couch and sat down next to her. "Are you okay? Really?"

"I'll be fine. The doctor said I just needed something stronger. I have to go back to see her next time I get a migraine. She wants to see how the new pills work." Lucy took a bite from her sandwich. "Thanks for stopping by."

"That's what friends are for," said Sabrina.

"Did you get off with Beau last night?" Lucy asked Wendy in between mouthfuls of tuna.

Wendy laughed. "I had the same conversation with Sabrina already. No, I left early. I think Beau left with that blonde woman."

Sabrina ran her fingers through Lucy's hair. "I told you he wasn't to be trusted."

"At least I answered the doctor's question correctly then."

"What do you mean?" asked Sabrina.

Lucy laughed and finished up the last of her sandwich. "She wanted to make sure I wasn't going to get pregnant before she gave me my new migraine tablets."

"Lucy!" screamed Sabrina. "Stop it."

"Shhh," said Lucy. "You'll give me my headache back."

11

"Come on in, Beau. Take a seat." Peter Ramsey sat back down behind his desk as Beau strode over to the seat in front of his desk. "Glad you could spare me a few minutes."

"What's up, Peter?" Beau straightened out his trousers a little and brushed away an imaginary piece of fluff.

"You know we have corporate here today, don't you?"

Beau nodded. "Yeah."

"Well I got a call last night from Clemmons that they're giving you the whole of the West Coast."

"What?" Beau tried to keep back a huge smile.

"Yes, the West Coast. All the way from San Diego to Seattle, and over to Boise and Las Vegas. Looks like someone has been watching you."

"Wow. Is it because of the sale the other day?"

"Who knows? They work in mysterious ways in corporate. You should know that by now. Bottom line is that they are making you Vice-President of Sales for the West Coast."

"Do I get another office?" This time Beau let the smile escape and he laughed out loud.

Peter sat back in his chair and smiled. "We don't have another office, Beau."

"I know, I was only joking. Just relieving the tension a little. You know."

"Oh, right."

"So what does this new job entail?"

"No idea. A bigger territory I guess. More planning and more travel. Less face time with the customers."

"Really? Oh well. I guess if that's what I've got to do."

"You'll be fine. Corporate obviously have their eye on you. Just don't mess it up."

"Right." Beau got to his feet. "That it?"

"Yes. Don't go breathing a word of it though. The suits will be here around ten I'm told. You're joining us for lunch. I'll see you later."

Beau nodded again, turned around and left the room and made his way back to his office. Another promotion. Things really were going better than he had expected. This had to be the work of the Anons. They certainly had kept their side of the bargain. Beau walked over to his chair and sat down. He pushed the pile of paper to one side and put his feet up on his desk. He smiled and pushed back a little in his seat and stared up at the ceiling. West Coast VP of Sales. Maybe the company was expanding. He didn't even know some of these other offices existed. He was going to need more staff. Maybe promote a few of the others in the office too. Maybe Wendy could take on a little bit more. He had been hard on her earlier in the week during their sales visit but she had dealt with him well. And she knew her stuff. Yes, maybe she would make a good director here at the office. He'd have to talk to the suits about that. Beau allowed himself a laugh. What was he thinking? He was going to be a suit now too.

"Well, Tempest, what do you think?" the gray haired Clemmons asked over lunch.

"Quite honestly I'm flattered, sir."

"Nonsense. By all accounts you've earned it." Clemmons allowed himself a little laugh. "All accounts."

Beau and Peter laughed along with Clemmons and tried to relax a little. Beau took another bite of his halibut and chewed thoughtfully.

"We bought out three companies on Friday," Clemmons continued. "All hush, hush at present you understand. It'll hit the press soon enough."

"Three companies?" Peter asked. "Which ones?"

"None you've ever heard of I'm sure," Clemmons replied. He leaned over a little closer to Beau. "But you're going to find out all about them for me."

"I am?"

"One in Las Vegas and one in San Diego. The other one can wait for a week or two. I want you to make trips down to see them. They're expecting someone from corporate, they just don't know who's coming."

"What do they do?"

Clemmons smiled. "That's for you to find out, Beau. You're going to need one of your technical people with you. Just go down, ask a few questions and make a few notes. I'm sure you'll like what you see."

"You don't know what they do? Why aren't the techies in corporate going down?" interrupted Peter.

Clemmons sat back in his chair a little and spooned some mashed potatoes into his mouth. As he chewed it over he let his gaze wander across to Peter. "Will you excuse us for a few minutes, Peter?"

"Sure, no problem." Peter put his fork down on his plate, took his napkin from his lap and placed it on the table. "I need to go to the restroom anyway." With a questioning glance at Beau he got to his feet and walked off towards the restroom.

"Sorry," continued Clemmons, "but there are a few things still on the hush, hush you understand." Beau nodded. "These companies we have bought out are very small and each doing some very special things. We need someone we can trust to work alongside them and make recommendations of which parts we can fold into our operation. I've been told by someone on the inside that you're our man."

"I am? But I don't understand."

"Let me just say this, Beau. There are skeletons in every closet and anonymous people can make things happen." Clemmons got to his feet. "I think I need to take a trip to the restroom too. Won't be long."

Skeletons in the closet? Just what was Clemmons implying? Beau took another bite of his halibut and watched as Clemmons walked across the room. Maybe someone at corporate knew about the Anons. Maybe there was more to this than he had realized. "Shit," he said out loud as Peter returned to the table. "Oh, shit!"

* * *

"So what's with the suits being here today?" Tim asked Sam as they sat in the coffee room during the lunch hour.

"No idea. Beau didn't say anything to me if that's what you're asking?"

"I was. Really? Nothing?"

"No. I didn't even know they were coming in today."

"They? I only saw one of them."

"No, there's two. One went to lunch and the other's still sat in Peter's office with the door closed. Not to be disturbed so I hear."

"Odd."

"Very. There's obviously something going on we don't know about." Sam took a sip of his coffee and let the cup stay close to his lips.

"Do you think we've been sold or something?"

"Could be. Certainly something is going on. There's been a lot of changes recently. Let's just hope we're not being downsized."

"Downsized? What's this?"

"Didn't see you come in, Wendy."

"Obviously." She wandered over and took a seat next to Tim. "What have you heard?"

"I haven't heard anything, Wendy. I was merely speculating a million things." Sam took another sip of his coffee. "Besides, you work for the man. What's he said?"

"Nothing. He has been in his office all morning. Even turned down a meeting I was supposed to have with him. But I guess we'll find out soon enough. We all just got a meeting invite to the large conference room at five today."

"Five? That's a little late. Definitely sounds like bad news," Tim said, getting to his feet. "Better go read the details."

Sam and Wendy got up from their seats as well and followed Tim as he walked back to his cubicle. "See you at five," Sam said.

* * *

"Thanks for attending at late notice," Clemmons said to the overflowing conference room. "I'll try not to take up too much of your time."

Wendy elbowed Sam and motioned towards the older man in the corner. "He's the other suit," she whispered.

"I know."

"But you don't know who he is, do you?"

"You do?"

Wendy nodded. "That's the president."

"The president? Harry S Fornton the third?"

"Yep. And he never comes visit the offices."

"I just have a few things I wanted to say," Clemmons continued. "Last week Zygote Technologies purchased three smaller companies in the fields of bio-technology and nano-technology and we will be incorporating several of their ideas into some of our products over the next twelve months. I wanted to tell you all this so you are not surprised when the press gets onto our story and rumors start to circulate." Clemmons glanced over at the president and waited for his nod. "There will no doubt be a lot of negative fall-out about our company. There are certain areas of the press that don't understand the things we do here and how we are moving technology forward into the twenty-second century. But I want you all to know that we are proud of the work you all do and we want you all to stay and reap the rewards of this burgeoning company. So I want to go on record today and tell you all that for each one of you that are still here in one year's time you will receive a fifteen percent bonus of your annual salary. Furthermore, if you are still here in three years you will receive another fifty percent bonus and be vested in a quarter of one percent holding in the new company." He paused to let what he had said sink into the room. Clemmons watched as people looked at each other in disbelief. He smiled. "And you all thought we were going to fire you."

Several people in the room laughed out loud. Clemmons waited for the noise to die down before continuing. "But, there are going to be some changes and I won't lie. Some of you aren't going to like them and some of you are going to leave this company. That's why I wanted to give you these promises now, up front. It's your choice." He waited again while the murmurs died down. "And one final thing. As of today I am pleased to announce that Beau Tempest is promoted to Vice-President of Sales of the West Coast. He will personally be overseeing some of the transitions of the new companies and will no doubt be reorganizing his department accordingly." Clemmons stood back and raised his hands. "Let's show our appreciation to Beau for all the great work he's done so far."

"Vice-President? He was only a Director for a week," Wendy said under her breath to Tim as they all applauded him out loud.

"I know," Tim replied. "I wonder what job you'll get now?"

"Yeah, right. I'll be lucky to keep my old one. He hates me. This could be his excuse to let me go. Or make me leave of my own accord. Remember what Clemmons said? *Some of you will leave the company.*"

"Thanks Wendy. Now we're all going to be worried." Tim stopped applauding and turned to face the front of the room where Clemmons was trying to regain everyone's attention. "Every day something happens in this place. Maybe it is time to find a different career after all."

12

There was a definite chill in the air as Wendy parked her car and walked across the parking lot early the following morning. The weather warned of scattered snow in the lowlands and for once it actually felt like it may snow a little. Wendy involuntarily shivered as she approached the entrance door and looked back over her shoulder. The parking lot seemed as full as usual. Perhaps others weren't taking the snow story seriously. She pulled open the front door and stepped inside. At least it was warm in the office. Wendy unbuttoned her coat and turned down the corridor towards her desk. She dropped her coat off on the back of her chair and headed back towards the coffee room.

"Hi there, Sam. You're in early today."

"Morning Wendy. Yeah, thought I'd better get a head start. We may have to leave early and who knows what changes will be instigated today."

Wendy smiled and poured herself a coffee. "Did you speak to Beau about all this at all?"

Sam waited for Wendy to sit down next to him before answering. "We did speak a little about it last night at Paddy's. Although it was more of a mini-celebration of sorts than anything else. Beau seemed a lot more relaxed once the suits were back at the airport."

"Well? What did he have to say?"

"Nothing of value really, and certainly nothing about you if that's what you were hoping to find out."

Wendy took a sip from her coffee. "No, I was just asking, that's all."

"Besides, I think you'll be fine. You won't get any pressure from him today for certain." Sam smiled. "Let's just say he will probably be a little delicate this morning. He had a few too many Tequilas last night."

"Beau got drunk?"

"I don't know about that but he certainly seemed to be on fine form. We got talking to a group of girls that came in and well, one thing led to another, and the shots came out."

"Did Beau get off with another girl?"

"Wendy! No, actually we both left for home together. I think Beau just wanted to unwind a little. We didn't even really talk about the office last night."

"Can I ask you something, Sam?"

"Sure. Although if it's personal I reserve the right to lie!"

"No, seriously. You know Beau pretty well, don't you?" Wendy put her coffee cup down and waited for Sam to nod an affirmation. "He must tell you things. About what he wants and what he likes?"

"He keeps a lot of things to himself, Wendy. I met him in our final year at college but back then I didn't know him that well. He had a reputation for being a bit of a loner, although he also had had some run ins with several of the women. He was the one that convinced me to join him here at Zygote. Just after he joined. I left another company down in Southern California to come here. I'd only been there a month too."

"So he's always been pretty persuasive then?"

"I guess so. You know what he's like, Wendy. He has an enchanting personality. You can't help but like the guy. Even when you want to hate him."

"You're right about that, Sam."

"And I may be his best friend at the moment but there are lots of things I don't know about him. I don't know anything about how he grew up and his family. I don't know much about his school life. He keeps a lot of things private."

"And his girlfriends?"

"That's another interesting topic. He hooked up with a girl in college and dated her for a long time. They always seemed to hang out together, go to concerts and things. I never saw them intimate though, not once. It always seemed a bit odd to me."

"You mean he's gay?"

"No, I don't think so. There were rumors he'd slept with other girls and his girlfriend seemed happy enough."

Wendy finished off her coffee and squeezed the paper cup in her hand. "So why did they split up?"

"She just sort of disappeared one day."

"What do you mean?"

"Well, like I say. One day she was with him and the next day she was gone. It was right after college. He even brought her here to Melrose I think. I assumed they were going to get engaged. Then one day I spoke to him and asked how she was doing and he said she was gone. No other explanation or anything. He's never spoken about her since."

"She left him?"

"Like I said, I don't know. She just disappeared and Beau won't talk about it. Since then he's dated a few girls I think, but nothing serious. He's certainly not been looking to date guys. And he doesn't appear to be that way to me at all."

"Did you ever try and contact the girl after she left? To find out her side of the story?"

"I didn't have any contact details and Beau would never say where she went. I assume she went back home. Somewhere in the mid-west I think." Sam sat back a little in his chair. "Anyway, I don't know why I'm telling you all this. It's not really relevant to here."

"No, but it's interesting. Besides it may explain a little about the way he is. I need to know as much as I can if I am to keep my job working for him."

Sam laughed. "You'll be fine, Wendy. I think he trusts you. He wouldn't have taken you on that sales call if he didn't."

"Did he say that?"

"He didn't need to. And no, he didn't say anything about it either if that's what you're going to ask." Sam got to his feet and pushed the chair back. "Anyway, I need to get back to work. There's a lot of things to get through today in case the snow comes in later." He touched Wendy on the shoulder. "I'll see you in a while. And stop worrying. Everything will be fine."

Wendy watched Sam as he left and continued to scrunch up the paper cup in her hand. Everything will be fine. She hoped so. After the things that Sam had just told her she definitely needed to change her tactics. A relationship with Beau definitely didn't seem a good idea. His track record with women wasn't good. She didn't want to be another failure in that long line. Besides, she needed the job too much. And if she was to make her bonuses she had to concentrate on the job and not on Beau. No, it was better to completely forget that idea. She got up from her chair and walked over to the trash can to throw the cup into it.

"Morning, Wendy!"

Wendy looked up. "Good morning, Beau." She felt a flush run across her face. "Busy day today." She didn't wait for an answer and quickly rushed off back towards her desk.

"Wendy? Hang on a sec," Beau said, rushing after her. "I need to talk to you about some of the changes I want to make."

Wendy stopped just short of her desk, took a deep breath and turned to face him. "Sorry."

"No problem," Beau replied, wandering over to stand next to her. "It's just that there's a lot of things to talk about. I really need to get this department organized. I've got a lot of travel plans to make as well." He took a step back and rested an arm on the walls of her cube. "Tell you what, why don't you come by my office in an hour. About nine-thirty?"

"Sure."

Beau let his arm drop and walked back towards his office. Wendy took another deep breath and picked up her coat from the back of her chair and hung it up on a hook. Hopefully it would be a good conversation. She was only just getting adjusted to her new position. Much more change wouldn't be good for her. She straightened her hair slightly, took a seat at her desk and turned on her PC. Anyway, first things first, she needed to see what emails needed answering.

"Take a seat, Wendy," Beau said a little later in the morning as Wendy entered his office. "I've been thinking about a few things and I'm going to need your help."

"My help?"

"Don't look so surprised. You know I'm going to have to rely on you for a lot of things. You're the person in my team with the most seniority here and the one who knows most about what we do. Isn't that true?"

"Well, I guess."

"Of course. So I'm going to need to rely on you when I go out of town."

"You're not staying here?"

"Yes I'm staying based here, it's just that I need to go visit the new companies we've acquired. Well, at least two of them anyway. And I'm going to have to go to Vegas in the next week or so. So when I'm gone I'm going to leave you in charge. You'll need to report in to me daily and let me know how things are going, but I'm going to want you to run the sales team. Do you think you can do that?"

Wendy sat open-mouthed in the chair and remained silent for a moment before replying. "I guess. I mean, I hadn't thought about it. What exactly will you want me to do?"

"Just co-ordinate the sales visits and make sure everyone is keeping busy. You know, nothing too difficult." Beau laughed. "Just teasing, Wendy. Lighten up a little. I told you things were going to have to change around here. And besides, who knows, there may even be a promotion in it for you if things turn out well."

"Of course. No problem, Beau. I can handle that."

"Right then, that's settled. We'll talk more a little later. Right now I've got a few phone calls to make."

Wendy took the signal to get to her feet and she left Beau's office and walked back to her desk. A possible promotion. Wow, things were definitely looking up for her. No need to even think about dating Beau now. That wouldn't be required. She allowed herself a broad smile as she opened up her email once more. Maybe things would work out really well at Zygote Technologies.

"Wendy, time to head out I think," Tim said later that morning, stopping by at her desk. "It's started snowing and it looks like it's going to be pretty heavy. Peter said we should all try and work from home."

Wendy looked up from her PC. "Okay. I'll pack my things up. Thanks." She watched Tim walk away and sat absentminded for a short while as her PC shut itself down. "Maybe I'll make some plans at home," she said to herself. "I'm sure Beau would be pleased with that." When she was sure everything was switched off, she stood up and pulled her coat from its hook and put it on. Then she turned towards the lobby and strolled off with a huge smile on her face.

13

Eleven-twenty-five. Lucy stared up at the clock. Out of the window she could see the first heavy flakes of snow falling. She got up from her desk and wandered over to the window. At least it didn't seem to be settling and hopefully it wouldn't last too long. She stared up at the dark gray sky and looked for a break in the clouds. Oh well, at least it was warm in the office. She walked back to her desk and continued with some coding.

Twelve-eleven. She looked up again from her work. It was still snowing. Looking around her, the office seemed to be mostly empty. Maybe people had gone for an early lunch. She got up and wandered down the corridor towards the break room. Nearly everyone had left. She stopped by Naveen's desk. "Where did everyone go?"

"Home I think. They all said the snow was not going to be stopping for a while and it was best to go home."

"So why are you still here?"

"I have things to be doing."

"Well, no one told me to go home. Great." Lucy walked back towards her desk and looked out of the window. The snow was already settling on the ground and she could see the streets were mostly deserted of cars. "Great. Well I guess I should go home too." She grabbed all her things from her desk, put her laptop in its bag and threw her backpack over her shoulder.

Outside it was cold and the snow swirled around her as she walked towards her car. There were already a couple of inches of snow on the windscreen and she ran around the car as quickly as possible brushing it off. Inside her car she turned it on and waited for the heater to kick in. The wipers swished back and forth across the windscreen brushing off fresh snow. With a little hesitation Lucy's car reversed out of its parking spot and turned to face the road. Fresh snow crunched under the wheels as the car mostly kept its grip in the parking lot. Soon she was on the main road and driving towards the freeway. At least the roads weren't too bad yet. The constant traffic was keeping them mostly bare and wet. Within ten minutes she had reached I-520.

"Damn it," she shouted out loud as her car joined a long line of others crawling along the freeway. "What's up with these people?" Twelve-forty-two. The snow continued to fall as her car inched along the freeway. She turned the radio on just in time to hear the weather report. "Great. It's a bit late to tell me not to get on the freeway now." Lucy switched radio stations and found some music to listen to. Then she wound down her window a little to stop the inside of the car from getting fogged up. At last the traffic was moving a little faster. Twenty miles per hour. She looked at her watch. Twelve-fifty-eight. At this speed she wouldn't be home for another hour. The snow continued to fall.

Finally the traffic started to thin out a little as Lucy reached the exit for Melrose. She spotted a gap in the traffic and moved across the freeway towards the right-most lane. She accelerated into a space and then braked so that she didn't get too close to the car in front. The car twitched a little and Lucy tried to correct it. She over-steered and the car started to get a little sideways on her. She hit the brakes again causing the car to spin around. Then she hit the gas to try and straighten it up only for it to spin around even more. She sat helplessly as the car slid across the freeway and came to a halt in a bank of snow at the side of the road. She put the car into reverse but it was no good. She was stuck. "Damn it!"

Lucy took a deep breath and gripped the steering wheel hard. She slowly pressed the gas once more but she could feel the wheels just spinning. And it was not going to do any good to try and drive forwards further into the snow bank. Finally she put the car into park and turned off the engine. She opened the driver's door, unbuckled her seatbelt and stepped outside to inspect the damage. The front of the car seemed to be okay. No obvious dents but she was certainly stuck. The front wheels had gone over the edge of the roadway and she wasn't strong enough to push the car backwards. It was going to need a tow truck. She leaned up against the side of the car and watched as the traffic drove by.

She was still about two miles from home, but she was going to have to leave the car. No tow truck was going to come out in this weather. It would have to wait until tomorrow. There was nothing else for it. She pulled open her door and reached inside for her backpack.

"Need some help?"

Lucy pulled her head back outside the car and turned around. A car had stopped in front of her and reversed back a little. Lucy smiled at the man that was walking back towards her. "You're a godsend," she replied. The man was wearing a gray jacket over a pair of faded jeans and at this moment looked the most wonderful thing she could have imagined.

"You look like you need some help," the man repeated. "I saw you spin out and thought maybe I could help. This weather always catches people out." He patted Lucy's car with his hand. "And this car's not built for the snow. It's a wonder you got this far."

"Thanks. Actually I've had this car a while and it's never let me down before."

The man laughed. "I'm Ben." He extended a hand towards Lucy.

"Lucy."

"Nice to meet you, Lucy." Ben wandered around the front of the car before returning to stand next to Lucy again. "I'm not going to be able to get it out of there."

"No, it'll need a tow truck. I was going to walk home."

"Do you live far? I can give you a ride."

Lucy laughed. "A ride? I don't know if I should accept rides from strangers."

"I can always let you walk if you want. It may take you a while. Especially in those shoes."

Lucy looked down at her feet. She had forgotten she was wearing her heeled work shoes. "Yes, I guess you're right about that. No planning ahead." She laughed. "I guess it won't hurt. I live close by anyway. Less than two miles. Near to Melrose city center."

"I'm going your way then. Come on, let's get back in the warm." Ben reached out a hand. "Here, give me your backpack."

Lucy handed Ben her backpack and followed him to his car. She waited while he opened the door for her and she climbed inside. "Nice," she said as he got into the driver's seat.

"I haven't had it long. Actually I wanted an SUV so that I could go up into the mountains. It seems to handle the snow pretty well." He pulled his door shut and handed Lucy her backpack. "So, where to?"

Lucy gave Ben directions and he pulled back into the traffic and took the off-ramp from I-520 towards Lucy's apartment. Ten minutes later they were parked outside. "Thanks. I really appreciate it," Lucy said, opening the door and stepping down. "Thanks again."

"Hold on, wait a moment." Ben leaned over towards Lucy. "Can I get your number? I mean well, if you don't mind that is. Maybe we can go for dinner after you've got your car back."

"I don't know, it's just that…"

"Please? What you see is what you get. I promise I'll behave."

Lucy laughed. "Alright. But just dinner. We'll see how it goes." She gave him her number and shut the car door. She watched Ben drive away before she hesitantly walked towards the apartment. After a few near slips she was safely inside.

"Where have you been?" asked Sabrina. "I was home hours ago.

"It's a long story." Lucy slumped down in the chair next to Sabrina. "I crashed my car."

"What?"

"It's okay. It just sort of slid off the road. It's stuck in a snow bank. I'll get it towed tomorrow. A nice guy gave me a ride home."

"Really? Do tell." Sabrina leaned forward in her seat. "What does he look like?"

"I don't know. Mid-twenties I guess. Tallish. Dark hair. Interestingly dressed. Good sense of humor. And most of all he appears to be a gentleman."

"A gentleman," Sabrina repeated, laughing. "Not many of those in Melrose. And what do you mean, interestingly dressed?"

Lucy laughed. "He had on a dark gray jacket over faded jeans. Very odd I thought to myself. That's all."

"And what's his name?"

"Ben."

Sabrina nodded. "Yeah, he sounds like a Ben."

"What's that supposed to mean?"

"Nothing. You know. Just sounds like a Ben." Sabrina got to her feet and wandered over to the kitchen. "Tea?"

Lucy nodded. "Yeah, he seems nice. He's going to take me to dinner."

Sabrina filled the kettle and put it on the stovetop. "He didn't waste much time then."

"He wasn't like that. He was just, you know, normal. I think…" Lucy stopped mid-sentence as her phone started to buzz.

"Well, answer it then," Sabrina shouted out, watching as Lucy just stared at her phone.

"I think it's him."

"Answer it!"

"Hello… Yes, this is Lucy… Hi… Fine, no problems. I'm just making a cup of tea." Lucy stuck out her tongue at Sabrina who was making faces from the kitchen. "That's good… Yes, I know… When?... Sure, that would be fine… I'll look forward to it. Bye."

"Well?"

"We're not going for dinner."

"He dumped you already?"

"No, he suggested maybe going for a walk on the trail first. He said we could talk more that way."

"In this weather? Are you crazy?"

"Well obviously not until it stops snowing and it warms up a little. He said at the weekend."

"And you're okay with that? Maybe he's cheap and can't afford dinner. I mean, you did say he dressed weird too."

"He must have some money he was driving a nice new SUV."

"Maybe he spent everything on that and there's nothing left to spend on you."

"Will you shut up, Sabrina? Is that tea ready yet?"

14

Ten-twenty-two. Still plenty of time to get ready for her date. If she should call it a date. Lucy and Ben had already spoken a couple of times during the week. He had even offered to take her back to her car the morning after the snow storm but Sabrina had already helped her out. Thankfully the roads had been clear and a tow truck soon got the car out of the ditch at the side of the freeway. Also thankfully, there hadn't been too much damage. The garage had fixed it up a day later and Lucy already had the car back home again as she sat in her bedroom contemplating which of her heavy sweaters to wear on her upcoming walk with Ben.

The week had gone by fairly quickly and uneventfully. Lucy had also complained to her bosses that no one had told her that everyone was going home early. For some reason she had been left off a critical email distribution list, along with four other people, and so Nyble Storage had had to update its emergency procedures to make sure it never happened again. They even offered to pay for the damage to Lucy's car which in the end had made things a lot better for her. Sabrina had also suggested she think about getting a new car; something that would suit her better for the Melrose winters. This was something she hoped to talk to Ben about today on their walk.

Ten-thirty-three. The crimson red roll-neck sweater. Probably the best compromise between warmth and fashion for a first date. The weather woman had said that temperatures would struggle to get above forty-five on this Saturday morning and there was a chance of drizzle later in the afternoon. She just hoped the walk wasn't going to be too long.

"Lucy, he's here," Sabrina said, poking her head around Lucy's door.

"I'll be there in a couple of minutes."

Sabrina gave Lucy a thumbs up and pulled the door closed behind her again. Lucy smiled. She guessed she must have Sabrina's approval. She picked up her coat, put a brush through her hair one more time, made sure her touch of lipstick was okay and finally said a small prayer before she opened the door and walked out into the living room.

Ben got up from the couch where he had been sitting. "Hello Lucy. You look great. Sorry the weather isn't any better."

"Hi Ben. Thanks. It was difficult knowing what exactly to wear. They said it may drizzle this afternoon."

"No problem. I even brought an umbrella although I don't really think we'll need it." He stood awkwardly by the couch. "Are you ready?"

"Sure." Lucy didn't know whether she was supposed to hug Ben or not. In the end she just ushered him over towards the door. She saw Sabrina trying to suppress a huge smile in the background. "See you later, Sabrina."

"I managed to get my car fixed," Lucy said as they walked towards the trail. "My company even paid for the damages."

"They did?"

"Apparently they left me off an important emergency distribution list. That's why I was left at the office after everyone else went home. I think they felt guilty for my spin out." Lucy waited to cross the road as a few cars went by. "Sabrina said I should use the opportunity to buy a new car."

Ben and Lucy crossed the road and made their way onto the trail. It seemed mostly deserted. "It does look very dated, Lucy."

"I know, but I'm not sure if I can afford a new car. I was going to ask you, was yours expensive?"

"You're very direct aren't you?"

Lucy blushed. "I am?"

"Girls don't normally ask the price of a man's car on a first date. At least I believe that to be a rule." Ben laughed. "It's okay, I'm just teasing you."

"It's the English in me. We're always kind of direct."

"I thought the English were shy people."

"It's a myth we pass about. It protects us from the world and allows us to get everyone else's secrets from them."

"Really?" Ben stopped and stared at Lucy. "This is part of your plan to get to know all about me without me realizing?"

Lucy laughed. "It was. I think I've just given the game away." She continued to walk the trail again. "By the way, where are we going? I've only walked this trail a little bit before."

"Well, if we walk about four miles along here we'll come to a big pub where they make their own beer. They do good food too. I figured we could have some lunch there and then walk home again."

"One hour there, one hour for lunch and one hour to walk home? You're confident aren't you?"

"I am? Is that too long for a first date? I figured it was like going to the movies and having some food. Only this way we get a chance to talk too."

"Lighten up will you? I can see my humor is going to take a time for you to get used to. That is if you're not completely square?"

"No, I'm not. At least I don't think I am." They both moved over slightly on the trail as a small group of cyclists rode past.

"It's a bit cold to be out cycling, don't you think?" Lucy asked.

"Not really. It keeps you really warm. I would usually be cycling the trail on a Saturday. That is if I wasn't walking it with a woman."

"You cycle?"

"A lot. How about you?"

Lucy shook her head. "No, not me. I think I'd be on the ground more than on the bike."

"So what do you do to stay fit then?"

"Ah, so personal questions from you too now?"

"Well, no, not really. I'm just…"

"Relax Ben. Just teasing."

Ben smiled and the two of them continued to stroll along the trail exchanging trivialities of conversation as they went. Eventually they reached the pub that Ben had mentioned and they went inside and were seated at a table near the window for lunch.

"Four hundred and ninety-nine a month by the way," Ben said.

"What is?"

"The car. It costs me four hundred and ninety-nine dollars a month to lease it."

"I can't afford that much. A couple of hundred at most is all I can afford."

They both ordered a beer and some appetizers from the server and unbuttoned their coats as they warmed up a little after their walk.

"I never did ask you," said Ben, "exactly what you do for a job?"

"I'm a programmer. For a cloud storage company." Lucy noticed the confused look on Ben's face. "What?"

"Cloud storage? Okay so I know I'm not into all this technology stuff, but what is cloud storage? Don't tell me people have found a way to store clouds now to provide rain whenever they want to?"

Lucy covered her mouth as she burst out laughing. "No. That's hilarious." She took a sip of her beer and set it back down again. "The cloud is just a term for somewhere on the Internet. It's a place where people can keep work they are doing without having to keep it on their own personal computer. It's just called the cloud. So cloud storage is the ability to look after anything you do without it being on your PC. Then you can access that information from wherever you are in the world, from any PC that is connected to the Internet."

"Well thank you for the lesson, professor," Ben said. "I feel suitably schooled."

"Sorry. It's just what I do."

"No need to apologize. Actually I really do know very little about technology. I am in the car industry. I'm an assistant manager at the Chrysler dealership downtown. That's why I drive the car I do. I get them at a very reduced price. Otherwise I couldn't afford it."

"So you were just trying to impress me?"

"Sorry if I misled you."

"Relax, Ben. You're going to have to work out my sense of humor." Lucy fingered her glass a little as the server arrived with their appetizers.

"I guess that's a good sign then. You're already talking about the future."

Lucy smiled. "Maybe."

* * *

"So, what was he like then?" Sabrina asked after Lucy plopped into the chair next to her.

"Alright."

"Only alright? That Mister Hottie was only alright?"

Lucy laughed and ran a few fingers through her hair, twisting it a little as she did so. "He was nice. Kind of different. He works at a car dealership."

"He sells cars?"

"More of a manager really, learning how to run the business. He was sent here by head office to learn about things. He knows nothing about technology though. In fact there wasn't really a lot of things we had in common."

"So it's not going anywhere then?"

"I didn't say that."

Sabrina leaned forward in her chair and grabbed a hold of Lucy's arm. "So tell me then, will you? You drive me crazy with all this suspense."

Lucy laughed and slapped Sabrina's arm away. "I haven't made up my mind yet. He's also really big into cycling apparently. He wants me to go on a cycle ride with him when it gets a little warmer. I'm not sure if I want to do that. But he also wants to go snowboarding in the mountains. I told him that sounds like fun."

"He sounds a bit of a fitness geek."

"He seems pretty fit." Lucy smiled again.

"And he kissed you?"

"Sabrina!"

"Well?"

"We hugged and he kissed my cheek. He really does seem a gentleman."

"Or maybe he doesn't fancy you."

"Don't say that, Sabrina."

"It's just a possibility. You know most men just want to get in our pants."

"No, he just seems to be nice, that's all. Besides, we're going to go on another date next week."

"So you like him then? That's good. You won't need to go after Beau anymore."

"I'd forgotten about Beau. Maybe I should go on a date with him too and then I can decide which one I prefer most."

"Really?"

"Just teasing, Sabrina. You know I'm not like that. No, Beau can wait. He can be in the wings in case things don't work out with Ben."

"Don't ever tell Beau that. I don't think he's a stay in the wings kind of guy."

"Well, these men need to know their place. After all it's us girls that run this world!"

"Amen sister," Sabrina shouted. "Let's drink to that."

15

"What's up Sam? Come on in." Beau put his pencil down and sat back in his chair as Sam came into his office and closed the door behind him.

"Just wondered if you had time for a chat, that's all." Sam sat in the chair on the other side of Beau's desk and crossed his legs. He picked up a paperweight from in front of him. "You've been so busy recently and it feels like some of the fun has gone out of our friendship. I just wanted to make sure everything was still okay?"

"Everything's fine, Sam. I'm just a little busy with the new job and all the responsibilities. I have so many staff and new projects that I haven't had a chance to even relax for a minute. I'll try and find some time for us at the weekend."

"Sure."

"Anything else?"

Sam put the paperweight back down on the desk. "Anything else? You're dismissing me already, Beau?"

"Well I said we'd talk over the weekend."

"Maybe some of the rumors that are going around the office are true." Sam got to his feet. "Try and carve some time out for me at the weekend."

Beau got to his feet. "Sit down. Sit down. Sorry, you're right. You're my best friend. Sit down." Beau waited to sit again until Sam had retaken his seat. "Now what do you mean, rumors?"

"Just what I hear in the office. That now you're in charge everyone is worried about their job and about how you might fire them all."

Beau laughed. "Fire them? Most of them don't even report into me. Why would I fire them? If anyone would it would be Peter. He's the head of the office. I may be a Vice-President now, but I certainly haven't been given a task to fire everybody." Beau wiped a little sweat from his face. "Who's been saying this?"

"People, Beau, just people. I'm not going to tell you who's been talking. You know I wouldn't do that."

"But why do the staff think I will be firing people?"

"You've got to admit you've got a little scary recently. Even Wendy worries every time you ask her to do anything."

"She does? She seemed fine last time I spoke to her."

"Look Beau, it doesn't really matter about who, it's more about the what." Sam ran his fingers along the edge of Beau's desk and examined the dust that had collected. "The point is you're always gruff and direct now. You're not your old laid back self. I sometimes think it was no wonder your last girlfriend left you."

Beau got to his feet. "That relationship is none of your business. I wish I hadn't even told you." Beau pointed a finger at Sam and continued speaking. "I hope you haven't been spreading rumors about me around the office either."

"Chill, Beau. Chill for goodness sake. I may know that you and women aren't exactly the best combination in the world, but I'm not going around telling everyone." Sam leaned back in his chair. "Although Wendy did ask about your ex-girlfriends the other day."

"Sam!"

"Chill. Seriously, Beau. You need to relax a little. We all work together, remember? There's bound to be a little talk about one thing or another in the office. No harm."

Beau crossed to the side of his desk and walked towards his office door. "I think perhaps you should leave, Sam. Before I say something I'll regret. Look, we're at work now and you're interrupting my flow for the day. I don't want to get into an argument with you, so let's chat again later in the week. Like I said."

Sam got to his feet. "Sure, Beau. Sure. Just chill out a little and remember you've got humans working for you, not damn software programs." He waited for Beau to open the door and walked straight out of the office without giving Beau a second look.

Beau closed the door behind Sam and returned to his desk. "Shit! Why did he have to bring all that up?" He threw himself into his chair, picked up and snapped his pencil in two and threw the pieces into the trash can.

The only downside to having Sam working at Zygote Technologies was that he knew a little of Beau's past; the time before he had started work. Still, he didn't know everything. And he certainly didn't know the complete story about his ex-girlfriend. Thank god. By the time Sam came to Melrose, she had gone. At least as far as Sam was concerned. That seemed such a long time ago now but only just over a year had passed. So much had happened in that time. Anyway, enough about that. He had more serious things on his mind.

Somehow he had to get rid of Peter. If he was going to lead the company and do all the things he wanted to do then he needed Peter out of the picture. He just wasn't sure how that was going to happen. Beau smiled. Unless the people at corporate already planned to do that for him. But he doubted it. No, he was going to have to take matters into his own hands.

Beau reached into his drawer and pulled out another new pencil from the large supply that was stacked inside. As his mind wandered, he doodled all over the paper blotter sat on his desk. He pulled himself to and stared down at what he had been drawing. His blotter was covered with pictures of demons. At least they looked like demons. They had evil faces with two horns and tongues that lollopped idly from big mouths. Some had bulging blood-stained eyes and others spiky hair and short beards. All in all there were about ten of the demons. An involuntary shiver worked its way down Beau's spine. What was he doing? Why was he drawing demons? And then he noticed. In the middle of the sheet of paper. There were a group of people, much smaller than the other faces, and these people had limbs hanging off them and were in various stages of decomposition. He couldn't tell who they were from their faces, but they were clearly people from his office. He knew that somehow. "My god," he muttered to himself. "What am I doing?"

Beau stumbled to his feet and threw the pencil down. He walked backwards towards the window and clung onto the wall. Then he turned around, walked over to the window and stared out into the parking lot. There was no denying it. He had somehow become an evil person. He was not an innocent young man any more. Something had changed him. He knew what it had been. He even knew when it had been. No matter how he tried to deny it. Now there was no turning back. Now he craved more power and he was going to let nothing stand in his way. He had to be in control. He nodded to himself. Yes, Peter was going to have to go.

Beau crossed back to his desk and picked up the phone. He dialed an extension and there was a voice at the other end. "Yeah, sorry Sam. I don't know what came over me. You're right of course. As always. Let's meet for a drink tonight. Seven-thirty?... Great. See you at the Queen's Arms?... Thanks, bye." He put the phone back down and sat in his chair. Then he tore off the paper blotter sheet, screwed it up into a ball and threw it in the trash. "Time to plan the rest of my week."

* * *

The Queen's Arms was not like most other pubs and bars in Melrose. In fact it was known for its eclectic staff and clientele. Beau often chose it as a meeting place if he wanted to go somewhere local where he wouldn't bump into anyone he knew. He had arrived at about six-thirty, just after the happy hour rush had died down, and secured himself a small table in the corner of the room that made up the bar area. The pub was an *over 21* place and it was nice to go somewhere and not to listen to the screams of children having dinner. A mostly empty pint of Speckled Hen sat in front of him as he jotted down a few more notes and watched the clock over the door that slowly ticked towards seven-thirty. The other thing about the Queen's Arms that Beau mostly liked was the fact that the servers left you alone. In fact they were known for it. To some it was a source of complaint, but to Beau it mostly suited him when he wanted peace and quiet.

"You're here already then?" Sam asked, sitting down next to Beau. "I thought I was early."

Beau glanced up at the clock again. "You are." He closed his notebook and slipped the pencil in his jacket pocket. "What you having?"

"What are you drinking?"

"Speckled Hen."

"I'll have one of those then."

Beau looked up and tried to catch the attention of one of the servers. He looked around the room but couldn't see any. There was only the barman and he was deep in conversation, polishing a glass, with one of the customers sat at the bar. "Looks like it may be a while."

"No worries." Sam slipped off his coat and put it down on the chair next to him. "Look, I'm sorry about what I said this morning."

"No. It was my fault. You were right. I've been in a different mood recently. I have to change the way I am perceived at the office. That's why I invited you here tonight. I need you to help improve my image at the office."

Sam laughed. "And how am I supposed to do that?"

"We'll brainstorm over it. A bit like in the old days when we both first started working. Do you remember?"

Sam laughed some more. "Those days involved a lot of alcohol, Beau."

"Well if we could only get served we could try it again." Beau looked around. "Where is that girl?" He finally caught the eye of the barman and threw up his hands in question. Beau turned back to Sam as the barman went off in search of the server. "I was thinking a little earlier just how serious this job has become. I've gone off track a little somewhere. That's why I need to speak to you. You're still on the good side."

"What would you like?" the gum-chewing server asked, impatiently bobbing by the side of their table.

"I'll have another Speckled Hen and my friend would like one too. Thanks." The server started to walk off. "And we would like menus too, please," he shouted after her.

"Why do you come here?" asked Sam. "You're never happy with the service."

"I know. I keep asking myself the same question. I think the only reason is the fish and chips to be honest. They are really good."

Sam smiled. "I know what you mean. Actually I like the shepherd's pie. I'll probably get that again. I usually do."

"So what's your secret?"

"To what?"

"Staying relaxed in the office. You never seem to be stressed or angry."

"I don't have the job you do, Beau. If I did I'd probably be a stress case too."

"But it's more than that, isn't it? I mean you have a great attitude on things at work. How do you do it?"

"I guess I leave my job at the office. I enjoy my time at home and then I…"

"Two Speckled Hens." The server put the two beers down, picked up the empty glass from in front of Beau and turned to walk away.

"Menus?"

"I'll be right back." The server smiled and Beau noticed the bright blue gum stuck between her teeth.

"It's okay. I think we know what we want. I want the fish and chips and my friend wants the shepherd's pie."

The server smiled again and walked off towards another table.

"Maybe I would have had something different," said Sam.

"You want to eat tonight or not?"

Sam laughed. "Yeah, I guess so. So anyway, like I was saying, I leave my job at the office."

"I don't know if I can do that. Especially if I am going to run the whole thing soon."

"You are?"

"Well, only if I can find a way to get rid of Peter."

"Beau? What are you saying?"

"Just supposing. Look Sam, I haven't come this far to stop now. I've been thinking too and I think it's time I took over the management of this office. And I need your help. Yours and some brainstorming with beer." Beau raised his glass. "Cheers. Come on, drink up. We've got a lot of planning to do."

16

Nine-thirty-six. Lucy still had a little time to get herself ready. She had persuaded Ben to join her in the weekly trip to church. She smiled to herself. He hadn't been at all keen to go either. In the end they had struck a deal. Ben would go with her to church in the morning and in the afternoon they would cycle along the trail to a couple of wineries. Thankfully the weather looked like it was going to cooperate. Lucy brushed her hair one more time and set the hairbrush down in front of her on the dresser. She leaned back in her chair and breathed in deep. It had been a busy few days with lots of unexpected twists and turns but maybe this year was going to turn out to be a great one after all. Maybe she had made the right decision to move here to Melrose. She had thought a lot about Ben the last couple of days too, and she had decided that although he wasn't her typical kind of guy, she was going to give it a go. After all, there were still lots of things about him she did like. And she felt relaxed when she was with him. There didn't seem to be any pressure.

Nine-fifty-five. Time to get serious about things. Lucy finished applying her lipstick and picked up her purse from the bed. After a final glance around her room she opened the door and made her way to the kitchen.

Sabrina was curled up on the couch, still in her pajamas, with a blanket pulled over her. "Morning," she yawned.

"Morning, Sabrina. Looks like the weather will be cooperating today."

"So you're actually going on that bike ride?"

Lucy laughed. "I guess I am. It'll be fine. I mean, it's only a few miles."

Sabrina pulled the blanket up higher and tried to tuck her bare feet into it. "Rather you than me."

"Thanks."

"There's some coffee made if you want some."

"Thanks but I'll make myself some tea. I still have thirty minutes before Ben gets here. Do we still have milk?"

"There should be some left."

Lucy put some water in the kettle and set it on the stove. Then she looked inside the fridge to hunt out some milk. "There's only a little bit left. One of us will have to get some more later. I'm going to use the last of it." She didn't wait for Sabrina's reply and started to make herself a bowl of cereal. A few minutes later she was sat in the chair beside Sabrina, sipping on her tea and eating her cereal. "What you watching?"

Sabrina looked up from her blanket. "Don't know. Some documentary on forensics. It seems interesting."

"It's a little gruesome for a Sunday morning, isn't it?" Lucy got up and took her empty bowl back to the kitchen. "Call me when Ben arrives." She took her mug of tea and wandered back into her bedroom.

"Lucy, Lucy! He's here. Come answer the door."

Lucy opened her eyes to the sound of Sabrina shouting from the other room. She wiped her mouth and jumped down from her bed, not stopping to look in the mirror. "Hi there, Ben," she said, opening the door.

Ben laughed. "Morning, Lucy. In a hurry this morning?"

"What?"

"Sorry, it's just your hair."

Lucy reached up a hand to brush her hair down and pulled Ben inside the apartment. "Sit down over there. Talk to Sabrina. I won't be a minute." She made her way back towards her bedroom, pushing Ben in front of her as she went. "Sit here."

"Hi," Ben said to Sabrina. "What you watching?"

Lucy shut her bedroom door behind her and went over to stand in front of the mirror. Oh well, it could have been worse. She took her brush from the dresser and ran it through her hair one more time. A minute later she was done. "You ready then?" she asked Ben, walking back into the living room.

Ben looked up from the chair. "Sure." He eyed Lucy up and down. "Very nice."

"You're driving, right?"

Ben laughed. "Oh yes, I'm driving."

"See you later, Sabrina," Lucy shouted out as she and Ben left the apartment. She turned to Ben. "And don't look so worried. It's only a church."

Ben and Lucy arrived at church about ten minutes later and made their way to a seat on the left hand side of the very large room. Ben looked nervously around the room before sitting down next to Lucy.

"I've never been to church before," he said.

"Never?"

"No never. Not even for a wedding or a funeral."

"Well, there's a first time for everything." Lucy took a hold of Ben's hand. "And there's nothing to worry about. It's not like they're going to be calling you out for anything. Just relax."

Ben smiled and squeezed Lucy's hand. Maybe church wouldn't be so bad after all.

"Will you stop laughing?" Lucy kicked the wheel of her bike for what seemed like the hundredth time.

"Just get on it, will you?"

"I'm trying."

"Do you need me to help you? Or perhaps you need some training wheels?" Ben laughed out loud again.

Lucy let out a mock scream and climbed on the bicycle once more. She sat back on the seat and pedaled a few more steps before wobbling and nearly falling off again. "It's impossible."

"It's a bike, Lucy. You've ridden a bike before. Stop worrying about it and just ride."

"Lucy looked up at Ben. "It's been years since I've ridden a bike okay, and somehow my center of balance seems to have changed."

Ben laughed again.

"Ben!" Lucy blushed. "That isn't what I meant at all."

"I didn't say anything."

"Don't. Don't say another word. If you do then I'm going to put this bike back inside and shut myself away in my bedroom." She looked at Ben and dared him to speak but Ben remained silent. Then Lucy tried once more to cycle down the path. Finally with a wobble and a weave she managed to stay on the bike and headed off into the distance. Ben quickly raced off after her.

"See, it's not so difficult."

"We haven't discussed stopping yet."

Ben slowed his bike down as Lucy attempted to weave around two people that were walking on the trail, nearly knocking one completely from her feet. "Sorry," he called out as he passed. "My girlfriend's new to cycling."

Lucy waited until Ben caught her up again. "Girlfriend? Did you just call me your girlfriend?"

"Aren't I?"

Lucy looked straight ahead again and tried to concentrate on staying roughly in the middle of the trail. "It's a bit early to say. I haven't decided yet."

"Well if you want to get safely to the wineries and back you had better make up your mind. A lot can happen to an unfortunate cyclist between here and there."

Lucy laughed. "We'll see."

Steadily Lucy got her confidence back as she continued to ride along the trail and soon she was cycling as straight a line as Ben and avoiding the walkers with ease. Fifteen minutes later they climbed the path that led from the trail and dismounted their bikes.

"Which winery do you want to go to first?" Ben asked. "There are at least half a dozen here."

"You choose. I've only been to a couple before. I don't know a lot about wine really."

"That makes two of us then." He climbed back on his bike. "Come on. This way."

Lucy and Ben spent the next hour or so visiting a couple of the wineries and tasting the various wines that were on offer. Ben bought a bottle of 2008 Syrah from one of them and put it into his backpack. Soon they were back on the trail again, headed for Lucy's apartment.

"We'll have to drink this with a nice steak meal," said Ben. "Maybe I'll cook for you next weekend if you'll let me."

"You cook?"

Ben laughed. "Yes, I cook. I have to. I live on my own and no one else is going to cook for me. Actually I'm pretty good. I do a mean burger."

"You said steak."

"I can do steak too."

"Maybe it's better if I cook the meal," Lucy said, swerving to avoid a walker at the last minute and nearly knocking Ben from his bike.

"You concentrate on the cycling and I'll concentrate on the cooking. You never know, you might like it."

Lucy smiled. "Okay."

"You want a quick drink before you have to go home?" Ben asked.

"We've just been at the wineries."

"I know, but we only had a few sips of wine. Besides the ride home will have flushed it out of our systems. I was thinking we could stop at that Irish pub in Melrose."

"Paddy's?"

"Yes, that's the one. I've never been there before."

Lucy laughed. "It's sort of my local."

"Okay. Somewhere else then."

"No, that's not what I meant. Sure, we can stop there for a quick drink. This cycling has made me quite warm. A cold beer would be good before I go home."

"I'll race you to the end of the trail then," Ben shouted, sprinting off into the distance.

Lucy got up out of her seat and raced off after Ben. She chased as hard as she could but she was a good ten lengths behind Ben when he finally pulled up. "That was unfair," she said, out of breath. "You started before me."

"Maybe you'll beat me next time."

Ben and Lucy cycled up to the road and had soon parked up their bikes outside Paddy's. Inside they found a table in the corner and waited for the server to come and take their order.

"It's happy hour all day today," the server said, opening a menu to the back page and putting it down on the table in front of them. "Can I get you started with a drink?"

"I'll have an IPA," said Ben.

"Me too," said Lucy.

Lucy squeezed up next to Ben and held the menu up for them both to read it. "I'm actually a little hungry."

"It's all that exercise. What do you want?"

"How about some potato skins?"

"That sounds good."

Lucy put the menu back down on the table and took Ben's hand in hers as they waited for the server to return with their drinks.

17

The past week had been packed full of twists and turns for Beau. Suddenly he had been propelled into upper management in the office. Now he was the focus of attention of the corporate office. Everything was starting to come together. The only thing that stood between him and complete control of the office was Peter. And he and Sam had discussed that the other evening. He smiled to himself as he remembered some of the crazy ideas they had talked about. In the end Beau had decided the best way forward was to try and discredit Peter somehow. He had asked Sam to do a little background investigation for him and then, once he had enough information, he would make his move. In the meantime he had to position himself to be indispensable to everyone. He also needed to change his attitude a little. Sam had said that people were thinking that power was going to Beau's head and they were getting more cautious around him every day. That was going to have to change. He jotted down a few notes on the pad on his desk.

"There's a letter for you," the girl from reception said, handing Beau a small manila envelope with a non-descript postmark.

Beau seized the envelope and waited for the girl to leave. He took a letter opener from his desk drawer and slit open the top of the envelope. It was very odd to get a letter nowadays, especially one addressed personally to him. He opened it up and looked inside. There was a single sheet of paper.

Dear Beau,

I hope this letter finds you in good spirit. We have been waiting for the right time to write to you and believe that time is upon us. Hopefully the events of the past few weeks have made you realize we have a plan for you; a big plan.

Time has passed us by since I last spoke to you and during that time many things have happened to us both. At our end we have had somewhat of a hierarchy shuffle and many of the old guard has departed for different ventures. Industry leaders from many long established companies have now reached the twilight of their careers and have stepped down to make room for new blood.

That has left me more or less in charge of the American Chapter and so I have been busy reaching out to several young and promising recruits who I believe will form the vanguard of our next push into making America once more a force to be reckoned with. I understand that this is an aspect of our society you know nothing about, but in time you will learn many things. You believe your talents make you unique, but you know so little about so much. There are others, household names, that possess the same skills as you. These people have shaped the American economy and become rich beyond belief at the same time. This too could be your destiny. Only time and your dedication to the cause will decide.

However, because of the current period of reorganization we are going through, I need you to tread carefully during the next few weeks and ask you not to do anything out of character or to take unnecessary risks. There are things in motion that will involve you soon enough and those things rely on you being seen to be as trustworthy as possible. I repeat again, do not take unnecessary risks. Do not give in to those base urges to take another for yourself. Now is a period of reflection and planning. I say this for your own good. If anything were to happen to you to cast suspicion upon you then we will be forced to take alternative actions and those will have the most unfortunate consequences for you. To date you have seen only the rewards that come from being one of the Anons, but there is a darker side of which you know nothing. You do not want to be at the wrong end of these people.

Still, enough of this talk. I trust you are enjoying being in a new position of power? You are probably wondering how I know of such things, indeed you are probably wondering why I even care. Suffice it to say that nothing happens without my planning or involvement. From the moment I first saw and met you I have been following you very closely. I know of all your assignations and the lives you have plucked. I am not saying this as a means of threat. That is not our way. I am merely saying that nothing you do goes undetected.

And so, onto a few matters concerning your current employ. You will soon be asked to take a visit to Las Vegas, to investigate the workings of another company there. This trip will coincide with a small get together we are holding for people such as yourself. During your stay in Las Vegas you will be invited to come visit us and try out for a most coveted of positions, one within the inner sanctum itself. Such a position will confer powers onto you that even now you could only imagine. Do not take such an invitation lightly. There is a strict hierarchy within the Anons and you are currently firmly embedded in the second tier. Absolute power comes from being in that first tier and you are now just a step away. Your actions over the next few weeks will determine your ultimate future. I am hopeful you will prove worthy of the time I have invested in you. Indeed, the founding fathers would no doubt hope that too. Beau Tempest, you are at the precipice of something amazing and unbelievable. Something that is bigger than any dream you could ever have. Do not take anything I have written lightly.

And one other thing. There is a woman in your company, now within your team if all things have worked out successfully, that is also ready to take that first step on the road to success. I have not yet had the opportunity to visit this woman and even she does not yet know of her destiny, but you should have already noticed the potential in her. Just ensure you invite her with you to Las Vegas and do not get tempted into any physical relationship with her. This would end in disaster. Not just for her, but for you too. You do not yet understand the extent or consequences of your talents.

I am indeed looking forward to seeing you again soon.

Yours, Ted

Beau stared down at the letter and reread it one more time. Then he folded it up and put it back into the envelope. He folded the envelope a couple of times and slipped it into his jacket pocket. There were parts of the letter that confused him completely. Tiers of power? Powers beyond belief? Just what was being promised to him here? Being a part of the Anons and killing women for their knowledge and souls was where it all ended as far as he knew. Now, suddenly he was being told there was more to it than this. Just what was going to be asked of him? Just what had he gotten himself into?

And then there was this other woman in the office. Who was being alluded to here? There were only a few women that worked with him and the most obvious one was Wendy. Surely the letter wasn't referring to her? Wendy was just a good support person who he was now training to be a sales woman. But there really wasn't anyone else he could think of that could fit the references in the letter. Wendy was going to become one of the Anons? Just like him. That really didn't make any sense. Still, who was he to question things? And what about this talk of a physical relationship? Dangerous? Beau smiled. At least if the woman was Wendy, there was no worry about that happening. She was definitely not his type at all.

Beau started scribbling on his blotter again. More demons and people. And now he was going to have to put his plans regarding Peter on hold. The Anons had made that very clear. And no more assignations either. It was going to be a slow couple of weeks. Still, at least he could go ahead with his plan to gain better support in the office.

Beau picked up the phone. "Sam, you have a minute?... Thanks." He put the phone back down and tore off the top sheet from the blotter, screwed it up and threw it in the trash. "Come on in, Sam," he said, looking up from his desk and seeing Sam at the door. "Take a seat."

"What's up?"

"It's about what we were talking about the other night at the Queen's Arms. I have had a change of heart. You were right, I need to concentrate on getting the people here to better understand me. I don't need any sidetracking and more upheaval."

"You sure? You seemed very determined the other night?"

"Yeah, I'm sure, Sam. This doesn't change anything between us though. Just so you know. I appreciate everything you do for me and I'm still going to find a good position for you here in the office."

"That's not necessary, Beau. I'm only..."

"I made a promise and I keep my promises. Besides, I was the one that originally brought you here to Zygote. It's the least I can do." Beau shuffled a few papers on his desk. "That's all, Sam. Thanks. I'll see you later."

"Thanks, Beau." Sam got to his feet and left Beau's office, closing the door behind him as he left.

"Been talking with the boss?" Wendy asked Sam as she passed him in the corridor.

"He just wanted to ask me a few things, that's all."

"What's going on with him then?"

"What do you mean?"

"Well, you're the closest to him. What's he had to say about the new position and the new plans for the office?"

"Nothing, Wendy. Really nothing. Actually I think he's finding everything a little overwhelming."

Wendy laughed. "Beau? I think you've got the wrong person there. Beau always knows what he's doing. I'm sure he doesn't do anything without planning it first."

"You're probably right, Wendy."

"So there is something then?"

Sam smiled. "No, like I said, Beau is just trying to find his place I think. Actually he's realized he needs to change his image a little if he's to keep the respect of everyone in the office."

Wendy laughed. "You're right there. I guess we'll just have to see how that turns out."

18

"Yeah, she seems to be quite taken with him, I have to admit."

"What's he like?"

"And you're asking me?" Sabrina laughed. "I don't know. Quite tall, dark, athletic. You know, mannish."

"Mannish? That's the best you can do?" Tim poured himself a cup of coffee.

"He's into cycling apparently. He took Lucy on a ride to the wineries on Sunday. After she took him to church."

"Oo. I'm sure he wasn't keen on that."

"No, not really apparently. Still, he went along anyway. It sounds like they got on alright as well. She was talking about going away with him for a weekend somewhere. He's a manager at one of the local car dealerships. Sounds like he has a good future ahead of him. And I actually think she's really quite into him"

"Who's into who?"

Sabrina looked up to see Beau standing in the doorway. "Nothing, Beau. We're not talking about you. Don't worry."

Beau walked over towards Sabrina and Tim. "Who were you talking about then?"

"No one," replied Sabrina.

"Lucy," said Tim.

"Lucy? That girl from Paddy's the other night?"

Sabrina glared at Tim and mouthed *thanks* to him.

"Yes, that girl," continued Tim. "She's got a new boyfriend apparently. That will keep you out of the picture."

"That's fine to me," Beau said, trying to sound disinterested. "One more woman off the market."

"Is that what you really think, Beau?" asked Sabrina. "We're just girls on the market to you?"

"I was joking. Lighten up. Sorry. Can't a guy make a joke nowadays?" Beau took a cup from the side and poured himself a coffee.

"It didn't sound like a joke, Beau." Sabrina threw her empty cup into the trash and left the coffee room.

"What's up with her?" asked Beau.

"Sometimes you're a little insensitive, Beau," replied Tim. "You do come across as a bit of an idiot from time to time."

Beau sat down in a chair and took a sip from his cup. "It isn't what I intended. I mean I did like that woman and of course it's disappointing she's dating someone else, but I'm not going to freak out about it. There are plenty of other fish in the sea."

Tim stepped past Beau and crossed over to the doorway. "Look Beau, we all like you but seriously, you need to lighten up a little. For everyone's sake."

Beau watched as Tim disappeared from view and took another sip from his coffee. Then he balled up his fist and banged it on the table. Why did he let these things get to him? He didn't know. All he knew was that Lucy was a girl he wanted to get to know and this jerk of a guy wasn't going to get in the way of him seeing her. He needed to find out who he was and make sure he stayed away from Lucy. A little gentle persuasion ought to do the trick. Beau uncurled his fist and took another sip. There couldn't be many young guys that were managers at a local car dealership. A little investigating and he could find that out. Beau smiled as he got to his feet and made his way back to his office.

* * *

"Dammit," Beau said, sitting upright in his chair as the local news ran a headline story. He had picked the wrong girl.

He needed to be more careful next time. Apparently too many people had missed that Jessica girl he had seen the previous week and police had already found the body. This time they were talking about it on the TV. But if they had found any of the other bodies then so far they hadn't spoken about it. Beau picked up the TV remote and turned up the volume to listen.

"Jessica Martin was twenty-one years old and lived on her own in an apartment in Bellevue. Police are asking people to help them build up a picture of her last movements. If you saw Jessica in the last week you are asked to contact the Bellevue police and give them that information. Police believe she could have been dead for up to two weeks, but have released little other information."

"Dammit." Beau turned off the TV and walked over to the kitchen to pour himself a whiskey. "Maybe the Anons were right. Maybe I need to tone things down a little for the time being. I can't afford to be found out." At least the police shouldn't have too many clues. Beau knew that the bodies he left behind were mostly unrecognizable. Mere shells. The fact that the police were able to identify this body as Jessica was probably just due to the fact that they knew she lived there alone. He doubted there would even be any decent DNA evidence to collect. At least that is what he hoped. He had stayed once and watched the body of one of his victims decompose in front of him. After he had finished with the girl there hadn't been much of the body left, but he had stayed anyway. He waited nearly twenty-four hours, just to see what happened. The sight had disgusted him. The flesh had turned to leather and had shrunk to fit the skeleton. What was left in the room he finally left looked more like a two thousand year old mummy than a twenty-four hour old murder victim. He really doubted how much the police could discover from a body left like that. Besides, the Anons had once told him that unless he was really careless he would never be discovered. There would never be any physical proof.

Beau sipped at his whiskey and sat back down in his chair in the silence. Was his whole life going to be defined like this? And what about the other Anons? They must be killing people too. Why didn't he hear more about these bodies and murders on TV? Surely if there were other Anons there must be hundreds of bodies that the police had found. Beau laughed to himself. The vision of all these bodies stacked up somewhere, all unsolved murders, made him smile. No, the police surely had no clues.

He needed to go for a walk. He needed some fresh air. Beau got up and pulled out a heavy coat from the closet and was soon on the main road, walking away from the apartment complex. It was already dark outside and a frost was beginning to form on the grass verges. The roads were mostly empty and he just wandered aimlessly for several minutes. Twelve-ten. Already past midnight. Oh well, time to return home and get some sleep. There were a lot of things that needed planning for the rest of the week.

As Beau turned into the street that led to his apartments he noticed a woman sat on a wall by the side of the road. "You okay?" he asked as he approached her.

The woman looked up and tried to focus on Beau. "My boyfriend buggered off," the woman said in a totally non-American accent.

Beau smiled and sat down next to the woman. "You live nearby?"

"I guess," the woman replied.

"Have you been drinking?"

"Maybe. I don't care. He wasn't worth it anyway." The woman looked up at Beau through blurry eyes. "You seem like a nice bloke though."

Beau looked the woman up and down. She was older than him, maybe in her early thirties. Her eye make-up was smudged all over her face and wisps of her hair covered her red eyes. "Can I walk you home?"

The woman giggled. "Such a gentleman. You don't see many gentlemen." She leaned backwards and nearly fell off the wall. Beau reached out and put a hand around the woman's shoulder to steady her. Then without warning the woman looked up at Beau and kissed him, straight on the lips. Her tongue found his and Beau immediately pulled back from her.

"Mary," he said. "I need to get you home."

The woman looked at Beau confused. "How do you know my name?" she slurred.

"Just a wild guess. You look like a Mary."

Mary leaned over and kissed Beau again. This time Beau let her tongue linger a little longer in his mouth before he pulled back. "I can't," he said. "You're drunk and I need to get you home."

"Just one more kiss. Please? Then I'll let you go. It's been such a bad night for me. I'll settle for a young bloke like you kissing me before I have to go home." Mary looked up into Beau's eyes and smiled.

"Just one kiss..." Beau replied as Mary cut him off before he could complete the sentence. Beau's tongue explored Mary's mouth and the two of them held each other close. Beau could feel Mary's hands running up and down his back. He pressed his mouth closer against hers and closed his eyes. "No!" he suddenly screamed out, pulling back and letting Mary go. "I'm not going to do this." He stood up and took a step back from Mary who was already in a state of confusion. Her body already looked weak and he watched as she lost the strength to sit properly on the wall. He watched as she tumbled backwards over the wall and landed on her back in the dirt, eyes facing emptily upwards. Beau watched as Mary closed her eyes and allowed a broad smile to wash across her face. Then she twitched once, twice and fell silent. Beau took another step back. Without waiting another moment he walked away, back towards his apartment complex. He didn't think he had killed her. He hoped not, but it had been close. Another couple of minutes and she would have been his for the taking. As it was she was going to be very ill for a few days, not knowing how she had gotten like she had. But she had already been drunk and confused and would probably not even remember him. He hoped so. Beau turned into his apartment complex and walked silently towards his block. A few minutes later and he was sat in his chair, still wearing his coat in the dark. Things were going to have to change. The Anons had warned him. He had nearly messed up already. It was a disease. He enjoyed taking these women's lives. Things were getting out of control. He craved power and control and these women gave him those things. Just what alternatives did he have?

19

"Hi there," Lucy said, getting to her feet as the doctor entered the room.

"Back so soon?"

"You told me to come back when I had my next migraine."

"And you had one today?"

"Yes, this morning. It wasn't as bad as they are sometimes but I took an Almotriptan anyway. It seems to have helped clear it up."

"Your migraine wasn't as bad as normal?" The doctor motioned for Lucy to sit back down again and she set up the blood pressure monitor. "Why do you think that was?"

"I don't know. Maybe it was the tablets."

"Probably not. You said you didn't take one until after you had the migraine." The doctor took Lucy's blood pressure and removed the wrap. "Your blood pressure is a little elevated. Still, that could be the effects of the Almotriptan. Let me take your pulse." She took Lucy's hand and felt for her pulse on her wrist. "Seems okay." Then the doctor listened to Lucy's heart with her stethoscope. "Nothing to worry about. It seems these tablets are going to do the trick for you. Any questions?"

"Do I need to take these forever?"

The doctor smiled. "Probably not. Migraines quite often disappear in patients for no apparent reason after a period of time, usually after some life event. In any case I want you to continue taking these tablets whenever you have a migraine and if you need some more, just contact my office. Then I want you to come back to see me in twelve months time. We'll reevaluate the situation then."

Lucy smiled. "Okay. That sounds fine."

"So, no questions at all? Well in that case I'll let you get back to work. Thanks for stopping by."

Lucy got to her feet, thanked the doctor one more time and walked out of the room, back towards her car. Three-twenty-two. It wasn't worth going back to work now. She might as well just go home. Besides, she was meeting Ben in the evening. The extra time to get ready would be welcome. She shivered as she got into her car and started the engine. She still needed to ask Ben if he could help her get a new car. Well maybe not a new car, but definitely a different car. It was nice to be dating a man that knew about these sorts of things.

"Sorry I'm late," Lucy said, putting her arm around Ben's shoulder and sitting down next to him.

"It's okay. I haven't been here long." Ben squeezed Lucy's hand and pecked her on the cheek as she sat. "I've never been here before. Is the food any good? It's mostly things I'm not familiar with."

Lucy laughed. "It's an English pub. The food is a little different, yes. But it's really good, I promise." She looked down at the empty table. "Didn't you order a drink yet?"

"I did, yes. It took a while for someone to come. But the girl recommended a Bass."

Lucy laughed. "A Bass? Oh well, I guess it won't do you any harm."

"What do you mean?"

"Bass is a tourist beer. We serve it to Americans and pretend it's English."

"It's not English?"

Lucy squeezed Ben's hand. "Yes, it's English. Just not a good representative sample of our beer, I'm afraid." Lucy looked around and caught the server's attention. "Miss, can I get a pint of cider? Oh, and a smoked salmon appetizer please."

"Cider? You're not having anything alcoholic?"

Lucy laughed. "English cider is alcoholic. I can see you've got a lot to learn about my country."

"Sorry."

Lucy leaned into Ben and kissed his hand. "I'm only teasing. Just relax a little will you? Let's have a fun night tonight. No work tomorrow. I hope you like smoked salmon."

"I've had salmon lots of times."

"Scottish smoked?"

"Is there a difference?"

"I guess we'll have to see when it arrives, won't we? So tell me, what was your week like?"

"Pretty normal. I think I'm starting to understand how it all works at the dealership. Different people are motivated by different things. Most of the job is understanding how your staff works."

"Like any job I guess."

"Alright, Miss Academic, this is my first job."

"It's my first job too."

The server arrived with Ben and Lucy's beers and they each took sips of their drinks.

"How was your week?" asked Ben, as the conversation started to die out.

"It was great up until this morning. I woke up with another migraine. I had to take a tablet and go and see the doctor."

"You get migraines?"

Lucy nodded. "Yeah. From time to time. It's really weird. I never had them before I moved here but now I seem to be getting them quite frequently."

"Maybe it's the Seattle weather." Ben took another sip from his beer. "This is pretty good you know."

"Try this." Lucy handed Ben her cider.

"Mmmm. Interesting. A little sweet. I don't think I could drink a whole one of these."

"It's a great drink in the summer when it's really hot." Lucy looked down at the menu. "So did you decide what to have?"

Ben sat silent for a few moments before answering. "Maybe I should let you recommend something for me."

"Here's your salmon," the server said, placing a small plate of salmon pieces, crackers and cream cheese on their table. "Are you ready to order?"

"In a few minutes," Lucy answered. She turned to face Ben. "Try a little." Lucy spread a little cream cheese on a cracker and then peeled off a small thin slice of salmon and placed it on the cracker. She handed it to Ben. "Either bite it or eat it whole. It's okay either way."

Ben took the cracker and put it all in his mouth, chewed it and swallowed it down. "Not at all what I imagined. It's very nice. Delicate."

"Good. So what about dinner then? Steak and kidney pie?"

"That sounds disgusting," Ben replied, while trying to pick off another small slice of salmon.

"It's wonderful. Maybe I'll have that and you can have a taste."

"That sounds a better idea. Perhaps I should just have the fish and chips."

"Chicken."

"It's alright for you. I don't know what I'm eating here."

"Did you grow up in small town America, Ben?"

Ben stopped loading a cracker and looked up at Lucy. "I guess so. Does it really show?"

"Lighten up, Ben. You're very serious sometimes. I was just teasing you."

"Oh, okay. But seriously, yes I did grow up in a small town and coming to Seattle is the biggest thing I've ever done. I've never been to a foreign country or anything like that. I think that's why I like my cycling. I can do that and be on my own. I don't have to talk to anyone or make conversation."

Lucy snuggled up next to Ben and kissed his cheek. "I'll soon have you acclimatized into society!"

"Thanks!" Ben took another cracker and ate it. "These are really nice you know."

Lucy stopped the server as she went by. "Miss, we'll have a steak and kidney pie with chips and a fish and chips, please." She turned to Ben. "If you don't stop them yourself in here you never get served. It's funny really, although they're American, it's just like being in a real English pub."

"What, the service?"

"Yes, the service. They just can't seem to get it right here. Still, the food is great so I have no choice really." Lucy took another sip from her cider. "So, tell me about where you grew up. I want to know what it was like."

"I don't mind walking you home," Ben said, a little later that evening. "Actually it's nice to get a bit of fresh air and the walk will certainly help to burn off a few calories."

"It's got nothing to do with you actually wanting to walk me home then?"

"Of course... Yes... I want to walk you home. I enjoy being with you."

Lucy put a finger to Ben's lips. "Stop talking." She reached an arm around his back and pulled him close to her. Then she kissed him on the lips.

Ben pulled back from the kiss and looked at Lucy. "Are you sure you want to do this?"

Lucy pushed her mouth onto Ben's once more while aiming a kick to his shin. As he opened his mouth in response to the kick, Lucy reached out her tongue to explore him. Suddenly the two of them were kissing, not caring about the looks they were getting from several people falling out of the pub. Lucy pulled Ben close to her and enjoyed the rush that was coursing through her. She felt him respond to her and she started to tingle as he kissed her passionately. After what seemed like several minutes, Lucy released her kiss and stepped back. "Are we good now? You know where we stand? Do I have to spell it out any more?"

Ben smiled and put his arm around Lucy's back. "I'm good." He kissed her once more before releasing her. "I guess I'd better walk you home now. I think we've put on enough of a show for these people tonight."

Lucy smiled and linked arms with Ben, happy to be out with him in the cold evening. The memory of his kiss lingered and she could still smell the perfume of his hair as they walked. "So what are your plans this weekend?"

"Well, I thought that tomorrow I'd go for a ride and then there's some shopping... Oh, I see. You mean, are we doing anything?"

"You're catching on." Lucy laughed and squeezed Ben's hand.

"I guess the cycle can wait. What do you want to do?"

"Well, I'll probably have a lie in tomorrow morning so you can have your ride if you want. Maybe we can go to the movies or something tomorrow afternoon? If you like."

"Sure, that would be great." Ben smiled as they continued to walk towards Lucy's apartment.

"Call me when you get back from your ride then. Besides it'll give me time to go grocery shopping too." Lucy rubbed her free hand along Ben's coat sleeve and leaned into him as they entered her apartment complex.

"Well, I guess this is it then," he said, letting her arm drop from his.

"Yes, no coffee tonight Ben," she laughed. "You'll have to make do with a parting kiss." She half stumbled backwards, pulling Ben as she walked. A few steps later and she was backed against a wall with Ben pressed to her. Her lips sought out his and they kissed again. She let her hands wander across his back and down towards his butt and she squeezed him tighter as her hands found a resting place. Ben responded by kissing her even more intensely and running his hands down her face. He stepped back a little and let his hands wander to the front of her coat. He undid a button and pushed a hand inside. Lucy gasped as his fingers moved across the sweater she was wearing. She squeezed his butt and pulled him back towards her. Their mouths continued to grind and they kissed until they were breathless. Finally she moved her hands to his back and released her mouth from his. She took a deep breath and hugged him tight. "Tomorrow. Call me tomorrow." With a final burst of energy she pushed him away and sprinted up the stairs to her apartment. Then without looking back she opened her door and disappeared inside.

Ben turned around and leaned back against the wall. He closed his eyes and smiled. The date had gone better than he had imagined.

"So that's him," a voice in the distant shadows muttered, under his breath. "Well, now I know just what you look like." Beau turned and walked away, already deep in thought of how he would win Lucy for himself.

20

Beau stood with his bike by the side of the trail and waited. Hopefully it would work out today. He had stood there yesterday as well but it had been a waste of time. He hadn't come. Still, the weather was better today and hopefully he would be out for some exercise. Beau looked off into the distance at the empty trail and waited. Some athletic cyclists passed by, in a group of six, but that wasn't who he was waiting for. Eventually he spotted him. He was sure it was him, and he wheeled his bike onto the trail and stood by the side of it. As the cyclist approached, Beau became more certain and started to flag him down. "Hey there," he called out.

The cyclist pulled to a halt beside Beau and put a foot on the ground. "What's up?"

"It's my tire. I think I've got a flat and I've got no gear. Do you have anything?"

"Probably. Let me see what the problem is."

Beau watched as Ben dismounted from his bike and eyed him carefully. He was a little taller than he was and maybe even a little fitter. Still, that was no concern. "Thanks so much, I'm new at this sport."

Ben laid his bike down on the verge and stooped down to look at Beau's bike. "I think you've just got a flat. Do you have a pump?"

"No, I don't have anything, I'm afraid."

Ben motioned back down the trail. "There's a cycle shop in town. The easiest thing to do would be to take it there. It's only going to take you twenty minutes or so to walk."

"Really, thanks. That's great." Beau extended a hand. "I'm Beau."

"Ben," Ben replied, shaking Beau's hand.

"Ben?" Beau continued, "Are you the Ben that's dating Lucy? Lucy Weatherington?"

Ben dropped his hand to side and took a step back. "You know Lucy?"

"She didn't say? Yeah I met her in the pub the other week. We were planning on going out on a date but then I heard some guy named Ben stepped in."

Ben took another half step back. "Look, I don't know anything of this. I met Lucy when she had some car trouble. I didn't know anything about you. I certainly didn't come between anybody."

"It's okay. It's just how it all turned out. It's just a coincidence meeting you on the trail like this. It's a small world. No hard feelings." Beau extended his hand again to Ben.

"Sure," Ben replied, shaking Beau's hand. "Well, I guess I'd better get on my way. You know where you're headed?"

"Yeah, thanks." Beau gripped Ben's hand tighter. "But not so fast. I really like Lucy. I was hoping to date her and I'm not happy about the way you stepped in. You had better treat her right, or there's going to be a disagreement between us. Just so you know." Beau smiled and let Ben's hand go.

"Is that a threat or something?"

"No. Not a threat. Just reality. You mess with Lucy and you mess with me."

Ben looked squarely into Beau's eyes and balled up his fist as he spoke. "Look Mister, I don't know you and I've never heard of you before, but what I do in my private life, with whoever I please, is none of your business."

Beau smiled. "But it is my business. I'm someone who gets what he wants. And I'm not sure whether you're okay or not."

Ben laughed. "Okay? It's none of your goddam business. In fact I'll go further. If you interfere with my dating Lucy I'll personally see to it that you are amply rewarded."

"You're threatening me now?"

"Yes, I am. Just so we're clear. I am threatening you. If you get in the way of my dating Lucy I will personally take you to one side and make sure you don't date anyone again." Ben bent down and picked up his bike. "So, crawl back to your hole and stay there." He got back on his bike and started to pedal off, continuing up the trail. "Have a great day."

Beau cursed under his breath as he watched Ben cycle off into the distance. That hadn't gone at all as expected. He had obviously pushed some kind of button and he had underestimated Ben completely. Obviously this was going to call for more serious measures. And he wasn't going to let some jerk get in the way of his dating of Lucy. Because now he was more determined than ever to date her. Beau pushed his bike back off the trail, and walked back towards his apartment. No, this was going to take a little planning, but he was definitely going to have to do something. He kicked the back wheel of his bike as he walked. "Damn that man!"

* * *

"You're very quiet this evening," Lucy said as she sat across the table from Ben in The Fish Plaice.

"Just thinking, that's all."

"About what? Are you having second thoughts about us?"

Ben laughed. "No, not at all." He cut into his salmon and put a piece onto his fork. "I just had a really weird encounter this afternoon. On the trail, when I was cycling." He put the fork to his mouth and ate the salmon.

"What sort of encounter?" Lucy replied, looking across at him while trying to push some salad onto her fork. "Like an alien encounter?"

"I'm being serious, Lucy. It was really weird. Do you know someone called Beau?"

"Beau?"

"Yes, Beau. I'm sure he said his name was Beau."

"The only Beau I know is one that works where Sabrina works. But I don't know him personally."

"Well, it's probably him then." Ben ate some mashed potatoes and stared down at his plate.

"Well? What happened?" Lucy put a hand on Ben's and squeezed it slightly. "Did something happen?"

"It was most weird. This guy stopped me on the trail and asked if I could help him with his bike. He said he had a flat. Anyway, then he introduces himself as Beau and I tell him I'm Ben. Then he launches into this spiel about you and how he was supposed to be dating you and not me. He even sort of threatened me."

Lucy laughed. "You're not serious, are you?"

Ben nodded. "Yep. Totally."

"Wow! Two men fighting over me."

"Lucy!"

"Sorry. Yeah, that is a little weird. But like I said, I hardly know the guy. I haven't even spoken to him one on one. Are you sure it's the same guy?"

"I don't know. All I know is that his name was Beau. He's a little shorter than me, dark hair, nice complexion, classically good looking I guess."

Lucy laughed again. "Yes, that sounds like him. But I don't understand. Like I said, I haven't even talked to him. I heard he was interested in dating me, but that's all. I wouldn't worry about it."

Ben put his other hand on Lucy's. "I'm not going to. After all we're happy, the two of us. Aren't we?"

"You know we are." Lucy tried to reach across the table to kiss Ben, but the two of them couldn't quite reach. She laughed again. "Later. Now let's finish our dinner."

"I'm sorry, but I need to get an early night tonight," Lucy said as Ben walked her home later that evening. "It's going to be a long week at work."

"Are you playing hard to get with me?"

"Of course not." She reached over and gave Ben a peck on the cheek. "But really, I am tired this evening and I need to get some sleep. We'll get together again in the week."

She squeezed his hand tight and put her mouth up to his ear, "And I promise I won't be so tired next time!"

Ben turned his head and kissed her on the lips. "That's a deal."

They continued walking arm in arm until they reached Lucy's apartment. "I'll call you tomorrow," Lucy said, giving Ben a last kiss and rushing up the stairs to her front door. She put her key in the lock and let herself inside. Then she closed the door behind her and leaned back against it.

"You're home early tonight," Sabrina said from the couch.

"Yeah. It was a bit weird."

"What do you mean?" Sabrina listened as Lucy told her all about the incident with Beau and Ben. "Do you think it was really like that?"

"I don't know. What do you think? Either way, it's a bit odd. I mean, I can't see Ben making it up. He doesn't even know Beau. I don't even know Beau."

"Should I say something to him?"

Lucy shook her head and crossed over to the couch to sit down next to Sabrina. "No, I don't think so. I mean, what good will it do? It's something that will blow over I'm sure. It's not like Beau and Ben are going to have a duel over me."

Sabrina laughed. "Like in the old days. I don't know, Lucy. I'd like to see that."

Lucy punched Sabrina on the arm. "Shutup!"

"Two men fighting over you. Whatever next? I can't even get one girl to date me."

Lucy gave Sabrina a peck on the cheek. "You'll be fine, Sabrina. You'll see. In the meantime I really do need to get some sleep. It's been a long week."

Sabrina watched Lucy as she got to her feet and headed off to her bedroom. "So you really don't want me to say anything to Beau?"

Lucy turned her head to face Sabrina. "No. It'll be fine. I'm sure nothing will come of it." She put a hand to her mouth and blew Sabrina a kiss. "See you tomorrow."

21

"Hi there. I'm sure we've met before," Beau said, putting a glass of white wine down in front of the young woman.

"We have? I don't think so. I would have remembered." The woman picked up the glass of wine anyway and took a sip from it.

"A few months ago, at Mariachi's I think. You were at the bar with another woman, dressed in red I think."

The woman took another sip and smiled. "Really? Such a memory. But it seems you are the only one that remembers this encounter." The woman turned back to face the bar and smiled to herself as Beau took a seat next to her.

"Well maybe I can jog your memory a little," Beau said, running his fingers through the woman's long blonde hair. He breathed in deeply and took in her aroma. He wasn't supposed to be out tonight. He wasn't even supposed to be talking to woman. The letter he had received from the Anons had made that clear. But he couldn't help himself. Not tonight. So many things had happened this evening and he just had to take a little pleasure for himself. Maybe if he just spent some time with this woman it would be sufficient. Beau leaned in close to the woman's ear. "Melody, isn't it?" It was always so easy to start this conversation.

The woman put her glass of wine down and turned to face Beau. "Yes, Melody. You really do remember? I am so sorry, it's just that I don't remember meeting you. Maybe I had had a little too much to drink that night."

Beau laughed. "Maybe." What did they know? It was so easy. Just like taking candy from a baby.

"But not to worry, you're here now. And what is your name?"

Beau took a swig from his bottle of beer and put it back down on the bar. "Beau. Beau Tempest."

"Such a romantic name." Melody smiled and fingered her glass of wine. "And what brings you here to Bellevue?"

"I work locally. I just had to unwind a little tonight. To tell you the truth I only usually come out on weekends. I am new to the area and I just needed a drink tonight. And when I spotted you at the bar, well I couldn't not say hello. Besides it is good to have someone to talk to."

"You're new to the area. Don't you know many people?"

Beau shook his head and picked up his bottle once more. "I'm not really much of a partygoer. And my job, well let's just say it takes up way too much of my time."

"I see. Well Beau, let us both unwind a little tonight and keep each other company." Melody picked up her glass of wine. "Cheers!"

Beau breathed in deeply once more and took in Melody's scent. Already his heart was beginning to race a little. Already he could imagine the pleasure of devouring her body later in the evening. He licked his lips. "Cheers!" He took another swig and ran his eyes over the woman's shapely body. His eyes lingered for a moment when they reached her legs. Bare legs that were showing well above the knee. He swallowed.

"I do believe you're checking me out," Melody said, waving a hand in front of Beau's face. "You could at least make it less obvious."

"Sorry." Beau snapped back to reality and looked up at Melody's face. "I was a little obvious, wasn't I? It's just that, well, just that…"

"You don't have to explain. Actually I'm flattered. You do know I'm older than you, don't you?"

"You are?"

"Oh yes, young man. Seriously older. Still, I like the compliments."

Beau leaned back a little in his chair to get a better look at the woman. "Twenty-five?"

Melody laughed and took another sip of her wine. "Keep going."

"Thirty? Surely you're not thirty?"

"A little more."

"Now you're just messing with me. You're not over thirty."

"Thirty-four," Melody replied. "I guess I'm holding out pretty well."

Thirty-four, Beau thought to himself. Thirty-four. Maybe this wasn't such a good idea after all. Women of that age had all sorts of connections. They would definitely be missed. Someone would miss them too soon. He had made a mistake. "Yes, very well," Beau stammered. He had to find a way to depart gracefully. It had been a bad idea to come out after all. "But maybe I should let you enjoy the rest of your evening."

Melody placed a hand on Beau's. "Nonsense. No need to leave so soon. You seem such a nice young man and we've only just been introduced. Let's have another drink. My treat."

Beau let the woman's hand linger on his and tried to breathe in her scent once more. Her name wasn't even Melody. The woman was playing with him. "Sure." Just one more drink then he would have to leave.

"Barman," Melody said. "Another round of drinks. On my tab." She squeezed Beau's hand. "I'll be right back."

She let go of Beau's hand and stepped down from the barstool. She picked up her bag and he watched as she headed off towards the rest rooms. Maybe he should just pay his tab and leave. That was probably the right thing to do. But there was something about this woman. Something he couldn't quite place. He nodded to the barman as another beer was put down in front of him. "Hey, excuse me, does this woman come in here regularly?"

"Never seen her before," the barman replied before wandering back down the bar.

Beau smiled. Maybe she wasn't a local after all. Maybe she was from out of town. That would be better. He finished his first beer and set the empty bottle back down on the bar top.

"That was quick," Melody said, returning to her seat and moving the second glass of wine a little. "At least the service is good in this place."

"So, do you live locally?"

Melody finished her first glass of wine and kept the empty glass in her hands. "No. I'm just visiting. My first time here actually."

"I'm an idiot, aren't I?"

Melody put her glass down on the bar and laughed. "No. Quite cute actually. Very impressive about the name thing. Do you do this sort of thing often?"

Beau blushed and was suddenly caught on the defensive. "No. Not at all. I'm really quite shy. I don't know what came over me. Look, I'm sorry. It's best I leave. Sorry to interrupt your evening."

Melody reached out her hand to cover Beau's again. "No harm done. Actually I'm enjoying your company. You don't really have to leave yet do you?" She reached over and kissed him on the cheek.

"I guess not," Beau replied. Maybe the evening would work out after all.

"Come on, just ten minutes and a night cap," Melody said, a little later in the evening as they strolled towards her hotel. "I promise I won't eat you!"

Beau smiled. "Ten minutes." He couldn't decide. Was this a good idea or not? He really didn't know how well this woman was known and the barman would probably remember him if the police showed photos. This was dangerous territory. He would just have to have the night cap and maybe just kiss a little. That would have to make do.

"I'm right here," Melody said as the approached a large hotel a few minutes walk from the bar. "Just walk in with me and we'll go straight to my room." She took a hold of Beau's hand and squeezed it tight. "Come on." Beau followed alongside the woman as she led him through the hotel lobby and into the elevator. A few minutes later and they were in her room. She took off her coat and threw it on a chair. "Help yourself to a drink from the mini-bar. I'm just going to freshen up."

Beau watched her go into the bathroom and wandered over to the mini-bar. He took out a whiskey and unscrewed the small bottle. Then he wandered back to the large chair by the bed and sat himself down.

"You've made yourself comfortable then?" Melody said, leaning over Beau.

"Sorry?" Beau opened his eyes. He must have dozed off for a few minutes. He stared up at Melody and swallowed. She had changed out of her clothes and was wearing a long black silk nightdress. He tried hard not to let his eyes wander.

She reached out a hand and pulled Beau to his feet. Then she took a few steps back and fell backwards onto the bed, pulling Beau on top of her. "Did you pour me a drink too?" she asked as she put her arms around him and rolled over until she was on top of him. She sat up, sitting on his stomach, stared down at him and unbuttoned his shirt a little. "I can't have you at an advantage can I?"

Beau looked up at the vision that was sat on him. He could already feel himself warming towards her. Thirty-four or not, this woman was more tempting to him than any of the others he had been with. "I only opened the one whiskey." He tried to sit up a little but she pushed him back down on the bed and then undid a few more buttons on his shirt. He closed his eyes briefly as he felt her warm fingers caress his naked chest.

"Not to worry. We don't need any more drinks." She said. "I have a surprise for you. Close your eyes."

Beau smiled and closed his eyes. Actually he was the one that had the surprise for her. He took a sharp intake of breath as he felt her breath on his ear. She nibbled at it briefly and he could feel the movement of her soft body on his. One of her hands caressed his chest again. As he felt her breath move onto his face he opened his mouth slightly in anticipation of that first kiss. That kiss that would seal her fate. He waited.

Beau screamed.

22

The visions in Beau's head wouldn't stop. It was like someone was forcefully stamping all over his mind and stripping pieces away. He balled his hands to a fist and tried to move them but was completely powerless. His eyes jerked open and all he could see was Melody's hair which was covering his face. Thoughts of sex and passion raged through his body and he could feel himself responding to her movements. But it hurt. It hurt more than he could have imagined and he was powerless to stop it. He screamed in silence again and lay powerless on the bed as Melody stripped him bare of whatever she wanted. Then it was over. She rolled off him and lay on her back next to him. For a few minutes they both laid there in silence, neither speaking nor moving. Finally Melody turned her head towards Beau and spoke.

"Not quite what you were expecting was it?"

Beau sought for the words to answer. His mind was still fuzzy and things weren't forming as they should. "Triple time. Bath in the morning." He closed his eyes and tried to refocus. "What was that?"

Melody sat up next to Beau and pulled up her nightdress to cover her shoulders once more. "You are not the only one, Beau Tempest. It is important you understand this. You were warned to control yourself during the next few weeks and here I find you, not listening to sound advice. I could so easily have killed you."

Beau struggled to comprehend what he was hearing. "You are an Anon?"

Melody laughed. "Of course I am. And one who is a lot more powerful than you. You are just a child and you have so much to learn. I was your test and you did not pass. I fear you are not yet ready for the next level of responsibility."

"What does that mean?"

Melody swung her legs off the bed and crossed over to the bathroom and went inside. Beau tried to sit up but his head pulsed with pain. He lay back down on the bed once more and closed his eyes. A few minutes later he heard the bathroom door open again and he opened an eye to look. Melody was fully dressed again and walking towards him. "I am leaving now. You will be contacted again. In the meantime I suggest you listen to what you have been told. You have had your one chance. There will not be another." She pulled a small bag from under a chair and threw in a few bits and pieces. Then without another word or a glance at Beau she was gone.

* * *

Two-forty-seven. The bright light of the alarm clock ate into Lucy's mind. Intense pain throbbed in her head and she squeezed her eyes as tightly shut as she possibly could. She needed to go and get one of her migraine tablets but it would have to wait a little while. Right now it was all she could do to keep from throwing up and screaming. She tried to control her breathing and her thoughts and grabbed the pillow to cover her face. After what seemed like forever she struggled free from her bed and stumbled into her bathroom to get a tablet. She swallowed it down and fell back into bed again. Two-fifty-one. It was going to be a long night.

Five-twenty-two. Lucy couldn't understand why she was getting all these migraines. And they seemed to be coming with greater frequency than before. She was going to have to do something about it. The Almotriptan seemed to mostly do the trick but this time her headache still lingered. She thought about getting up to go to the office but decided against it. It was going to be better to spend the day at home.

Hopefully she could do some work a little later on her laptop. She struggled out of bed and slipped on her dressing gown and made her way to Sabrina's bedroom. She knocked and pushed open the door. Sabrina was sat on her bed sorting through some clothes.

"You look a mess," Sabrina said, looking up at Lucy.

"Thanks. I feel a mess too."

"Another migraine?"

Lucy nodded. "I think the meds have taken the worst of it away but I'm going to stay home today. I just wish I knew what was causing it."

"You going to go to the doctor's again?"

"She didn't have much to say. I think it might be related to living up here. I mean it never happened before. Perhaps I need to seriously think about getting a job somewhere else." Lucy crossed over to Sabrina's bed and sat down. She rubbed her temple with two fingers.

"Don't talk like that," Sabrina replied, putting an arm around her roommate. "I'm sure it's a temporary thing. You'll see."

Lucy smiled. "I hope so." She touched a hand to Sabrina's and got back up again. "Anyway, just wanted to let you know I'll be at home all day. I'll see you this evening."

"Look after yourself." Sabrina waved a small goodbye as Lucy left the room. "And don't forget to eat something." Sabrina continued to sort through the clothes on her bed and then started to get ready for her week at the office. As she moved about her room she wondered just what this week would have in store at Zygote Technologies. So much had happened in the past few weeks. The whole organization had been turned upside down. Hopefully it would be a quieter week. She smiled as she walked into her bathroom to take a shower.

"She's at home again this morning, poor thing," Sabrina said, sitting with Wendy at the office a few hours later. "Another migraine. She seems to be getting a lot of them."

"And she's been to the doctor's?"

Sabrina nodded. "Yeah. She's even got some special tablets."

"Oh yeah, I remember. Those elmo whatsits."

Sabrina laughed. "Yes, those ones. I have to say though, I am really worried about her. I hope she hasn't got anything seriously wrong with her. Perhaps she should go and get a second opinion from another doctor."

"It wouldn't do any harm," Wendy said, getting to her feet to drop her empty coffee cup into the trash. "And if they did find something, at least she'd know."

Sabrina got to her feet. "Yes, I think I'll mention it to her this evening. It can't be any fun having to cope with migraines every week."

"Good idea. I'll see you later. I need to get back to my desk. There's a presentation planned for tomorrow with a new customer. Beau left me strict instructions on what I needed to get done. I'd better at least get it half-completed this morning." Wendy crossed over to the doorway. "You haven't seen him yet, have you?"

"Not this morning, sorry."

"Weird. He's usually in the office well before now. Maybe he's got a day off and I didn't know, or maybe a meeting somewhere. Oh well. See you." Wendy walked back to her desk by way of Beau's office but he wasn't there. She sat down at her computer and checked through her email. Nothing. She clicked a few folders and opened up the Word document she was working on for the presentation. There was still a lot to write. It was going to take her most of the day. She leaned back in her chair and stared at the screen. Maybe the document would write itself. She smiled to herself. She didn't even know why Beau wanted this document anyway. Everything was in the original project folder. He'd said it was something to do with not offering the customer all the features this time, but she wasn't so sure. She thought it was something to do with that project one-eighty-five. It seemed a lot of the future of the company was being based on the success of that project. Wendy had noticed several memos spun up around it. She had even heard that some people back in corporate were working to rewrite several sections of the code. There were lots of things that Beau wasn't telling her. She was going to have to speak to him about that. After all if they were going to work closely together then she needed to know a little more about what was going on with all the projects. She turned back to her PC and made a note to ask Beau later.

Random thoughts continued to run through Wendy's mind. Maybe Beau had a date with a woman last night. Maybe that was why he was late today. Maybe it was that blonde girl at the club. Probably. She had been way too cute to pass up. And Beau liked a pretty girl. She was sure about that. Wendy was just going to have to be content with being Beau's right hand woman. A promotion would be nice. She smiled as she remembered the hint at one Beau had made previously. A pop-up in the corner of her laptop screen caught her attention. An email. She switched to her email program and opened the new email. From Beau. He was finally in the office. She got to her feet and wandered down the corridor to his office. "Good morning."

Beau looked up from his desk. "Good morning, Wendy. Come in and shut the door."

"My God, Beau. Are you alright? You look like you got hit by a car."

"I'm fine. Just had a rough night. I didn't get much sleep."

Wendy sat down in front of Beau's desk. "Not much sleep? It looks like you haven't slept for a week."

"Yeah, and it feels like it too," Beau muttered. "Still, haven't got time to dwell on that. I need to talk to you about that presentation for tomorrow. Change of plan. I've decided we'll go with the original stuff. We need to be more aggressive. There's no space for companies that don't want to be fully onboard. You okay with that?"

"Sure. No problem." That would save her a lot of work. "Anything else you need?"

"Coffee?"

"Just this once, Beau. But don't make it a habit. It does look like you're in real need of one this morning." Wendy got to her feet and left Beau's office before he could say anything else. Wow. She had never seen him like that before. He looked wrecked. Maybe he had had a tough business meeting. Or maybe it was that blonde girl. Wendy laughed out loud at the thought. "Looks like he got eaten alive by her," she muttered to herself.

23

"What's up, Lucy?" Sabrina asked as they sat in the living room pretending not to watch the latest reality show.

"It's Ben. He didn't call me yesterday or today. And I left messages for him too."

"That's odd."

"It is. We were supposed to be going out tonight."

"Did you try calling the car dealership?"

"Yeah. Just now. They said he hasn't been into work this week. No one has seen him. It's not like him at all." Lucy got to her feet and crossed into the kitchen. "Want a hot drink?"

"No thanks. I'm good." Sabrina got up from her seat and walked into the kitchen to stand next to Lucy. "So what are you going to do?"

"I don't know. I don't know where his parents live or anything, so there's no one else I can contact."

"And did you try his apartment?"

Lucy filled a kettle with water and put it on the stove. "I don't know where he lives exactly."

"Well what about the car dealership? Did they try?"

Lucy took down a cup from the cupboard and placed a tea bag inside. "I didn't think to ask."

"Let me do it," Sabrina replied, reaching across the counter to pick up her phone. "Which dealership?"

"Use my phone, it's the last number I dialed."

Sabrina put down her phone and walked across the other side of the kitchen to get Lucy's. She hit redial as Lucy leaned back anxiously against the kitchen counter. A few minutes later and the phone call was complete. "They sent someone out to his apartment today apparently. They even got the landlord to let them in. There was no sign of him and nothing was amiss. Looks like he just went off somewhere." She crossed over to Lucy and put her arms around her. "Sorry. I don't know what else to say."

Lucy leaned her head into Sabrina's shoulders and closed her eyes for a moment. "It doesn't make any sense. We were having fun and he didn't say anything about going off. There must be something wrong."

"He'll be back. Perhaps he just had an emergency crisis or something. Or maybe he had a bicycle accident and is in the hospital."

Lucy broke free of Sabrina and stepped back. "My God, you could be right. I need to call all the hospitals. He might have come off and be concussed or something."

Sabrina put her hands on Lucy's shoulders and stared into her face. "Calm down, Lucy. I'm sure he's fine. You can't go calling all the hospitals. Let's think about this rationally. If the police found someone they didn't know it would be on the news." The kettle began to boil on the stove and Sabrina let Lucy go. She poured some water into Lucy's cup. "Let's watch the end of our program and then the news will be on. Perhaps there will be mention on there. If not then tomorrow we can think of another plan."

Lucy walked the two steps over to her tea and squeezed out the bag. "Okay. Sure. I just hope he's alright." She picked up her cup and walked back to sit down in her chair to watch TV.

"My God, Sabrina," Lucy said a little later as they watched the local news. "Are you thinking what I'm thinking?"

Sabrina and Lucy sat in silence as the news reporter spoke about the possibility of a serial murderer in the Seattle area. Three bodies had been found in the last few weeks and the circumstances behind the murders were very similar. The police weren't releasing the exact details but in each case it had been a young woman that had been killed. Three pictures were put up on the TV in case anyone knew anything about the women.

"It's all women, Lucy. Ben is a man."

"I know. But what if Ben is the murderer?"

"Do you really think so?"

"No."

"Exactly. Ben's not that kind of person, is he? Why would he go around murdering women?"

"I don't know," replied Lucy. "But he is missing now. And at exactly the same time as they announce the murders. Is that just a coincidence?"

"I'm sure, Lucy."

"Well, as much as I want it to be, I'm going to have to call the police."

"What do you mean?"

"The police. I'm going to call them to tell them that Ben is missing and that maybe there's a connection with the murders."

Lucy, you can't do that. You don't have any evidence and besides, the two things are probably totally unrelated."

"They probably are, but it also means the police will track Ben down. And that's got to be a good thing, right?"

"I suppose so. But it seems a bad way of going about it."

"I need to know, Sabrina." Lucy put the ends of her hair in her mouth and chewed them, watching the rest of the news in silence. "I just need to know."

* * *

Wendy stared at her computer screen one more time. She couldn't be sure. She tried to remember but the memory had been very brief. It may be her, or it may not be. She tried to remember.

Wendy had seen the evening news and the pictures of the three missing women. One of them looked familiar and for a while she hadn't been able to place her. But then an hour or so later it had come to her. It looked like the woman from the nightclub. The one that Beau had been dancing with. She was almost sure. She had gone to the website on her computer for a better look at the picture. And now she was staring at it, full screen. And she needed to be sure. Absolutely sure.

She tried to remember that night; Beau dancing with the short blonde woman at the club. But they were fleeting moments and she couldn't be sure. She picked up her phone and dialed a number.

"Beau? Hey sorry to disturb you, but I was just watching the news. Did you see it?... Yeah, the murders... I know, terrible. Look, there's one thing I wanted to ask you. It's stupid but I've got to ask... Sure... Those three women. One of them looks just like the woman that was dancing with you at the nightclub a couple of weeks ago... Yeah, you remember?... I'm not saying that. I just wondered, did you take a close look?... You should. Maybe you can help the police with some information about her... Just take a look. I'd hate to think that some guy is walking free out there and you had the knowledge to put him away... Yeah, me too... Okay thanks, Beau. Sorry to disturb you. Just take a look, okay. I'll see you at work tomorrow. Bye..."

Wendy hung up her phone and sank back into her chair. Beau seemed very touchy about it. He probably didn't like being disturbed out of working hours by Wendy. But this didn't seem the sort of thing that should wait until the morning at work. Besides, if Beau could help the police then they would all sleep better at night. It may not even be that girl anyway. It just looked like her. Wendy got up and walked into her bedroom, sat on the bed and pulled off her slippers. But if it was her then what was it all about the other day? She remembered back to the day last week when Beau had been late getting into the office. She had assumed Beau had been out with the short blonde girl then. But he couldn't have been. The police said she had been murdered a few weeks ago. So who had Beau been out with? She laughed to herself. Did it really matter? What Beau did in his spare time really wasn't any concern of hers. She was becoming a little obsessive. She needed to calm down a little. If she was to get promoted at work then she should concentrate on just doing her job. What

Beau got up to in the evenings wasn't really her concern. That is, unless it was murder. She laughed again. No, Beau was no murderer. Certainly a womanizer, but no murderer. A shiver went down her spine as she briefly imagined him kissing her passionately in the office. Stop it. It was time to get some sleep. She pulled off her clothes and made her way into the bathroom to take off her make-up. She would apologize to Beau in the morning.

* * *

Beau slumped back down in his chair. Damn that woman. How could he have been so foolish? Taking a woman home in front of everyone at the office. Hopefully no one else remembered. But what about other people at the nightclub? What if they had seen them leave? What if there had been security footage? Shit! Beau kicked the coffee table and cursed out loud. How could he have been so careless?

He got up and walked over to his desk in the corner of the room. He pulled up his personal email and typed out a few sentences.

Need advice. Looks like I may have left a trace in a recent assignation. Awaiting instructions.

He hit *Send* and watched as the message disappeared from his screen. It was only the second time he had sent an email to the mysterious mailbox address that he had been given a year or so ago. Hopefully the Anons could tell him what to do.

Beau got up and wandered over to the kitchen and poured himself a large whiskey. Too many things weren't going as expected recently. First the discovery of the bodies, although that was to be expected. But for Wendy to recognize Jessica; that wasn't a good thing. And then Melody. That had certainly been a learning experience. He had found out what it was like to be the victim. It had put a new perspective on things. And it had taken him days to recover from that small adventure. There were things going on that he was not privy to. Just what did it mean to be a top tier member of the Anons? What powers did they have that he didn't? What was their ultimate purpose? He took a big gulp of his whiskey and slumped back down in his chair. Damn!

24

It had been a rough day for Lucy. She had contacted the police about Ben in the morning and they had come to talk to her at the office. It had led to some explaining to her colleagues and there was still no news of Ben. The police had taken all the information Lucy had given them but in the end didn't seem that concerned about him. It was as if they already had a suspect in mind for the murders. Lucy got home early and went straight to her bedroom and lay down before dinner.

It was already dark when Lucy awoke. She rubbed her eyes and sat up on the bed. Six-twenty. She had missed several hours of work again today. She turned on the bedside light and pulled her laptop out of her bag. She needed to check her emails in case there was anything important from the office that needed addressing before tomorrow.

She yawned as she waited for the login screen. Finally she opened her email and scanned through the messages of the afternoon. Nothing important. Relieved, she closed the program down and opened up her private email. It had been a couple of days since she had checked it. So few people actually had her private email address that usually the only thing in the email box was spam. But not today. Halfway down the list of emails was one from her best friend back in England. She clicked on it to open it.

Dearest Lucy,

It's been so long since I spoke to you. It seems that now we are working we never get the chance to catch up. My job in the Civil Service is keeping me totally busy. But I recently got a small promotion and I've been transferred to another office. The details are included at the end of the email.

But enough about work, how are things in America? Do you still like it there? Is Seattle nice? I heard it rains all the time there. Probably just like London has been this winter. We've had a really wet few months here. Everyone is ready for it all to be over as soon as possible. It's funny isn't it? Everyone in England always talks about the weather. But what can you do, it changes so much every day. I was thinking that maybe in the spring you could come over? I have a really nice flat just outside London now and there's always room for you to come and crash like in the old days at Uni. Gosh, I can't believe how long ago that all seems now. Do you remember that party in Chelsea? You know, the fancy dress one? I have never laughed so much all night. I miss those times we had.

Anyway, the reason for my email is that I ran into someone the other day. You'll never guess who? Of course not. Anyway, I was waiting at the station at Kings Cross and I literally bumped into Terry. You remember Terry from school? It has been years since I saw him. He's really changed a lot. He still has that ginger hair though. That's the bit that made me recognize him. He said I looked completely different. Anyway we got talking about old times. I went for a drink with him and missed my train completely. He's still working near home, some kind of contract job designing medieval weapons for an historical society, and we talked about a lot of old friends.

It was really great to see him again. I hadn't realized how much I missed him. He seems quite reserved nowadays, not at all like I thought he would be. Still, he's been through a lot these past years. Those days as kids certainly were life forming! So, I just wanted to let you know that we have started dating! What do you say to that, eh? You said I'd never see him again. You shouldn't have doubted me. I knew we were fated in some way.

Anyway, drop me a line back and let me know what's happening. I'd love to see you soon if you can. I don't know if I can get over there this summer; work's going to get in the way. But see if you can come over. Like I said, you can crash at mine.

Love you and miss you,

Susan xxx

Lucy smiled and reread the email over again. It had been several months since she had heard from Susan. That had been her fault as well. She hardly ever wrote to her. She flagged the email and closed down her laptop. She'd reply to her in the morning when she was thinking straighter. She got up from her bed and went into the bathroom to see how much of a mess she looked. Yes, definitely some work to do. She pulled off her clothes and started to rearrange herself.

"How did it go?" Sabrina asked when Lucy finally emerged from her bedroom in her dressing gown.

Lucy told her about her visit from the police and what they had said. "It seems they're not that worried about Ben. They said he's most likely just gone somewhere. Then they showed me photos of those women again. The ones that were murdered. But I told them I had never seen any of them. To be honest, they all sort of looked the same. I asked how they died, but they wouldn't tell me any details. It was a waste of time really. All that happened was that I ended up missing half my day at work. Oh well."

"Did you eat yet? Of course not. Lucy, you never eat. You're going to disappear one of these days. How about we get a Chinese or something tonight?"

Lucy slumped into a corner of the couch and folded her legs under herself. "Sure. Chinese sounds fine. I'll have some of that Mongolian Beef with broccoli."

Sabrina got up and crossed to the kitchen. "I'll give them a call and go and collect it. Maybe you want to open a bottle of wine while I'm gone. I think there are still a couple left in the cupboard."

"Yeah, okay." Lucy sank back further into the couch and closed her eyes. At least Susan was happy. Hopefully Ben would turn up soon too.

"Lucy? Have you been asleep?" Sabrina asked, returning to the apartment about thirty minutes later.

Lucy rubbed her eyes and tried to move her legs. "I guess. Sorry."

"No problem. I've got the Chinese."

Lucy winced as she straightened out her half-sleeping leg and carefully got to her feet. "Wine, right?" she crossed over to the cupboard and pulled out a bottle of cheap cabernet as Sabrina opened up the packages of Chinese food and put plates on the kitchen counter. A few minutes later they were engrossed in their food.

"I'll clear these away later," Lucy said, pushing her plate across the coffee table. "It's nice to be able to relax at the end of a long day."

"It is," Sabrina agreed. She put her plate on top of Lucy's and poured them both a little more wine. "You okay?"

Lucy took the glass from Sabrina and took a sip before putting it down once more. "Yeah. It's just so frustrating. Not knowing where he is. I just don't understand why he didn't let me know." She wiped a tear from her eye and put her hands to her face.

"Hey, come on. It'll be alright." Sabrina put her wine glass down and put an arm around Lucy. "You'll see. He probably had some kind of family emergency and had to rush home. When it's all over he'll call you up again."

"I guess."

Sabrina pulled a tissue from the table top and handed it to Lucy. "Come on. You'll see."

Lucy looked up from her hands and smiled. As Sabrina handed Lucy the tissue she leaned in and kissed her. On the lips. For a brief second Lucy responded but then she suddenly pulled back. "Sabrina!"

"Oh my God, what am I doing? I am so sorry." Sabrina jumped to her feet and sat down in the other chair. "Lucy, I'm sorry. I wasn't thinking for a second. I just got caught up in the emotion and wanted to cheer you up. For God's sake, say something."

Lucy laughed. "I guess that broke the tension anyway." She wiped her eyes with the tissue and sat up straight in the couch. "Actually it was quite a nice kiss."

"It was?"

"It was also the only one you're ever going to get. To be clear. Forget about it, okay?"

"I'm so sorry, Lucy."

"Like I said, forget about it. It's been one of those days. We're both not ourselves." Lucy picked up her glass of wine and took another sip. "You've probably been angling to kiss me for the past six months anyway."

Sabrina blushed. "Like I said. I'm sorry. I just forgot myself for a moment."

"You need to get yourself a girlfriend, Sabrina. Otherwise I'm going to have to move out."

"You are? Don't say that."

"I'm just teasing you. But seriously, you do need to find someone. Otherwise you're going to drive me crazy. Let's go out at the weekend and see what we can find for you, okay?"

"Sure. That would be nice. I'll invite Wendy from the office too."

"Is she gay?"

"No, but I think she'd like a good time out. That's all I'm saying."

Lucy got to her feet and picked up her glass of wine. "I'll clear this stuff in the morning. I need to get some rest. Goodnight Sabrina."

"Goodnight Lucy." Sabrina watched Lucy disappear into her bedroom with her glass of wine and shut the door behind her. "Crap, what was I thinking?" she said to herself. She laughed and took a sip of her wine. "I really do need to get laid though. The life of a nun doesn't suit me at all."

25

"You okay?" Sabrina asked Lucy as she walked into the kitchen to make herself some breakfast.

"Yeah, I'm fine."

"We're still friends?"

"Of course we're still friends. Why wouldn't we be?"

"Well I was a little stupid last night, that's all."

Lucy laughed. "It's quite funny really. It's been building for a long time. Now that you've got it out of your system, maybe you'll be fine about it."

"I guess so. I really don't know what came over me. I've never seen you as a girlfriend before, honest."

"Right! Here, have some coffee, there's a pot made."

"You made coffee? You must have forgiven me."

Lucy gave Sabrina a big hug and finished making her breakfast. "Shut up."

"I was thinking," said Sabrina. "We could go look for Ben or something if you liked?"

"What do you mean?"

"Well, I'm sure we can find his address and go look for him. A little detective work and we may discover where he comes from too. It would give us something to do. You never know, by the time we have looked he may even be back home again."

Lucy took a sip from her tea. "Sure, why not? Nothing to lose. It'll have to wait until after work though. I can't afford to take any more time."

"Okay." Sabrina picked up her cup of coffee and bowl of cereal and walked back to the living room. "I'll make some enquiries at lunch time and try and get back early from work. I'll pick you up here at four-forty-five or so. Does that work?"

"I'll be here," Lucy replied, wandering back into her bedroom to continue getting ready for work.

"He lives just around here apparently," Sabrina said later that evening as they drove through Melrose. "There should be an apartment complex on the right."

"There it is. Lofty Meadows."

Sabrina slowed down and turned into the complex. They drove around for a little while until they found the correct building. "A-five, right?"

Lucy looked at the piece of paper. "That's what you wrote."

Sabrina parked the car and the two of them got out and walked back across the parking lot towards the apartment building. There was a light drizzle in the air. "It doesn't look like anyone is at home."

"We're not expecting anyone to be are we?" asked Lucy.

The apartment was on the ground floor and the two women walked around it and tried to peer through the windows but there was nothing they could see. "We could try breaking in," said Sabrina.

"Probably not a good idea."

They stopped outside his front door and stood in silence. "What car does he drive?"

"Blue," replied Lucy. "A blue SUV."

"That's most helpful," laughed Sabrina.

"It's not here. I would have seen it. Also the police would have too."

"So what are we going to do then?"

"I'll ask a neighbor. They might know something." Lucy walked the few steps to the next apartment and banged on the door. A dog barked. "Hi," Lucy said when the door opened and an older woman with a small dog in her hands appeared. "We're friends of Ben, who lives next door and just wondered if you'd seen him recently?"

"Ben?" the woman replied, checking the two women out, "Don't know him. The man next door keeps himself to himself and so do I. Sorry." She closed her door and the two women listened as the dog went mad, barking at full volume.

"What next then?"

"We could do a sweep of the area," suggested Lucy. "Just drive around and see if we spot his car. There have to be stores and things."

"And you are sure you can spot the car?"

"I know what it looks like. I just don't know what it's called." The two women walked back to Sabrina's car and drove back to the main street. Soon they were cruising the area looking for any signs of his car but after twenty minutes or so decided the task was pointless. "Let's just go home. It's too dark anyway and we're not going to find the car."

Sabrina drove through a strip mall and turned the car back towards Melrose. "I forgot to tell you. I found out his parents now live in Chicago. That's as close as I got though. One of the guys at the dealership said he had spoken about them a few times. He goes home to visit them occasionally apparently. But he always tells the dealership in advance. They said it was most odd that he would just disappear."

"I guess we could try and find them from the Internet. It might be a long job though."

"Probably," agreed Sabrina. "I think we're stumped, Lucy. We're just going to have to wait and see what happens. Sorry."

"You want to go get something to eat? I can't be bothered to cook tonight. Besides, I don't think there's much indoors."

"Paddy's?"

Lucy nodded. "Yeah. Why not? As long as we don't drink too much it'll be fine.

Fifteen minutes later Sabrina had parked the car and they were walking into Paddy's. "Good, it's not too busy." They found a table in the corner and waited for the server to ask them what they wanted.

"What are you going to eat?" asked Lucy as they sat and waited for their drinks to arrive.

"Probably some wings. I'm really quite hungry. You want to share?"

Lucy scanned the menu again. "No, I think I'm going to have the cob salad. I may steal a wing from you though." She rearranged her purse next to her and sat back against the seat. "What am I going to do, Sabrina?"

"There's nothing you can do, is there? It's just a good thing you haven't known him for a long time."

"That doesn't really make it any easier. He's still my boyfriend. We were just getting to know each other really well."

Sabrina smiled. "You did already?"

"Sabrina! None of your business." Lucy blushed and looked away.

"So you didn't yet then? Oh well."

"How do you know?"

"Your face gave it away."

"If you must know, I'm still a virgin. I've been waiting for the right man. And as a Christian I believe that's important."

"Lucy, I can't believe we've never had this conversation before. If I'd had known that…"

"Shhh. The server's coming."

"Thanks," Sabrina said as the server put their drinks down on the table. "I'm going to have the hot wings and she's going to have the cob salad. Thanks." She waited until the server had left before continuing. "Cheers, Lucy. You know, we've never had this discussion before. I don't know why not."

"It's not something I usually talk about. That's why."

Sabrina took a sip of her beer and put the glass down again. "I haven't always dated women you know?"

"What?"

"Actually I've slept with two men before, too."

"You have? I thought you'd always been gay."

"I got drunk one night at college. Let's just say the evening was a little experimental."

Lucy laughed. "What happened?"

"I'm not telling you the details, Lucy. But I will say there were several of us in the bed at the same time." She took another sip of her beer. "Actually the whole experience confirmed my choice of women as partners. Those men are so messy and noisy!"

"Sabrina! What are you saying?"

"You know. Messy!"

Lucy nearly choked on her beer as she laughed out loud. She wiped her mouth and put her beer back down on the table. "Oh, that's horrible. I hope it's not like that with Ben."

"It won't be. I'm sure with two of you it will be a totally different experience. Like I said, it was the only experience I've got to compare it to."

"When did you finish with your last girlfriend? I don't think I've ever seen you with anyone."

"It was nearly a year ago now. She lives locally. I still see her in the street from time to time. She's got a new girlfriend now. It wouldn't have worked out anyway. Actually she was my previous roommate."

"So, that was your plan after all?"

"No, I told you. Last night was a mistake. Although when I placed the ad for a roommate I did half want someone else like that. But it's okay being single. At least I don't have to do everything different just to please someone else. You'll see. Soon Ben will be telling you to do this and change that."

"I don't think so. He doesn't seem that kind of guy. I hope he turns up soon. I do actually miss him."

"And you never slept with him yet?"

"No Sabrina. Like I said. That's not what I do. It's going to have to be the right guy."

"But you've kissed him, surely?"

Lucy smiled. "Oh yes!"

"Thank God for that then!" Sabrina broke Lucy's gaze as the server arrived with their food. "Let's eat. I'm starving already."

Lucy picked at her salad and gazed around the bar. It was about half full. "Is that the guy from your office over there? Beau?" She nodded towards the direction of the bar.

"Oh my God, it is. Let's make sure we don't catch his eye. The last thing we want is him coming over here."

"Why's he drinking on his own?"

"I don't know. Actually there are a lot of things I don't know about him. And to be truthful I don't want to know a lot about him. I think you're well out of it, not getting involved with him. He would certainly want to be in your pants on day one."

Lucy choked down a piece of lettuce. "Sabrina! Stop it, will you? Change the subject. I'm trying to eat."

"He is attractive though, in a Neanderthal kind of way. Don't you think?"

Lucy nodded. "Yes. He has a certain way about him. Confidence. He even looks quite refined. But he also looks like trouble. I've never dated anyone like him before. I can tell that already." She chewed on another piece of lettuce. "Anyway, what am I saying? I don't even want to date him. I just want Ben to turn up safe and sound as soon as possible."

"To Ben, and all other nice people," Sabrina said, raising her glass. "We need some nice people in our lives."

"To Ben," agreed Lucy. She took a drink from her beer and slowly put the glass back down on the table again. She was missing him already.

26

Beau tipped his glass at the server and waited for a refill on his whiskey. He still had time for one more before he had to walk down the street to Mariachi's.

A man's laugh caught his attention and he turned his head to see a group of three middle-aged men sitting at a table at the end of the bar. English. He could easily distinguish the accent. Melrose was full of people from different countries and that was one thing that he liked about the city. It was easy to be anonymous in a city of foreigners. He smiled. The guy was obviously enjoying himself. The man sat opposite the one who was laughing was gesturing with his hands. "Supplies!" The whole table erupted once more. It must be nice not to have a care in the world. At least it seemed that way to him. He turned his head back to the bar again as the barman put down another whiskey in front of him.

"More water?"

Beau nodded. "Sure. Thanks." The barman took his glass and returned with a full one. Beau took a drink of the water and looked along the bar top. It was full. That was another thing he liked about Paddy's. Most days the bar was full. Today it was Tuesday and it looked like a Friday as far as the customers were concerned. There was something about an Irish bar. He nodded his head to a man at the end of the bar and took a sip of his whiskey.

He glanced at his watch. Still another twenty minutes or so before he had to leave. He had received a reply from his contact at the Anons today and was meeting him very soon. Hopefully they would be able to explain just exactly what was happening. There was too much uncertainty at present. And after his last encounter with that Melody, he wasn't sure about anything. Had that been a real test or was it something else? He needed to know. He also needed to know what their plans were with him. It was all getting a little old. Sure it was nice to be boss of the office and to make decisions, but now it seemed like there was something bigger. Something else that he needed to understand. Beau picked up his whiskey and finished it in one. He took a twenty dollar bill from his pocket and placed it on the bar. With a nod to the barman he got up and turned to leave. He smiled at the loud Englishman who was still belly laughing at the end table and squeezed past a couple who were patiently waiting for a table. Pushing the door open he stepped into the cold evening air, pulled his coat tight around him and set off for Mariachi's.

The man with the newspaper and cloth cap was already seated at a table in the corner of Mariachi's. It was like something out of an old spy movie but it was the method they always used. Beau pushed past a large man that was wandering towards the bar and crossed to stand next to the man at the table. He didn't recognize him. "I'm Beau."

The man nodded in response and waited as Beau removed his coat and took a seat opposite him. "Good evening."

After ordering a drink from the server, Beau studied the man in silence. He was in his forties with graying temples and was wearing a crisp white shirt. He carried a look of distinguished elegance and seemed the type of person that would be at home in any situation. "You can call me Larry," the man said after a while. "What is it that brings me here this evening?"

"I need to know, just what is going on?" Beau replied, studying the man to see if there was anything else he could learn about him. His accent was definitely more east coast but it had been tempered with travel. He didn't wear a wedding band and his skin was lightly tanned.

"It's been an interesting few weeks for you, hasn't it?" The man smiled. "You met Melody I understand?"

Beau tried to remain calm as the memories rushed through his head. He nodded. "I did."

"Not quite what you were expecting, was she?"

"Why did she do it?"

The man laughed. "Now that's an odd question. I was expecting more along the lines of surprise there were others."

Beau picked up his glass and stared at it briefly before responding. "I guess I always thought there must be others. After all I was visited before and things were explained to me. I just wasn't expecting it to be used against me."

"Used against you. Now there's an interesting way of putting it. It was more of a, shall we say, lesson so that you understand just what you are doing to the people you meet. Lest you begin to take it all too lightly. Remember, you are killing people, Beau."

Beau put his glass back down on the table. "I know."

"Killing is not something that should ever be taken lightly. I fear you have forgotten the seriousness of what you are doing. You have been so caught up in the reward that comes with the knowledge that you have forgotten just what you are truly doing." The man took a sip from his soda. "There are consequences to everything in life, Beau. I wish that we controlled everything and did not have to worry about others, but that is not the case. Police investigate murders and arrest people and lock them away. It would be unfortunate if you were one of those people. The gifts you have need to be used carefully if you are to be successful."

"And what is success?"

The man laughed. "I am success."

Beau waited for the man to say something else but instead he remained silent and just sat watching Beau.

Finally he spoke again. "I have everything I could ever want. A large house, a boat, vacations anywhere in the world and more money than you could count."

"And a wife?" Beau asked, looking down at the man's empty finger.

"You know that presents complications, Beau. How would she survive? But I have my women. Many."

"How?"

"You are getting ahead of yourself. First you need to understand a little more about the Anons and what we do." The man leaned forward and lowered his voice a little more. "We are a group of people that are comprised of special souls, much like yourself, drawn from all walks of life. There are some of us that are a little different from the rest of society, freaks of nature if you like, and we have skills that we have learned to nurture over the years. In ages past people called us werewolves, vampires, monsters. There were many names. And we were the things that legends were made of. In reality we are just freaks of nature in much the same way as someone born with an extra finger or toe. Except that in our case our difference makes us dangerous. Careless use of our skills will lead to our deaths but careful and planned use will lead to our fortune. Why do you think it is that some people rise to the top and yet others do not? Luck? Money? Sometimes a combination of those things will help you. But to get to the very top it takes more. It takes the knowledge, power and the life force you will get from the souls of others."

"And why would I want this?"

"You have heard of many of these people, Beau. These super-people of society. They are household names. Steve J, Bill G, Larry P. They have all been members of our society at some time or other. Freaks of nature. But the current guard is getting old. Their time is limited and we need to nurture new members. Being an Anon doesn't give you an extra lease on life. In fact it is more likely you will die younger than most. But it does give you an extraordinary power and wealth that you can use to shape the future of mankind. We need people like you, Beau. We need your knowledge and insight and vision. We need your hunger for success. But you must control it. You must direct it. Otherwise it will be wasted."

"So what am I supposed to do?"

The man smiled. "You are not yet quite ready for the next step. And you will also need a partner."

"But you said we cannot get married."

"Not a marriage partner, Beau. A partner you can work with to help you get to the top. Every successful Anon needs someone they can rely on to set things up for them. But it needs to be someone who is ultimately disposable if necessary. This partner is another who has the skills, just not in the same abundance as us."

"And you have someone in mind for me?"

"We do. But we will talk more of that later. In the meantime I need to remind you of a few ground rules. It seems you have become a little careless of late."

"I've learned my lesson."

"Maybe, but I want to spell things out for you, Beau." The man took another sip from his soda and took an envelope from his pocket. "Read this tonight and again in the morning, until you have memorized its contents. Then destroy it. Burn it." He handed the envelope to Beau. "The message inside is the same as I am going to give you now. Number one. You are not to take any more women within a fifty mile radius of your home. Number two. You are to find out everything you possibly can about Zygote Technologies and their secret client list. Number three. You will obey without question any direction given to you by another, higher ranking, Anon." He waited while Beau slipped the envelope into his pocket. "There are other items in the list but these are the most important ones." He picked up his cap and folded it up before putting it in his coat pocket. "Oh, and one more thing. Every time you kill a woman you are to send us a message. The address is in the envelope. We need time, place, circumstances. This is most important. We will be leaving nothing else to chance and we have to leave no traces. There are people that do these things for us. Do I make myself understood?"

Beau nodded.

"Good. Then I will take my leave. You will be contacted again soon. Don't get up."

Beau sat back and watched as the man who called himself Larry got up from the table and left. Beau picked up the newspaper that he had left behind and opened it up. The front page boldly proclaimed *Police looking for serial murderer*. A large red circle had been drawn around the headline. A shiver ran down Beau's spine as he refolded the newspaper and put it into his coat pocket. He put another twenty dollars on the table and left the restaurant as quickly as he could.

27

"Take a seat, Wendy." Beau waited while she closed the door to Beau's office and took a seat in front of his desk. "How's it going?"

"Alright. There's a lot to do though. I think we may have to recruit some extra people if we are to keep up with all the new orders."

"That's one of the things I wanted to talk with you about, Wendy." Beau opened up a file that was on his desk. "You remember me saying I had to go to Vegas to look at the new company we've acquired down there? Well, it looks like I need to go sooner rather than later. As you say, things are heating up, and there's lots of opportunity for new business coming. We need to know what our options are with this new company; just what software developments they have to offer. So anyway, I'm going to be leaving for Vegas in the morning, for the rest of the week."

Wendy smiled. "And how does this affect me?"

"You're coming too."

"What?"

"Yeah, I know I didn't make myself clear before. There have been a lot of things to arrange. And then the trip has been a bit last minute. Anyway, I've already got you tickets booked and we fly down first thing in the morning. Is that okay?"

Wendy sat speechless for a moment before regaining her composure. "Yeah, I mean sure. I mean, certainly. No problem at all. If you think I'm the person for the job then I'm ready for it."

"Yes, this is a change in responsibility, Wendy. Like we spoke about before. It's just come a little sooner than I imagined. But there's no time to wait at present. There are matters that need attending to. So anyway, get all the project files together and make sure we have a copy of everything on your laptop. I'll email you all the trip details later this morning and I'll meet you at the airport tomorrow morning. Okay?"

Wendy nodded. "I won't let you down, Beau."

"I'm sure you won't." As Wendy got up to leave, Beau held up his hand. "One more thing, Wendy. Sit down a second." He leaned forward. "You've heard the saying, what happens in Vegas, stays in Vegas?"

Wendy smiled. "Of course."

"Well, this trip is going to be a little like that. Except this trip is based upon work, confidential work. You're not to share what we do down there. Do I make myself clear?"

"Of course."

"Good. Oh, and one last thing. Bring some party clothes. We're not going to Sin City without at least going out on the town once."

Wendy laughed. "Certainly." She got up to leave once more. "Oh, and by the way, sorry for that phone call the other night. About those murders. It's just that that woman looked like the one from the club. Like I say, sorry."

"No problem, Wendy. I'm glad you phoned. She did look a little like the girl from the club and I was thinking maybe I should contact the police just to let them know I saw her. Thanks." Beau closed the file on his desk. "See you later." He waited until Wendy left the room before taking another file from his bag. He opened it up on his desk, took out a small slip of paper and unfolded it. "Number Six. You are to take Wendy Baumberger to Las Vegas when you go. This journey needs to be undertaken as soon as possible." He refolded the piece of paper. "Only seven and eight to go. I wish I knew exactly where all this was leading." He leaned back in his chair and closed his eyes. Perhaps at last he was going to find out his true destiny.

*　*　*

There was a slight fog as Beau drove to the airport early the following morning. His one carry-on bag was sat next to him on the passenger seat of his Mercedes. He had plenty of time. The flight left at seven-thirty and it was just before six. Wendy would probably already be there waiting for him. He still couldn't believe that she was to be his partner. At least that is what he supposed. It hadn't been made totally clear to him, but the instructions had been apparent enough. He was to take Wendy with him to Las Vegas. What else could that mean? Still, he supposed it could have been worse. Wendy seemed a reliable enough person and she was certainly intelligent. The phone call about Jessica still worried him though. But if she was to be involved in the things he did then maybe that wouldn't matter. What did the Anons have planned?

He turned into the airport parking garage and found a space as far away from other cars as he could. A few minutes later he was in the terminal and walking towards security. Wendy was in line a few places in front of him. She was only carrying her purse and laptop; obviously she had already checked a bag. Women! Why did they need so many things for a three day trip? He nodded to her as she looked around before going through security and a few minutes later was standing next to her as she waited for him on the other side.

"Good morning, Beau. I thought I was going to be late. It was a tight squeeze getting everything into my suitcase."

"Morning Wendy. Shall we grab a coffee?"

Wendy nodded and they made their way towards their gate, stopping off at a Starbucks on the way. Thirty minutes later they were boarding their flight and preparing for the two hour flight down the coast. "I brought everything I could find. There were even some projects I found in a folder on the network that I didn't know we were working on. It seems that extra access you gave me opened up a set of locked projects."

Beau looked at her in confusion. "Locked projects? Extra access? I didn't give you any extra access, Wendy."

"You didn't? That's odd then. Last week I didn't have access to these folders on the network and now I do. Anyway, I downloaded the information and took a look through them. Seems we are working on some very exciting things. I'll send you the summaries when I get Internet access again."

"Okay." Beau sat back in his seat and tried to relax. Suddenly he felt out of control. Things were happening that he wasn't driving. Who was pulling all the strings? Maybe there was someone from corporate who was involved in all this. Maybe the man named Larry was from corporate. That might explain a few things. He was going to have to start making a list of questions.

"Beau?"

Beau looked across at Wendy. He had missed everything she had been saying. "Sorry Wendy. Just a lot on my mind. Let's talk about this later. I think I may need to try and get a little more sleep before we get to Vegas. I only got about three hours last night with all the preparation I was doing."

"No problem. I can do with the nap too. I got about the same."

Beau watched the short dumpy Wendy close her eyes and get herself comfortable in her seat. No, he could never have a relationship with that woman. She wasn't his type at all. Probably just as well she was going to be his partner. At least he would never be tempted. He smiled and closed his eyes too. Images of Jessica and the other women ran through his head. He needed sleep to take him.

Number seven. Beau tore the top off a small package in his pocket and poured the white powder into Wendy's drink. He watched as it effervesced briefly before dissolving into the soda. The day had gone pretty smoothly. They had arrived at the company before midday and spent a few hours meeting the existing staff. The executives had taken them both to lunch and told them in some detail about the current projects they were working on. Wendy had taken copious notes and asked several technical questions. He had been surprised at just how much she seemed to know. Then later in the afternoon Beau had had a few one-on-one sessions with the staff while Wendy had spent time with the engineers. Dinner had been a low key affair and they had decided to take the first opportunity they could to have a night out on the town. The concierge at the hotel had suggested Project Fifteen at The MGM as the hottest place in the city. The name itself had brought a smile to Beau's face. They had arrived about an hour and a half ago and spent some time chatting over the day and having a few cocktails. As the night drew on, the nightclub began to get full. Beau had already seen a few women he would have liked to have gone back with later. Another time. He smiled as he put the drink down in front of Wendy. "Here you go. Rum and coke."

Wendy nodded and continued to scope out the room. "It's fun here, isn't it? It's my first time at a place like this." She took a sip of her drink. "What you said before about what happens in Vegas, does that apply to the nightclubs too?"

Beau laughed. "Everything."

"Good. Because I think I may just have myself a good time tonight." Wendy took another sip and continued to look around the room.

Number eight, Beau said to himself in his head. There was still number eight to go. Unfortunately the good times were going to have to wait. At least for tonight. "Drink up, Wendy. Let's make the most of the evening." He raised his glass to hers. "Cheers."

"Cheers." Wendy took a long gulp of her drink and swallowed it down. "This is a strong one," she said. "Or maybe it's just that they appear to get stronger as the night goes on." She giggled.

"That could be it." Beau watched as Wendy finished her drink and put the glass back down on the table.

Wendy closed her eyes briefly before reopening them. "Very strong. I feel quite woozy."

Beau put his unfinished whiskey back down on the table and got to his feet. "Let's go get some fresh air, Wendy. I'm sure that's all you need." Beau helped the unsteady woman to her feet and put his arm around her shoulder. "Number eight. Come on, there's somewhere we need to go."

28

"Twenty minutes," Beau said into his phone as he walked, supporting Wendy, from the nightclub. "Yeah. Okay. Got that. Bye." He let the phone disconnect and slipped it back into his pocket.

"Where we going?" Wendy asked. Her eyes mostly met his but wandered from side to side a little.

"I thought we'd go to another place if that's alright with you?"

"Sure," Wendy slurred. "Letsh go."

Beau helped Wendy into a cab and gave the driver the address. Twenty-five minutes later they stopped in a residential area of the city. Beau paid the driver and prodded Wendy. "Come on, wake up. We're home." He smiled at the driver and half-pulled Wendy from the cab. She nearly collapsed onto the ground. He put an arm around her to support her as he watched the cab drive off. Hopefully the man would think nothing odd about his fare.

A door opened at the end of the driveway and a silhouetted man appeared. He waved at Beau. Beau turned into the driveway and walked as best he could with Wendy, staggering slightly as she moved her feet in different directions than him. "You didn't mention just how strong that stuff is," Beau said as he reached the man. "Help me with her, will you?"

The man stepped back to let Beau pass and smiled. "In there."

Beau leaned his weight against the part open door and pushed himself inside. There were three men sitting on chairs at the far end of a large living room. They were each wearing gray jackets over dark roll-neck tops, with dark pants. One of them had on a pair of glasses and seemed to be the one they all deferred to.

"Beau, glad you could make it. Tonight could be the night that changes your life forever. If everything goes as planned then from this day forward you will be entitled to call upon us at anytime for anything. You will become one of the elite."

Beau stood and stared at the men in turn. He didn't recognize any of them. He thought maybe the man who called himself Larry, or Ted or even Melody would be there. But he didn't know any of these people. Beau walked over to a large chair and carefully let Wendy collapse into it. "Hello."

"We are the gatekeepers," said the man with the glasses. "We make the decisions about who is a part of the Anons and who isn't. Some have tried to gain entry to the highest levels and many have been unsuccessful. Ultimately it is us who decide." The man stood up and crossed over to stand next to Wendy and looked down at her. "Hmm. She is a little out of it, isn't she? Maybe she is not as strong as we had imagined."

"Are you sure she is to become one of the Anons?" Beau asked. "It's just that she doesn't seem the type at all. And I'm sure she's never killed anyone before."

The man put an arm around Beau's shoulder and led him to the far end of the room. Another man handed Beau a glass of whiskey and invited him to sit down in a chair. "There are many who go through life not knowing of their potential. So it is with all things. Wendy is just such a person. She has had a few unsuccessful relationships to date. She thinks it is because she is not attractive, but she doesn't know that it's because of what she does to her men." The man sat down in the chair next to Beau. "Do you remember what it was like when you kissed Melody?"

A shiver went down Beau's spine. "I do."

"With Wendy it is similar but different. She is totally untrained and does not know how to direct her talents. So what happens is that the man feels totally confused and invaded after kissing her and decides never to date her again. Wendy, on the other hand, feels better than she could ever imagine, as if she has known the man all her life and is bitterly disappointed when he tells her they can't have a relationship. This repetitive cycle has made Wendy into what she is today. But today we will change all that for her. Today she will discover what her talents are really useful for." The man poured himself a small whiskey from a decanter and raised the glass to his mouth. "To success, Beau."

Beau took a sip from the glass and savored the taste of the single malt whiskey. "And what will become of Wendy after tonight?"

The man laughed. "Become of her? Nothing much will change. Except that she will understand what she can do and also that if she is to keep feeling that way she must support you in everything you do. As it was explained to you before, she will become your partner. With Wendy at your side you will rise up through the ranks of Zygote Technologies and become an industry leader to be reckoned with. Along the way you will also gain much wealth and knowledge and become one of the country's most respected businessmen. Doesn't that sound exciting?"

Beau nodded. "And there are no catches?"

The man laughed again and glanced briefly at the others. "There are always duties to perform from time to time, Beau. That is a part of being successful. But don't worry, you will find out these things in time." The man finished his whiskey and put the glass down on the table. "Come, let us get started." He stood up and waited for Beau to join him. "Let's see how this young woman is doing." The man walked across the room to stand over Wendy. "Wendy, wake up. How are you feeling?"

Wendy opened her eyes and blinked them into focus. There was an older man standing over her wearing glasses. The noises had stopped. She wasn't in the nightclub anymore.

She was in a chair in someone's living room. She tried to move her legs but they weren't reacting quite like she was expecting.

"It's okay. You're fine," the man said.

But she wasn't fine. Nothing seemed to work properly. She raised her hand to her face and found her mouth. She wiped a little drool from the corner of it and licked her lips. "Where am I?"

"Beau brought you here."

Beau. Yes, she remembered now. She had been out with Beau. They had been drinking. She didn't really remember much else though. "Beau."

The man reached out a hand to her and she took it. He pulled her to her feet and she fell into him. Her legs still weren't working properly. She looked past the man and saw Beau standing there. She smiled.

"We have arranged a special night for you, Wendy. Beau brought you to Vegas to have fun. Isn't that right?"

Fun? Yes that was it. They were supposed to be having fun. She nodded and leaned her head into the man's chest for support.

"Beau, come here," the man said. Beau took another couple of steps. "Here, take a hold of Wendy." He turned a little so that Beau could take Wendy from him. "Now show Wendy how much we appreciate her coming out tonight, Beau." The man waited while Beau took the unsteady Wendy from him. "Kiss her."

Kiss me? Surely she hadn't heard that correctly. Why would Beau want to kiss me?

"What?" asked Beau.

"Kiss her. Are you questioning our wisdom?"

Kiss me? Yes, she had heard it correctly but it didn't make sense. Nothing seemed to... Oh my god...

A bolt of lightning burst through Wendy's head and exploded into the deepest corners of her mind. Rainbow colors lit up her vision and she closed her eyes. Her fingers came to life and she reached her arms around him and held on tight. She pressed her mouth harder against his and let her tongue wander. He pulled back and she gasped for air. With her eyes still closed she sought him out again. She found his cheek and corrected her aim. Once more she found his mouth and relaxed as the electricity ran through her. Beau. My god, it had never been like this before. She never thought she would ever kiss him. But oh, it was worth waiting for. Better than she could ever have expected. There were so many things going through her head. She could hardly keep her legs from collapsing under her. She wanted him. She had never wanted anyone as much as she wanted Beau right now.

What? Where did he go? She felt herself falling and managed to catch herself as he stepped back from her. She opened her eyes. The older man was pulling Beau back. Why? What was going on? She tried to mouth some words but nothing came. The man took a hold of her arm and pulled her forward. She watched as Beau disappeared from view. They left the room and walked up a hallway. The man pushed open another door and led Wendy inside. A young man was asleep on the bed.

"Go to him, Wendy. He is yours. He has been waiting for you." The man let go of Wendy and stepped back. She heard the door close behind her.

Go to him? Who was he? She crossed over to the bed and peered down at the sleeping man. He was young, about her age, tall with dark hair. He had a half-smile on his face and seemed happy in his dreams. She sat on the bed and touched his hand. A smile washed over her face as his fingers brushed against his. What harm could it do? The man had told her. She bent down and kissed his cheek. It was a little rough and unshaven but she didn't mind. She turned her cheek to rest against his and let her tongue brush his lips. What harm could it do? She reached out an arm to steady herself and pulled herself on top of him. Her face hovered over his and she touched a finger to his closed eye. They flickered and opened and she smiled. "I have come for you," she whispered as she lowered her mouth to his.

As she kissed him he responded, slowly at first but then with passion. It was a feeling she had never experienced before. It was as if she knew just what he was thinking. She knew what he was going to do before he did it. She could feel his first thoughts; worry that he was betraying someone. Then he changed his mind and kissed her passionately. She could feel the desire in his thoughts. His hands pulled at her and wrapped around her. She knew he was hers. Somehow she just knew. She rolled off of him and onto her back. Then she sat up and pulled off her dress. She waited for him to undo her bra and she pulled his pants from him. She had waited twenty-three years for this moment and nothing was going to stop her now. Soon he was on top of her, kissing her, loving her. She was going to explode. Everything in his head was also in her head. He was giving his very soul away to her. She moved with him and took everything that he was offering. Memories, photos, desires, plans for the future. She took them all and when there was nothing left she screamed out and fell back on the bed. He fell on top of her, lifeless and spent. She closed her eyes and smiled. What happens in Vegas surely didn't have to stay in Vegas.

29

"You okay?" Beau asked Wendy as they drove to the office the following morning.

"Yeah, just a little headache. Seems I overindulged last night. My head is still trying to recover I think."

Beau laughed. "It takes a while, Wendy."

"What do you mean?"

"What you did last night. Afterwards it always takes a little while to recover and get your strength back."

Wendy looked at him inquisitively.

"Not that. The head thing. I do know what you went through last night, Wendy. You're one of us now, part of the Anons. You do know that, don't you?"

Wendy contemplated her answer before she spoke. "Sort of. That is I know I am now part of a secret society and that what I did last night is something that is not at all normal. I know it's a special talent I have and I also know I'm to use it sparingly. Apart from that, it's mostly all very vague. To be honest, I really was out of it last night and some of my memories are still a little fuzzy."

"Don't worry; I'll help you through it. You're going to have a lot of questions but I'll try and answer them all. Just remember that in the meantime you're now my partner and I'm going to start to rely on you for a lot of things, both inside work and outside. Also, this is not something you're going to talk to anyone else about. Ever."

"I think I get that bit Beau. I don't think anyone would even understand anyway. I'm still having trouble processing it all myself."

Beau turned into a parking lot on the outskirts of the city and parked the rental car in the visitor's lot. "You'll be fine." He reached into the backseat and pulled out his laptop bag. "You have everything? I think it's going to be a very busy day today."

"I'm good," replied Wendy, as she took a deep breath, opened her door and stepped into the hot Vegas day.

The remainder of the Vegas visit passed without incident and a tired Beau and Wendy returned to Melrose a couple of evenings later, laden down with all sorts of information they had gathered. Beau's Mercedes stopped at Wendy's apartment and she got out and retrieved her suitcase from the trunk. She waved a goodbye at Beau but he didn't return it. Two more steps and she was behind a line of trees and the car had disappeared from sight. She pulled her key from her bag and opened the door to her apartment and went inside. A few minutes later and she was sat, collapsed, on her oversized lounge chair, her suitcase propped up beside her. It had been a long week and she desperately needed some quality sleep. She yawned and closed her eyes. She just needed a quick nap and she would unpack.

The apartment was in darkness when she woke. The cable box glowed eleven-ten. Wendy stretched, pulled herself to her feet and walked into the kitchen, turning on the light as she went. She poured a glass of water and gulped it down. Her suitcase was still sitting in the middle of her living room with her jacket thrown on top. She smiled. What a week. She had gone to Vegas hoping for some new experiences and had come back a completely different person. Her life had been changed forever. A chill ran down her spine as she remembered the man that had died on top of her. Her talent. She could now officially love a man to death. What she would have given to know she could do that before. She smiled. No, not really. It was a terrible thing. As the man had laid there, almost rotting while she recovered, she had realized the enormity of just what she had done. She didn't need those men to tell her that she needed to be careful in future. Like she was going to do that every day. No way. But it had been disappointing to discover this meant she couldn't really have any long-term boyfriends. She would no doubt kiss them to death. No, she was going to have to make do with the occasional *assignation* as Beau called them. And even they had to be controlled and specially approved going forward. Just what had she signed up for? Oh, but the rewards. They were amazing. The feeling that had filled her head and her body. It had been totally worth it. She had been taken to new heights and she never wanted to come down from there. If this was how one person was supposed to feast upon another then she was totally for it. She smiled and crossed over to pick up her jacket. Absentmindedly she slipped it on, picked up her purse, and let herself out of the apartment. She needed a walk.

The streets were mostly empty except for the occasional person returning home from the pub or the cinema. She leaned up against a wall and watched people walk by. Then she saw him. He was a geek of a man but somehow he drew her attention. Wendy unbuttoned her jacket and went down on one knee as the man approached. "Hey, can you help me?" she said as he passed by. "I've dropped my driving license."

The man stopped and bent down to help Wendy look for it. As his head approached hers she reached out and kissed him. Just a small kiss, but a kiss nonetheless. Then she let him go and got to her feet. "What did you do?" he asked.

Wendy smiled. "Nothing. I just wanted to get your attention. You looked very nice, walking along the street towards me."

The man smiled and stood up next to her. "Really? Maybe you'd like another?"

"Just a small one. Why not?" Wendy took a step towards the man and put her lips to his. They kissed. Amazing. It was as if they were both lightning rods, letting a charge disperse itself between them. Wendy could read the man's thoughts and she wandered around his mind a little before untying herself and releasing him.

He fell back a step. "Wow! That was amazing. I didn't know you could kiss like that."

Wendy stepped in and gave him a peck on his cheek. "Anything is possible." Then she turned and headed off again before he had a chance to say anything. Ranjit. She had never kissed a Ranjit before. She had never kissed an Indian man before. But that hadn't stopped her this time. Nothing had. She just went ahead and did it. It had been like having a big appetizer and not needing the main course. She licked her lips and tried to remember the feeling that had flowed through her. Wow! She let herself back into her apartment and collapsed on her bed. Life was suddenly amazing. Now she could do so many things. She was even looking forward to going to work the next day!

* * *

"Sit down, Wendy. We need to talk."

Wendy entered Beau's office and walked over to a chair in front of his desk. "Something you needed to talk about?"

Beau got up, walked behind Wendy and closed the door. "Have you recovered from our trip to Vegas?"

Wendy smiled. She involuntarily licked her lips at the memory and the encounter the previous evening. "Yeah. I think so."

Beau took his seat again and picked up a paperweight from his desk. "Good. It's time to get down to serious business. I've been going over the notes we took at the Vegas office and I can see two projects that sound a good fit for our company. What do you think?"

Wendy watched as Beau turned the glass ball over and over in his hand. He had strong hands and he had probably used them to overpower many women. "That was my summary recommendation, Beau." Was he just going to repeat back to her everything she had already written? "Was there something in particular you wanted to ask?"

Beau smiled. "I was hoping for a little more detail. Why for instance do you believe the algorithms used in the nano-technology project will be useful to us?" He replaced the ball back on his desk and clasped his hands together.

"Everything to do with that project has to be highly optimized and with a high degree of artificial intelligence. Those are two elements we need here in Zygote too."

Beau nodded. "Interesting. This is why I need someone with your background, Wendy. I would never have come to that conclusion on my own." He laughed. "Actually, my technology skills would never even have identified these things."

Wendy smiled and relaxed in the chair. Beau had just given her a compliment. Even if he hadn't meant to. "Thanks."

"So, the question is, what are we going to do now?" Beau got to his feet and crossed over to the window. "I need you on my project, but I also can't afford to keep you in general day to day sales."

"You're moving me?"

"No, not moving you, Wendy. More of a reassignment and reorganization. I spoke to corporate this morning and they gave me the go ahead to make some changes here. As from tomorrow you are going to be Director of New Ventures Integration. I'm going to get you a couple of techies from around the office and the East Coast office is shipping me one of their people, but you're going to head up the department, under my direction. You will provide direct instructions to your department, but will not divulge where some of the information is coming from. Your department will analyze functionality in detail and suggest ways in which we could use the new technology in our existing products. Once those decisions have been made, you will hand over the algorithms and associated code to our developers for their integration. What do you have to say to that?"

Wendy continued to sit back in her chair in silence. Director. She had never imagined she would ever be a Director in a corporate company. And it sounded like the job was going to be very challenging and exciting. "I don't know what to say, Beau."

"Thank you would suffice."

"Of course. Thank you. I just wasn't expecting any of this."

"We're going to be a team, Wendy. Just like the Anons have said. You are my partner and right hand man. Together we will turn this company into something that our leaders can be proud of and along the way we will reap big rewards." Beau walked around his desk and stood behind Wendy. "I'm still working out the details of your new package, but don't worry, there's going to be a big pay rise for you." He placed a hand on her shoulder and squeezed it before letting go and returning to his seat. "Take the rest of the day to think about how you want to run this and put together your ninety day plan for me. We'll go through it in the morning, after I make the announcement about you."

Wendy got to her feet and turned back towards the door. "Thanks, Beau. I won't let you down."

"You won't," replied Beau, unaware his hand was already drawing more little devils on his desk blotter.

30

"Are you sure you've found nothing about him?" Sabrina asked the detective as they sat in a small side room at the Melrose police station. "He's been missing two weeks now. Surely someone has investigated it all?"

The detective shuffled some papers before replying. "Like I said, Miss, there's nothing I can really tell you. We've followed up on a few leads but there's very little to go on. He's not been home to his parents, and not to work either, so without some further information there's not much else I can say."

"But you do have him officially registered as missing?" Lucy asked. It had taken every piece of persuasion to convince Sabrina to come down to the police station with her that morning. Sabrina thought it would sort itself out and that if the police had any leads they would contact them. As it turned out, the police weren't really actively pursuing trying to find Ben.

"Officially no," the detective replied. "But unofficially we are keeping a lookout. You have to understand our resources are stretched very thin at the moment, what with this serial murderer business."

"I guess," replied Lucy. "It's just that it's so unlike him. He's always phoned me before."

The detective closed his folder and placed it squarely in front of him. "Anything else?"

Sabrina nudged Lucy and they got to their feet. "No. Thank you, sir," Sabrina said as they walked to the door.

The detective followed them out of the room and walked with them to the main lobby. "I'll contact you immediately if we hear anything. But I'm fairly confident he'll turn up soon. People like him always do." He held the door open for them and waited for them to leave before closing it again.

"What do we do now?" asked Lucy.

"Wait I suppose. There's nothing else we can do. The police know more about searching for missing persons than we do."

"I guess."

Sabrina put an arm around Lucy as they walked back towards their car. "Do you want to go for a drink?"

Lucy shook her head. "Do you mind dropping me at church? I want to say a prayer or two for him."

Sabrina squeezed Lucy tight. "Of course not. I'll tell you what, I'll come with you."

"You will?" Lucy laughed and leaned her head into Sabrina's shoulder. "You never come to church."

"Then a little church won't harm me then, will it?"

Sabrina unlocked her car doors and walked around the driver's side while Lucy got inside. She took some directions from Lucy and headed off towards the church. As she drove they both sat in silence reflecting on the events of the past few weeks. So many things had happened and it seemed like their worlds were falling apart. Lucy remembered the good times she had with Ben, how he held her close and made her laugh, and Sabrina reflected on all the changes that were happening in her life, especially at work. Ten minutes later Sabrina turned into the church driveway and found a place to park. "How does this work then?"

"What do you mean?"

"Church. What do I have to do?"

Lucy smiled. "It's just a church. There's not a service going on today or anything so it should be mostly empty inside. Maybe one or two other people praying. Just follow my lead."

Sabrina linked arms with Lucy and they both went through the entrance doors and stopped just inside. The church was bigger than Sabrina had imagined and there were rows and rows of chairs to sit on with a central aisle way. Lucy led Sabrina towards the front of the hall and found a chair to sit on. Sabrina sat next to her. She watched as Lucy bowed her head and closed her eyes. Sabrina bowed her head too and mouthed a few words of support for Lucy. Then she sat silently and waited for Lucy to finish. As she waited, she looked around the church. There were probably about ten other people there, all praying like Lucy. A man to one side looked like he was some kind of official, dressed in different clothes than everybody else. He was just leaning against the wall and watching. Eventually Lucy lifted her head and smiled at Sabrina. "Better?" Sabrina asked.

"I hope so. I just wish I knew what to do. Still, now it's in God's hands." Lucy took a hold of Sabrina's hand and squeezed it tight. "Come on, let's go get something to eat."

The two women got to their feet and made their way back out of the church. They were back in Sabrina's car and headed back towards Melrose when Lucy's phone began to vibrate. She picked it up and answered the call. "Hello, it's Lucy... Yes... Really?... What?... Sure thing. We'll be right there. Thank you. Goodbye." Lucy turned to Sabrina with a big smile on her face. "They've found something."

"What? Who?"

"The police. They say they've found something they want me to see."

"Did they say what?"

"No."

"Did they say it was good news?"

Lucy's face fell. "No. I didn't think to ask. I was just so pleased they had called. You don't think they've found a body do you?"

Sabrina glanced over at Lucy and tried to reassure her. "No. Why would they want to see you for that? I'm sure it's good news." She tried not to look at Lucy again and they both let the quietness inside the car grow as they drove back towards the police station. Sabrina hoped it was good news.

"Detective Stephens, please," Lucy said to the desk policeman as they entered the police station. "I'm Lucy Weatherington. He called me."

The man nodded and picked up the phone. The two women stepped back and impatiently looked around the lobby and waited.

"Thanks for coming so quickly," Detective Stephens said, entering the room looking slightly out of breath. "Bit of luck really. Come with me." He opened a door and ushered Lucy and Sabrina inside. "Just down here. We've had it a while apparently. No one really put two and two together. In fact I'm quite surprised we have it at all. This way."

Sabrina and Lucy looked at each other in confusion. "What are you talking about, detective?" Lucy asked.

"A bike. We had a bike handed in to us. Last week sometime." He opened a door to a small room. "In here." The two women went inside and looked at a bicycle that was propped up against a table. "That's the one."

Lucy took a slow walk around the bike and inspected it as best she could.

"Is it his?"

"I don't know," Lucy answered. "I only really saw it once. When we went on a ride. It's the same color though."

"Anything else?"

"The handlebars are the same. Oh, and the drinks carrier. I remember that." She inspected the seat closely. "Yes, I think that's the same seat too. It had a sort of notch in the side. Ben said he'd caught it in a fence once."

"So you're saying the bike is Ben's?" the detective continued.

"What do you think, Sabrina?"

"I never even saw it," Sabrina answered. "Sorry I can't help you on this one."

Lucy nodded and took another walk around the bike. "Where did you find it?"

"Like I said, it was brought in about a week ago. The ticket said a lady found it by the side of the trail, lying in some long grass. It could have been there for a few days already. We were actually surprised it got handed in at all. Normally someone just steals 'em when they find them. So this was a…"

"Do you have a black light, detective?" Lucy interrupted.

"A black light? I'm sure we do. Why?"

"I remember Ben saying that he wrote his name in fluorescent ink on the frame. Just in case it was ever stolen. If the bike is his then we ought to be able to see his name on it."

The detective nodded and went off in search of a light.

"Do you think it's his?" asked Sabrina.

"I don't know. I actually hope it's not. I'd hate to think how he came to lose it on the trail." She stopped and turned a little pale. "Do you remember how Beau threatened him that time on the trail? Do you think this could have anything to do with it?"

"I vaguely remember you telling me, Lucy."

"I know I did. I'm sure. But Ben did say he wasn't frightened of Beau anyway."

"This ought to do it," the detective said, returning with a long cylindrical light. He turned off the room's lights and turned on his. Then he slowly moved the light over the frame of the bike as the three of them looked for a mark. "Yep, there it is," the detective said after a moment or two. "That looks like it."

"It's Ben's signature," said Lucy. "It is his bike."

The detective turned the black light off and the room lights back on and remained standing in the doorway. "I think we'd better take a statement, Miss."

Sabrina put an arm around Lucy as they followed the detective to another room. "I'm sure he's alright, Lucy. At least they've found his bike now."

"But why would they only find his bike? He's either injured or kidnapped or dead. I know he is."

"Let's not go rushing to conclusions. There could be a really simple explanation."

As they reached the room where the detective was going to take Lucy's statement she tapped him on the shoulder. "It's Beau. He did it, detective. I know he did."

"Beau?"

"Beau Tempest," Sabrina replied. "A couple of weeks ago he threatened Ben on the same trail."

"You'd better tell me the whole story," the detective said, ushering the women into the interview room. "Seems like we've got something to go on at last."

31

Lucy had spent the last few days checking her phone in case there was any news. She hadn't been able to concentrate properly at the office and the only consolation was that she hadn't had a migraine for quite some time. She had also tried to stay out of Sabrina's way so that she didn't have to get involved in the same discussion or receive her sympathy for the hundredth time.

She lay on her bed and stared up at the ceiling. She had tried calling the police station earlier but Detective Stephens had been unavailable. And she was almost housebound. She didn't dare go to Paddy's or anywhere else local in case she ran into Beau and his colleagues. She just hoped the police had done their homework and interviewed him. Thoroughly.

She closed her eyes and tried to relax. But the same thoughts ran through her mind over and over again. What if Ben and Beau had met up again on the trail? What if they'd had a fight and something terrible had happened to Ben? But surely they would have found a body by now. He couldn't just disappear. She had a sudden thought. Unless he'd been dumped in the slough. Had the police looked there? Had they dredged it yet? Maybe she should call and suggest it to them. But surely they would have thought of that too. After all they were police detectives.

It was no good, all this lying down on her own wasn't helping. She just had the same thoughts going through her mind over and over again. She opened her eyes and sat up. She clicked on the TV and turned to the news channel. Perhaps there would be some development or other. Nothing. Not even a mention of the so called serial killer. She had a sudden pang of guilt as she imagined Beau as the serial killer. No, she didn't wish that upon him. She just wanted Ben back in her life. She clicked the TV off again and listened to the silence.

Sabrina pushed open Lucy's bedroom door and poked her head inside. "Lucy? You need to come into the living room. It's the police."

Lucy jumped up with a start and took a quick look at herself in the mirror. She put a brush through her hair and wiped her face a little. "Coming."

"Hello Lucy," Detective Stephens said as Lucy entered the living room. "Take a seat. There's a few things I want to ask you."

"Did you find him?" Lucy interrupted.

The detective motioned for Lucy to sit down. He waited. "When did you say the last time you saw Ben was?"

Lucy thought hard for a moment and replayed events in her mind. "It was when we ate at The Fish Plaice, a couple of weeks ago. He told me then how Beau had threatened him that morning. Like I said in my statement."

"You're sure of the date?"

"Yes, I'm sure. Why?"

The detective made a note in his notebook and looked back up again. "Some circumstances have come to light and I just need to be sure of the exact date." He fidgeted slightly in his seat before continuing. "And you never went on a trip or anything with him?"

"No."

"And he never mentioned going on a trip anywhere?"

"No." Lucy got to her feet and took a step towards the detective. "What are you getting at?"

"Sit down, please. I just have to check a few facts, that's all." He waited until Lucy was seated again before he continued. "The police in Flagstaff, Arizona contacted me yesterday about a body. The circumstances of the murder and the state of the body bore, shall we say, certain similarities to those we have been investigating in Melrose."

Lucy turned pale. "He's dead? Ben's dead? No, you can't be saying that."

"Of course we had to perform certain tests, but we're sure…"

Lucy screamed. "NO! No, you can't be certain."

Sabrina quickly moved to hug Lucy tight and muffle her screams. Lucy wept into Sabrina's shoulder. "You're sure it is Ben?"

The detective nodded. "Quite sure. It seems we had a little more to go on with this one than some of the previous victims."

"What do you mean?"

"I'm not at liberty to say that, Miss. All I can say is that we have confirmed the body in Flagstaff to be that of Ben's. It's being flown to Chicago as we speak. His parents are arranging his funeral for later this week."

Lucy continued sobbing into Sabrina's shoulder and nodded. Sabrina handed her a tissue and she blew her nose loudly. "We've got to go, Sabrina."

"Where?"

"To Chicago. It's the least I can do."

The detective flicked through a few pages of his notebook and wrote something down on another piece of paper. "Here you go," he said, handing the paper to Sabrina. "Ben's parent's phone number." He closed his notebook and put it back in his pocket. "We found his car too. Most odd. He was sat at the wheel, in the middle of the desert, dead. Not another print in the car. It was as if he had driven there himself. Of course, we know that not to be true. But even so, not many clues to go on." The detective got to his feet and walked towards the door. "My sincerest condolences, Miss. I'll let myself out. Terrible business, murder. Terrible."

Sabrina watched as the detective pulled the door closed behind him and then she gave Lucy an extra big hug. Lucy cried uncontrollably once more.

"Are you sure you want to do this?" Sabrina asked as they parked their rental in Ben's parent's driveway the following afternoon.

"I'm sure. I owe it to them and to Ben. It's the least I can do."

Sabrina turned off the car's engine and they sat for a moment in the car before getting out. The driveway had been cleared of snow, but there were still a few patches of ice as they walked towards the front door. Sabrina rang the bell and waited.

"Hello?" an older woman enquired, opening the door a crack and peering out.

"Mrs. Hansen?" Sabrina asked. "We're Sabrina and Lucy. I phoned yesterday."

"Wait there," the woman replied and closed the door once more. A couple of minutes later it opened again. A middle-aged man in dark pants and a white shirt greeted them.

"Mr. Hansen?"

"You must be the two girls that spoke to my wife yesterday. Come on in. Excuse the mess. We're not quite organized at the moment." Mr. Hansen opened the door to let the women in and showed them to a side room. "Take a seat. My wife will be out soon. Can I get you a drink?"

Sabrina and Lucy shook their heads and sat down on the couch to wait. Mr. Hansen disappeared again.

"It looks like they don't use this room much," said Sabrina. "It's got a lot of family pictures though."

Lucy was already up and walking over to a table that was against a wall. She picked up a photo. "It's Ben. Look. I think this was taken when he was at college." She crossed back over to Sabrina and handed her the picture.

"North Park University," Mrs. Hansen said, entering the room unnoticed. "Sophomore year. He was quite the handsome boy."

Sabrina handed the photo to Mrs. Hansen and waited for her to sit down in a chair opposite.

"You knew him well?" Mrs. Hansen continued.

"I was dating him," replied Lucy. "We'd only just started going out though."

Mrs. Hansen smiled. "He said he'd met someone. An English girl. That would be you."

Lucy blushed. "Yes, Ma'am. I just had to come to the funeral. It was such a shock."

Mrs. Hansen's face dropped and she let the photo fall to her lap. "Yes it was. The police have only just gone a few hours ago. Wanted all sorts of details. I didn't know what to say to them. He'd only been gone a few months. Off to that dealership in Washington. I don't know why he was in Arizona. He never said he was going anywhere."

"He didn't tell me either," said Lucy. "I was expecting to see him for a date actually when he disappeared."

"Would you like to see some more photos of him?" Mrs. Hansen got to her feet and walked over to the table. "We've been gathering a lot of them together. For friends and relatives to see of course." She picked up a large one from the end of the table. "No one offered you a drink? We can't have that." She put the photo back down again and walked towards the door. "You girls drink beer?"

"You don't need to," replied Sabrina.

"Nonsense, Ben would like to entertain you. He was like that."

"We shouldn't stay too long," Sabrina said, as soon as Mrs. Hansen had left the room. "I'm sure they have lots of things to organize for the funeral."

Lucy nodded. "I know. I just wanted to pay my respects. It adds a little closure being able to see something of his home life."

"Here you go, girls. Cold ones from the fridge." Mrs. Hansen handed the two women a beer and walked over to the table once more. "I've got a photo of him winning the college cycle race somewhere. That was his proudest moment. Here we are."

Lucy and Sabrina walked over to the table to take a look at the photo Ben's mother was holding. "He certainly loved cycling," Lucy said. "He even made me go with him one day."

"He tried to get everyone doing it," Mrs. Hansen replied. "Even me once." She laughed. "I'm going to miss him."

Lucy put her arms around Ben's mother and the two of them cried in silence before Lucy and Sabrina made their excuses to leave.

"I just don't understand it," Lucy said a little later after they had checked into their hotel room. "From everything his mother said, Ben didn't do much without telling her. He was the quiet type and didn't have a lot of different friends. It makes no sense why he would abandon his bike by the trail and drive all the way to Arizona. And then the police think he was murdered by the same serial killer that has killed those women in Seattle. It doesn't make any sense at all."

"What are you suggesting we do?"

"I don't know. But I can't leave it at this. I was just getting to know Ben really well and something very odd happened to him. I need to find out the truth. I'm going to have to confront Beau about all this when I get back."

"And why would you do that? Beau can't possibly be involved."

"It's all I've got to go on, Sabrina. Beau threatening Ben is all I've got. I've made up my mind, I'm going to talk to him about it as soon as we get back to Melrose."

32

"Are you sure you want to do this?" Sabrina asked Lucy as they sat and waited for Beau to arrive in Paddy's.

Lucy nodded. "Yes, I'm sure. I'm a little nervous, but I'm quite sure." She took another sip of her beer.

"Be careful. Don't have too much to drink. We don't want you getting out of control."

"And what does that mean? You think if I'm drunk I'll do something stupid?"

"I'm just saying, that's all. Just take it easy. We have no proof of anything whatsoever. For all we know Beau may deny everything. And remember, Beau has no idea you want to quiz him over Ben. He just thinks he's coming out with a few of the guys from the office."

"Relax, Sabrina. I'll be fine. I promise." She took a large drink from her beer and put the nearly empty bottle back down on the table. "I'm just going for a wee. I'll be back in a moment." Lucy got up from the table and headed off towards the restrooms.

Sabrina took a sip from her diet coke and waited for the party to begin. She wasn't looking forward to this at all. She had used deception to get people to come and unless she controlled the situation there would be a lot of arguing. She put her drink down and looked up in time to see the three men coming through the door. She waved to them as Tim led them over to the women's table.

"Hi Sabrina, you on your own?" asked Tim.

"No, Lucy's here. She's in the restroom."

"Lucy?" asked Beau. "Your friend Lucy's here?" His eyes lit up and a smile appeared at the corner of his mouth. He squeezed around the table and sat next to Sabrina before anyone else could choose a seat.

"She's been a little upset recently and needed cheering up. I thought it would be good to bring her out for a beer."

"We'll cheer her up," said Tim, sitting down opposite Sabrina. "And how's my cousin tonight?"

"You're cousins?" asked Beau.

Sabrina nodded. "You didn't know?"

"I guess there's a lot of things I don't know about the office." Beau ordered a beer from the server and leaned across the table. "Is Wendy here already too?"

Sabrina shook her head. "No. I thought she would be with you."

"Ouch," said Sam.

"She may work with me," replied Beau, "but she's not *with* me like you're suggesting."

"I wasn't suggesting anything." Sabrina laughed. She looked up as Lucy returned to the table. "I think you already know everyone?"

Lucy smiled and took her seat next to Sabrina and finished her beer. "What's it take to get another beer here?"

"I'll get you one," said Beau. "Same again?"

"Sure."

Beau got to his feet and walked off towards the bar.

"Are you okay, Lucy?" asked Tim. "We heard you've had a bit of a tough time recently."

"Yeah, I'm fine. Life goes on. I'll just have to find me another man." Lucy nudged Sabrina and winked. "Oh look everyone, here's Wendy."

Heads turned as Wendy approached the table. "You look, er, different, Wendy," said Sam.

Wendy took off her coat and took a seat next to Sam. "Thanks. I've had my hair done differently. That's why I'm a little late."

"You changed the color," said Sabrina.

Wendy giggled. "I know. I was feeling a little wicked. Besides, with my new job I figured I could afford to splash out a little and have a bit of a make-over."

"It looks good," said Sabrina.

"Yes, good," added Lucy.

"Wow, Wendy. What did you do?" asked Beau, returning to the table.

"She had her hair colored and got a new cut," answered Sabrina.

"It looks good," said Beau, retaking his seat. He leaned over towards Lucy. "Your beer will be here in a moment."

The server arrived with several drinks and put them down on the table. Wendy ordered a beer and Tim and Sam opened up a menu to take a look. Everyone was soon engaged in all sorts of private and public conversations. Lucy drank a couple more beers.

"Sabrina said you needed cheering up," Beau said, leaning across Sabrina to talk to Lucy. "Nothing too bad I hope?"

"Hmm? Yes, cheering up," Lucy replied. "Actually I wanted to talk to you."

Sabrina took a hold of Lucy's hand and squeezed it under the table.

"My boyfriend Ben said that you threatened him on the trail a couple of weeks ago." Lucy pulled her hand free of Sabrina's and wrapped it around her beer. "Is that true?"

"I did run into him, yes. But I don't recall threatening him." Beau picked up his beer and casually took a sip.

"What did you say then?"

"Actually I asked him if he could help me fix my bicycle and then he introduced himself to me."

"So you didn't threaten him?" Lucy finished another beer and clumsily put the bottle back down on the table.

"I may have said he was a lucky man to be dating you, but that's all. Maybe that he should take care not to lose you, but I never threatened him. That's not like me at all."

Lucy leaned into Sabrina. "Can I get another beer? Will you order me one?" She tried to focus her attention back to Beau. "You're sure about that?"

"I'm sure, yes."

Lucy giggled and turned to Sabrina. "He's quite hot, isn't he?" She spoke in what she thought was her quiet voice but instead could be heard by several tables nearby.

"I think we need to get you home," Sabrina said, trying to get Wendy to help her. "The beer has got the better of you today."

"I'm fine. I just need another one. Then this Beau can tell me more about what he's been doing." Lucy slumped slightly as Sabrina and Wendy got her to her feet and wrapped her coat around her shoulders.

"I'll just run her home," Sabrina said to Beau. "Sorry she's a little insensitive."

Beau smiled. "It's okay. I was actually quite enjoying it." He waved at Lucy. "See you again."

"Bye Beau. Beau bye. Bye bye Beau," Lucy giggled as Sabrina helped her out of Paddy's and into her car that was parked close by outside.

* * *

"My head feels like someone hit it with a hammer," Lucy said, coming out of her bedroom late the following morning.

Sabrina laughed. "Too much beer, Lucy."

"What time did we get home?"

"I brought you home early. About eight. You were certainly in a mood to get drunk."

Lucy put a hand to her forehead and winced. "And I'm paying the price this morning. I don't even remember getting home." She shuffled into the kitchen and poured herself a glass of water. "Eight o'clock? That was early."

Sabrina got to her feet and joined Lucy in the kitchen. "Like I said, you were intent on getting drunk. I think you had about six beers." She reached up into a cupboard and pulled down a bottle of aspirin. "Here, take two of these."

"Six beers? No wonder I feel like this then." Lucy took a sip of the water and swallowed down the aspirins. "Thanks."

She gulped down the rest of the water and put the glass into the sink. "And I didn't even get a chance to talk to Beau. And that was the whole point."

Sabrina laughed. "You did get to talk to him, Lucy. Don't you remember?"

Lucy tried to recollect the events of the night before. "No, I don't. What did he say about Ben?"

"Sabrina gave Lucy a big hug and let her go. "It was more of a case of what you said about Beau."

Lucy blushed. "What do you mean?"

"I think your exact words were, *he's quite hot, isn't he*?"

Lucy blushed even more. "No? Surely I didn't say that."

Sabrina nodded. "Yep."

"Shit!" Lucy burst out laughing and immediately put a hand to her head again.

"Well, I guess that's one way to get information out of him, Lucy. Break him down with charm."

"Shit! Now what am I going to do? That's so embarrassing."

Sabrina walked back to the couch and sat down. "The good news is he said he didn't threaten Ben; just told him he'd better take good care of you. I actually think Beau was just jealous about you. I know he can be a bit of a jerk, but I don't think he would actually harm anyone."

Lucy poured herself another glass of water and sat down in the chair next to Sabrina. "No, I don't think so either. Any fight between the two of them would have been a comedy. I'm sure neither of them could punch properly."

Lucy sank back in the chair and closed her eyes. "I do miss Ben. I hope the police find whoever is responsible for killing him." She wiped her eyes briefly and took another sip of her water.

"Who's that?" Sabrina asked, getting up as the doorbell rang. "Are you expecting anyone?"

"No. And don't let anyone inside. I'm not decent." Lucy hastily pulled her dressing gown tighter around her.

Sabrina went to the door and opened it a crack. "Yes, that's right. Thanks." She opened the door a little wider and pulled a large arrangement of flowers inside with her before closing the door once more.

"Flowers? Who's sending you flowers?"

"They're for you, silly." She crossed over to Lucy and handed them to her. "I wonder who they could be from?"

"Don't be so silly. I'm sure they're from Ben's parents or something." Lucy untied the wrap and peeled off the cellophane. Then she pulled off the small envelope that was attached to the main bouquet of yellow lilies and pink roses.

"Well?"

"It says, *I hope you're feeling better this morning. Let's have coffee some time.*"

"And the name?"

"No name, Sabrina. There's no name inside. But they have to be from Beau, don't they?"

"I think so, Lucy. I think you officially came onto him last night."

"Shit! That wasn't the plan at all. I'm not ready to date anyone else at the moment. I need to get closure on Ben."

Sabrina took the flowers back from Lucy and put them in the kitchen. "You don't have to see him you know. Just because he sent you flowers. You know how much of a player he is."

"But they are nice flowers and it was a thoughtful thing to do. Maybe I didn't give him the chance he deserves."

Sabrina took down a vase from the cupboard and started filling it with water. "On your own head, Lucy. Just be careful."

33

"So how's the new job, then? Still liking it?" Sabrina pulled up a chair next to Wendy and sat down with her coffee.

"It's really good. I'm so lucky. Things just seem to keep falling into place. A few weeks ago I was just in Support and now I'm a director with my own office."

"And it seems you're quite a popular boss from what I've heard around the office. Unlike a certain other person."

Wendy smiled. "He's not so bad. Once you get to know him."

"I hope so. Lucy's crazy about him. She won't stop talking about it. Ever since he sent her those flowers."

"Beau sent Lucy flowers?"

"At the weekend. After her embarrassing moment."

"That was quite funny. Was she alright?"

"She was fine after several glasses of water and some aspirin."

"Maybe Beau was just feeling sorry for her," said Wendy, fidgeting a little in her chair.

"I don't think so. There's nothing that he doesn't do unplanned. He knew what he was doing by sending flowers. He even wrote he hoped they could meet for a coffee."

"No!"

"What, Wendy? Are you okay?"

"Sorry. I was just thinking. Lucy's not the right kind of girl for him at all."

"You're not jealous are you?"

Wendy smiled. "No. Seriously. I'm completely over him. Besides he's my boss. That wouldn't work at all. No, it's just that as a potential dating partner, I'm sure Lucy could do a lot better than Beau."

"If you say so, Wendy."

"Hey, let's not fall out over this. I'm sorry. It's just my opinion that's all." Wendy flicked her hair back over her shoulder. "I was actually thinking about having a girl's weekend away. What do you think?"

"Who's going?"

"You, me and Lucy. We should invite her. I was thinking Las Vegas. I had so much fun when I went down there last time and it would be a great place to go and party for the weekend. What do you think?"

"I think that's a great idea, Wendy. I've never been there before and now you have the inside knowledge you could take us to all the hot places."

Wendy laughed. "I don't know if I know that many. But at least one or two. I'll tell you what, I'll find out some prices from Travel and let you know. Do you think Lucy will be up for it?"

Sabrina nodded. "I'm sure. She's been in quite the party mood recently. I think it's her way of letting Ben go."

"Still no news on that?"

"Nothing. I called the police yesterday to see if they were keeping anything from her but they had no news at all. At first they thought the person that killed Ben was the same as the person that killed the women in Seattle. But now they're not so sure. They think it might be two people working together. Something about *different technical issues*. I wasn't really sure what they were talking about to be honest. Anyway, they still don't have any suspects."

"That's too bad. It must be terrible for her. And by the way, I didn't tell Beau anything about it just in case you're wondering. There's no reason for him to know that Ben's dead."

Sabrina touched Wendy's arm. "Thanks for that. The last thing we need is Beau gloating over it and making a big play for Lucy. She's very vulnerable at the moment."

Wendy nodded. "I know." She got to her feet. "Anyway, sorry but I've got to get back to my office. There's a sales presentation I need to prepare for."

"Sorry, Wendy. I wasn't trying to hold you up. Really."

Wendy laughed. "I know. See you later. Let me know about Lucy and Vegas. Let's try for next weekend." Wendy turned away and walked a few paces along the corridor before stopping and leaning against a wall. She was just going to have to have words with him. She continued walking along the corridor and stopped outside Beau's office. She knocked and went in, not waiting for the invite. "We need to talk, Beau," she said, closing the door behind her.

"Make yourself at home," Beau said, looking up from his computer. "You can't just come into my office any time you want to you know."

Wendy sat down in a chair opposite Beau's desk. "I'm not here to discuss anything Beau. I need to tell you something. So listen up." She ran two fingers through her hair and leaned forward. "I heard you sent flowers to Lucy at the weekend?"

"What if I did?"

"You know you can't go out with her, Beau. You know the rules. We both know them now. We can't date people."

"Don't tell me what I can and can't do, Wendy. I managed well enough before you came on the scene and met the Anons. I've dated a few women before without problems."

"But Lucy's different and you know that. She's not just some woman. She's Sabrina's roommate and friend for one. You can't very well disappear her can you? There's no future in dating her so why even go there?"

"She's cute. She's blonde. I like her. She's funny. She has an accent. Are there any more reasons I need to give you? Maybe I just want to have a bit of fun and hang out with someone for a while."

"But you can't have a girlfriend, Beau."

"Who said anything about a girlfriend? Anyway, you don't know what the plan is. Maybe I'm supposed to be with her."

"Beau. Look, you can't…"

"Wendy! It's none of your business, okay? You are my partner. My junior partner I should remind you. And you are here to help me in whatever I feel necessary. You will do well to remember that. This job has been given to you as a privilege. It could just as easily be taken away from you I'm sure." Beau's face continued to turn a bright red in color.

"Go to hell, Beau," Wendy screamed, getting to her feet. "Sometimes you're the biggest ass on this planet. Don't threaten me over my job. You know it wasn't yours to give. The Anons chose me, not you, and you'll do well to remember that. I may be your junior partner but I can still give you advice. So grow up and think about your responsibilities." She turned towards the door and glanced back over her shoulder as she walked. "Think on that. I'll be in my office."

Wendy slammed Beau's door shut behind her and headed back to her office, ignoring the stares of several people who had heard parts of the argument and had come to investigate. She brushed past Sam, almost knocking him over, and turned into her office. "Shit!" she screamed at no one in particular as she sat down behind her desk. "That guy is a complete jerk."

"He is?" asked Sam, who had followed her into her office.

"I don't want to talk about it."

Sam pushed the door shut behind him and walked over to her desk. "You don't have to explain. I think he's a jerk sometimes too and he's my best friend!"

Wendy laughed. "Thanks, Sam. I needed that." She leaned back in her chair and put her hands behind her head.

"Are you okay?"

"Yeah, I'm fine. It's just that sometimes he makes me so mad. He knows exactly which buttons to push."

"At least you stand up to him. No one else does. People like you for that, Wendy." Sam placed his hands on her desk and leaned forward. "What was it about? Some project?"

"If only! No it was about Lucy, from the other night. He only wants to date her now."

"He does? Well he does seem to like them tall and blonde."

"That's not the point, Sam. Lucy is Sabrina's best friend and if he messes with her it'll cause all sorts of hell in the office. I told him he should go look elsewhere for a girlfriend."

Sam laughed and stood back up. "Rather you than me. No wonder he got mad."

"Oh yeah, he got mad alright. He even threatened me with my job."

"What?"

"It's okay. I can look after myself. He needs my expertise to win these projects and understand all the technology that's in those companies we've bought."

"What technology?"

Wendy's face dropped. "Sorry, Sam. I can't tell you about that. It's all secret at the moment. I'm sure it'll be common knowledge soon enough."

"Oh. I didn't know Zygote was doing secret work now."

"No it's not secret, just not ready for public consumption yet." Wendy looked down at her computer and clicked a couple of buttons with her mouse. "You're going to have to excuse me, Sam. Looks like there's something I've got to jump on."

"Sure. As long as you're alright. That's all I really wanted to know."

"I'm fine. But thanks."

"No problem. I'll see you later."

Wendy watched Sam as he left the office and closed her door behind him. She stared back at her screen and then pushed herself back in her chair a little. That hadn't gone quite as expected. But Sam was right, no one else stood up to Beau like she did. Maybe that was one of the reasons she was chosen, to keep Beau in check a little. Chosen. Just what exactly had she been chosen for? What was she supposed to do now that she was one of the Anons? How could being a director of Zygote Technologies be important to someone else? There had to be some payoff to be made. No one got anything in life for free. She was already beginning to dread the day that no doubt would come. Anyway, Vegas. She scooted her chair forward again and pulled up Outlook. She sent an email to Travel asking about flights and hotel reservations for next weekend. She would need to get Lucy on her own and try and convince her of the stupidity of dating Beau. A weekend in Vegas would be a great cover for that discussion. She smiled to herself. She was starting to become a little devious herself. Beau had better watch out. Vegas. She let a smile wash across her face as she remembered the man she had used. So many good things had happened to her since then. Perhaps she would get another chance to have a little more fun on her next visit. She just had to make sure that Lucy could never become Beau's next victim.

34

"Come on, Lucy. Hurry up. We'll be late."

"I'm nearly ready," Lucy replied from her bedroom. "Last few pieces." She stared at the pile of clothes on her bed one more time and cursed silently to herself. It was no good; she was going to have to leave a few of the pieces out. She had tried packing the case six times already and each time there had been things that didn't fit. Hot, she thought to herself. It's going to be hot. At least twenty degrees hotter than Melrose anyway. Two sweaters were tossed aside and she tried one more time. Nearly. Maybe one less pair of jeans. That would have to do it.

Lucy was excited to be traveling to Las Vegas. It was her first time and she was getting to have a real break, not just a day trip to somewhere. She was amazed her bosses had given her the time off, but she was owed vacation after all. Wendy had managed to get them cut price hotel rooms through her travel company and the air fare was really inexpensive. Maybe she'd have to think twice about a vacation again in the summer, but at the moment she didn't really care. Going away with Sabrina and Wendy was going to be fun. She smiled to herself. Wendy seemed to have changed quite a bit recently. Her new hair style had given her more confidence. Maybe she should try that too! And Sabrina had stopped bugging her about her relationships too. Hopefully she wouldn't bring it up in Las Vegas. She picked up her bikini and laid it flat on the bed. It had been a while since she had worn it but the thought of lounging in front of a warm pool watching the hot guys go by gave her brief goose-bumps. She picked it back up and stuffed it down inside her suitcase. "Just coming." She closed the top of the case and pressed down hard while she closed the zipper. Hopefully it wouldn't split apart on the journey.

"What have you been doing in there?" Sabrina asked as Lucy entered the living room pulling her case behind her.

"It took a while, okay. I think I may need a new case."

Sabrina looked at Lucy's case and smiled. "We're only going for a long weekend, Lucy. What are you taking?"

"You never know what you might need. I'm going prepared."

Sabrina picked up a small carry-on and made for the door.

"Is that it?"

"Bikini, book, black dress, some toiletries. What else do I need?"

"You make it sound so simple, Sabrina." Lucy followed Sabrina from the apartment and they made their way into the parking lot and put their bags in the back of Sabrina's car.

"I hope the traffic's not too bad. We're already later than I planned leaving."

"Relax, Sabrina. We still have plenty of time." Lucy messed with the radio until she found some music she wanted to listen to. "We're meeting Wendy at the gate?"

"Yeah. It seemed the easiest way. Less to co-ordinate." Sabrina pulled onto I-520 and moved over to the outside lane. "And we need to make an agreement about boys too. While we're in Vegas. If you take anyone back to our room you need to put the *do not disturb* sign on the door. Okay?"

"And the same goes for you with girls. I don't want to walk in on you with some naked woman."

Sabrina laughed. "Some chance. I've almost forgotten what it's like to have a girlfriend."

"I probably won't be going after anyone anyway. It's only a weekend break and I'm not into those one night flings.

Besides, I've got Beau to think about. I can fantasize about him when I'm laid in front of the pool."

"You need to stop thinking about him, Lucy. He's really no good for you. He's a jerk and will probably only use you. All he wants is to get into your pants and after he has done that he'll drop you and move onto someone else."

"How do you know that, Sabrina? Have you seen him do that before?"

"No, it's just what people say."

"People say a lot of things, Sabrina, but that doesn't make them true. Besides, he's a very successful man from what I can see. How many other people do you know his age that are Vice-Presidents of a company? He's a winner and he's going places. And if I can tag along for a little fun on the way, why shouldn't I?"

Okay, okay. Let's change the subject before we ruin our holiday mood." Sabrina merged onto I-405 and headed towards the airport. "Did you do any research on where we are staying?"

Lucy smiled. "I did. The hotel has two pools and a big outdoor jacuzzi. Also several very nice restaurants. Oh, and a nightclub. I don't think there's even a need to go outside the hotel. All in all it'll make for a nice lazy few days."

"Great. I am so looking forward to this. The last few weeks have just been crazy."

Lucy sat back in her chair and closed her eyes for a moment. "I know." She opened her eyes and turned the radio down a little. "I got an email from Ben's mother yesterday."

"What did it say?"

"Not a lot really. She thanked us for coming out. She said it was nice to meet us and I seemed like the sort of girl she'd like as a daughter-in-law."

"Wow. You were in there!"

"Yeah, I don't know if I was quite ready for that. Anyway, she also said she's spoken to the police a few times and they didn't have any further news for her. The case was progressing slowly but they hoped ultimately to be able to arrest someone for Ben's murder."

"That's it? Progressing slowly? That doesn't sound too promising."

"No it doesn't. At least they are still trying." Lucy turned the music up again and the two women listened to the radio in silence for the remainder of their journey to the airport.

"There she is," Sabrina said as she and Lucy made their way to their gate at the airport a little later. "I said we were late." They walked a little further before Wendy noticed them hurrying along. "Hey there, Wendy. Sorry we're late. Lucy had a little packing crisis."

"I was getting a little worried. They'll be boarding in a few minutes."

"I know. And then when we got here we hit all the long lines at security. Anyway, we're here now." Sabrina slumped down in a seat next to Wendy.

"You want mine?" Wendy asked to the standing Lucy.

"No, I'm fine thanks. We'll be sat for two hours on the plane anyway." She put her bag down next to Sabrina. "Watch that for me will you. I just have to go to the restroom."

"We're just about to board, Lucy."

"I won't be two minutes." Lucy skipped off the restroom, leaving Sabrina to watch her bag.

"I tried to talk to her about Beau," Sabrina said, as soon as Lucy was out of earshot. "But she's not having any of it. I think she's actually besotted with the guy. Maybe it's the shock of losing Ben or something, but either way she won't be warned off him."

"I'll have a word with her about him," Wendy replied. "I even had it out with Beau at the office. That was the commotion you heard about last week."

Sabrina smiled. "I guessed you were giving him a piece of your mind about something. People in the office like the way you stand up to him."

"Thanks. Someone has to though. Seriously. But anyway, he told me much the same thing. That he would see who he pleases and I should mind my own business. Still, I'm going to tell Lucy one more time. I just don't want to see her get hurt."

"Me neither."

Wendy suddenly sat up straight and rubbed her hands together. "I know. If we get Lucy set up with a guy in Vegas then maybe she'll forget all about Beau. I'm sure we can arrange something. After all, a tall skinny English girl in Vegas must be attractive to someone."

"Wendy!"

"You know what I mean!"

"Sshh. She's coming back." The two women burst out laughing.

"What's so funny?"

"Nothing, Lucy. We were just sharing a joke about someone in the office," said Sabrina, trying to stop herself from laughing.

"Hey, come on, they're calling our flight," said Wendy, getting to her feet.

Sabrina handed Lucy's bag to her and got to her feet. "Vegas here we come!" She linked arms with Wendy and Lucy and the three of them headed for the boarding gate.

"Hey Lucy, I did want to have a word with you," Wendy said a little later after Sabrina had gotten up from her seat and headed towards the back of the plane.

"If it's about Beau, I really don't want to hear it, Wendy."

"Just hear me out, Lucy. There are a lot of things you don't know about Beau."

"And you do?" Lucy turned her head away from Wendy briefly before turning back. "Look, I'm sorry. It's just that all anyone ever wants to do is give me advice about Beau. I just want to be able to make my own decision."

"I know that, Lucy. I really do. But I also feel I need to warn you about him. He's manipulative and controlling. And he always gets what he wants, at whatever personal cost to the others involved. Why do you think he has got so far at Zygote already? He walks over anyone in his way."

"You're telling me there are lots of buried bodies along the way?"

Wendy laughed. "There's a lot of truth in that. There's a reason why Beau doesn't have a girlfriend. Did you think about that?"

"Maybe I can change him. Soften him up a little. You can't fault me for wanting to try, can you?"

Wendy leaned closer towards Lucy and lowered her voice. "I'll tell you a secret, Lucy. I used to fancy Beau too. A lot. I used to dream of getting together with him. But you know it would never have worked. And not because we work together, but because I wouldn't want a relationship where I didn't have any say in it and it was all on his terms. That's what it would be like if you dated Beau. Seriously."

Lucy leaned back further in her seat and remained silent a moment before replying. "I hear what you're saying, Wendy. But at the end of the day it's my life. I thought I had found someone great in Ben and look what happened there. So this time I'm going to return the interest of someone who obviously would like to date me. And if I find out he's a jerk like everyone says then that's the way it is. But if I discover a man who just doesn't know how to behave around a woman then I'll teach him. Either way all I'm saying Wendy, is to give me a little leeway here. One date and I'll know a lot more about him."

"It's your choice, Lucy. I can only give you some advice taken from experience and that's what…"

"Sabrina, my turn," Lucy interrupted as Sabrina returned to her seat. "Excuse me, Wendy. Thanks."

"Did I miss something?" Sabrina asked as a red-faced Lucy squeezed past her and briskly walked towards the back of the plane.

35

"Let's just have some fun tonight," Sabrina said, trying to hold a fragile peace together between Wendy and Lucy. "We've spent the day at the pool and now we need to let our hair down. The least you can both do is come out with a positive attitude."

"I'm fine," said Wendy.

"Just let's not talk about anything back in Melrose," said Lucy. "Otherwise I'm going straight back to the hotel room."

"Okay. Wendy, you alright with that?" Sabrina waited until Wendy nodded. "Lucy, you'll relax a little?"

"Sure."

"Then let's go and have some fun then." Sabrina was relieved that at least the two women were talking again. The past day and a half had been very stressful with Lucy refusing to do anything that Wendy wanted and insisting on hanging out at the pool separately from her. Sabrina had been forced to try and get between them and up until tonight it had been a game she couldn't win. "What's the name of the club again, Wendy?"

"Project fifty-six. It's only down the street."

"We're walking?" asked Lucy. "I have my heels on."

"We can get a cab," said Wendy. "It's still quite a ways anyway."

The three women walked through the lobby of their hotel and got in a taxi that was waiting outside. Five minutes later and they were strolling through the lobby of another hotel and looking for the nightclub.

"Ladies," said a large bouncer outside the club, "this way. No cover charge for you three. The bar's straight ahead."

The women smiled, walked past the man and headed towards the bar.

"Quite a hunk, isn't he?" said Wendy.

"Probably not the smartest guy though."

Wendy giggled. "I don't care about that."

"Stop it," said Sabrina. "We haven't even got inside yet."

"Here's a table," said Lucy. "Shall we sit here?"

"Sure, this looks good enough." Sabrina sat down next to Lucy and Wendy took a seat to one side, trying to face out towards the dance floor.

"At least we got here before it is too crowded. Last time I was here it was totally packed." A waitress stopped by their table. "Rum and coke, please."

Lucy and Sabrina ordered beers and the waitress went off to get their drinks.

"Don't go too crazy on the beers, Lucy. We don't want a repeat of the other week."

"Seriously? Are you both just going to pick on me all weekend? I thought we were here to have some fun."

"You're right, Lucy. I'm sorry," said Sabrina. "Let's scope out some of the talent."

"There's a group of guys already watching us from over there," said Wendy, nodding her head towards the far side.

"They're just boys," Lucy replied. "If I'm going to dance with anyone tonight it's going to be a real man."

"Or a real woman."

"Speak for yourself, Sabrina," laughed Lucy.

"Watch out girls, here they come." Wendy straightened herself up and ran a couple of fingers through her hair.

"You girls look lonely. Can we interest you in some company?" The tallest of the three men stooped down to talk to the women. He looked just about old enough to be twenty-one.

"Sure. A drink is always welcome," answered Wendy.

The tall man turned to his friends, smiled and then squeezed in next to Sabrina. "I'm Joe." He turned to his friends who were taking their seats next to Lucy and Wendy. "This is Neil and Gabe."

"Hi," the other two guys said.

"I'm Wendy, and this is Lucy and Sabrina. We already have drinks coming. What brings you guys into Vegas?"

"We're with a bachelor party," replied Gabe. "But they are all resting tonight. Yesterday was a little heavy for them all. It's just us three left."

"Where are you girls from?" asked Joe

"Seattle," replied Wendy.

The waitress arrived with the women's drinks and Joe pulled out some cash and paid. Lucy and Sabrina took a gulp from their beers and smiled at each other.

"Seattle? The rainy city," continued Joe. "We're from Tampa."

"Your first time in Vegas?" Gabe asked Lucy. She nodded. "Having fun?" Lucy nodded again. "You don't say much, do you?" Lucy smiled.

"She's the shy one," said Wendy, trying to get the conversation going again. "I'm not."

"How about you?" Gabe said, turning to Sabrina.

"Oh. She's the gay one," said Wendy. Sabrina smiled.

"Shit!" said Gabe. "Nice job, Joe. One ugly one, one shy one and one gay one."

Wendy picked up her drink and threw it over Gabe. "You need to leave, assholes."

Joe laughed and pulled Neil to his feet as he stood up.

"Sorry love," Gabe said, wiping off his face. "You just lost out on the only chance you had of getting laid tonight anyway." He jumped to his feet and ran off after the other two who were beating a hasty retreat back to the other side of the room.

Sabrina burst out laughing.

"That wasn't funny," said Wendy. "He was a complete asshole. Really rude."

"Sorry." Sabrina covered her mouth and tried not to look at Lucy who was also nearly wetting herself. "It was funny though."

"And a waste of a good drink. I'm going to the bathroom and then I'm going to get myself another." Wendy got to her feet and hurried off in the direction of the restrooms. Sabrina stole a glance at Lucy and they both burst out laughing.

"Still think I'm the ugly one, do you?" Wendy asked, a lot later that evening as she sidled up to Gabe and put a hand on his backside. She squeezed and he jumped a little.

"Sorry love, I didn't mean anything by it. Can I get you a drink?"

"I'm alright for the moment." She looked around. "Where are your friends?"

"They left already. Ages ago. They left me drinking on my own. Still, it's good here. Lots of women to watch."

Wendy moved her hand to Gabe's other cheek. "And did you speak to any of them yet?"

"I was just going to finish my drink first."

"And then what?" Wendy squeezed again and then ran her hand inside Gabe's thigh.

Gabe gulped and turned his head towards Wendy. "I don't know."

"So, do you still think I'm ugly? You didn't answer my question."

"No, you're alright. I was just teasing really." He stepped back a little to get a better look at her. "You've got nice tits anyway."

"I'll take that as a compliment then." Wendy slipped her hand around Gabe's waist and pulled him towards her. "Would you like to touch them?"

Gabe's face turned a little pale as Wendy pulled his head towards her chest before letting him go again. He nodded.

"Let's get out of here then. Where are you staying?"

"Upstairs."

"Even better. Lead on, Gabe."

Gabe put his half-finished beer down and took Wendy's outstretched hand and led her out of the nightclub, back towards his room. "Where are your friends?" he asked.

"Enjoying themselves. They won't miss me. They were deep in conversation when I left them some time ago." She squeezed his hand. "Anyway, enough about them. We're going to have some fun tonight, aren't we?"

Gabe pulled Wendy along, stumbling slightly as he walked. After a few minutes they reached his room and he opened the door for her. "Sshhh. Don't make too much noise. You might wake the others."

Wendy stopped in the doorway. "You're sharing a room with your friends?" Gabe nodded. "We can't go in here then. I'm not that kind of girl." She took a couple of steps backwards and pulled Gabe towards her and shut the door. "Let's find a cupboard somewhere. There's bound to be a supply room or something." Wendy took Gabe's hand and led him down the corridor. Around a corner, nearly hidden from sight, she found a room that was unlocked. She pushed open the door, pulled him inside and threw him up against the wall. Within seconds her lips were on him and she was kissing him passionately. "No," she muttered as she felt his hands reach into her dress, trying to find her breasts. "Not tonight big boy." She took his hand and pulled it back towards his side and pushed her tongue deeper in his mouth, beginning to explore the edges of his mind as the magic did its work. She opened her eyes and watched as his burst open in surprise. She would have to be careful. This was a dangerous place to do anything foolish. She couldn't take everything from him. There were too many cameras that could be played back in the morning. As she pressed against him and wandered through his mind she could feel him pressing against her. He wanted her and yet he was confused at the same time. She smiled and then suddenly let him go. She took a step back from him and watched as he half-sunk to the ground still leaning against the wall. "Thanks Gabe. Have a great rest of your vacation. Hope your head's not too messed up in the morning." She opened the door to the room and spat on him as she left. He had it coming to him. It was just a shame they were both somewhere so public. She would have enjoyed using him up completely. Still, according to what she had learnt already, he would be sick with a terrible headache for days. Maybe that was even better. Wendy pressed the button for the elevator and waited for it to come. The trip to Vegas hadn't been so bad after all.

* * *

"You're going to have to go home without me," Lucy mumbled from under her covers the following morning. "My head is killing me. I didn't even think to bring my tablets with me either. I'm just going to have to sit it out."

"Did you drink too much?" Sabrina asked, sitting on the edge of Lucy's bed.

"No. This is one of my migraines. I never imagined I would get one here in Las Vegas. Seriously, I'll be fine. I'll just get a later flight. If you could ask the front desk to keep the room for a few more hours. By this afternoon I'm sure I'll be able to get up."

"I can stay. It's no problem. I'll just tell Wendy."

Lucy reached out a hand from under the covers and Sabrina took it. "Just go, Sabrina. You needn't change everything just for me. I'll be home later tonight. I'll give you a call from the airport and maybe you can come and get me from Seatac?"

Sabrina squeezed Lucy's hand. "Of course. Are you sure?"

"Just go. I'll be fine."

Sabrina let go of Lucy's hand and got up from the bed. "Okay. I'd better go and find Wendy. No doubt she has a story to tell. She must have found some guy. Typical. We were left on our own again." She crossed over to the door and picked up her bag. "Call me later, okay. Get some rest. I'll speak to the front desk. Bye." Sabrina left the room and walked down the corridor. "We're seriously going to have to get you examined by a neurologist," she said to herself as she waited for the elevator.

36

"Take a seat, come on in." Wendy held open the door as her small department filed into the conference room. She waited as the last of her group came in and took a seat before closing the door. She walked over to the long table and took a seat at the head. "Thanks for coming. I wanted to say a few words now that we have everybody here and we're ready to begin our mission in earnest." She looked around the room and studied the faces of her team one by one. There were six of them and each one was older than her, with more corporate experience. Still, that wasn't her concern. She had to move past that and remember that she was the Director.

"The New Ventures Integration group has been charged with discovering the pieces of other companies' proprietary intellectual properties that we can safely integrate into our products to make them better. As such you have all signed specific non-disclosures and I would remind you again that the work we do here is not to be discussed with anyone outside of this room with the exception of Beau Tempest. And by anyone I mean anyone. Not even Peter Ramsey or anyone else from corporate. You're all clear on that, right?" She waited until she had received nods of affirmation from everyone before continuing. "Okay. Today I want to talk a little about the company we have just bought in San Diego. Beau returned yesterday from a preliminary trip there and he has briefed me on a number of interesting projects they are working on. Although their main field of work is bio-technology, there are several overlaps that could help us expand more fully into our target market. Today I am looking for a couple of volunteers that are willing to spend some time in San Diego doing a little more detailed research for us. I would go myself but there are other matters I need to attend to." She scanned the room and waited as a few of the people whispered to each other. "Volunteers?" Four hands went up. "Rajeev, Cindy, Namitha and Tracy. Good. Cindy, Namitha, I think this could be your opportunity to show me just what you're capable of. Rajeev and Tracy, next time. Okay, that's mostly it for today. There will be an email coming out later that gives you all a little more background on some of our objectives. In the meantime, take a read of the PowerPoint I sent out yesterday." She got to her feet. "Thanks you can all go, except Cindy and Namitha. I'll have a separate word with you both." Wendy waited for the others to go before closing the door once more. "Thanks. Both of you. I want to say now that what you've volunteered for is not going to be pleasant. There are sights you're going to see in San Diego that you'd probably rather not see. There are certain elements of bio-technology that exist on the fringes of most people's morals. I just wanted to warn you now. Are you both okay with that?" She waited while they both nodded. "Good. I'll send you both an email later. In the meantime, go home and pack for two weeks and be back in the office by four o'clock. You'll be leaving this evening. Thanks."

    Wendy closed a folder that was in front of her and waited while the two women left the room. She sat back in her chair and breathed deeply. What had she gotten herself into? The report she'd read from Beau was most disturbing. Especially some of the photos. While she'd been enjoying herself in Vegas he had been in San Diego checking out Zygote's latest acquisition. She allowed herself a smile. Yesterday's trip back from Vegas had been mostly a blur. There were too many good memories to process and she had felt so empowered and full of life. She hadn't even minded that Lucy hadn't traveled back with them. In fact it had given her a chance to talk a little more to Sabrina and bond with her. Wendy picked up the folder, stood up and left the conference room. Then she made her way back to her office by way of

Beau's. She poked her head inside as she passed. "All done. No problems."

Beau looked up from his desk. "Good." He pushed some papers to one side. "Come in a moment, Wendy. There is something else I wanted to discuss with you."

Wendy stepped into the room and closed the door behind her. "What's up?"

"You have two people traveling down to San Diego?"

"Yes"

"And they know what they're likely to be confronting?"

"Not exactly. I told them it would be a challenge and said I would give them more information later. Is that okay?"

"However you choose to handle it, Wendy. You know that. Take a seat." Beau waited while Wendy sat down by his desk.

"I had a call this morning from corporate and it seems they are closing down one of their East Coast offices. The one that Cindy came from actually."

"Is there a problem?"

Beau laughed. "No, not at all. Quite the opposite in fact. They are offering several of the existing staff in that office transfers to here. It seems they want to ramp up your department. There is rumor of several other acquisitions in the works. They are talking about adding another fifteen people to your team."

"We don't have the room, Beau. I mean of course I'm pleased, but where are we going to put these people? We're maxed out in this office already."

"Corporate are negotiating to get some space next door. They hope to get it all up and running within four weeks. In the meantime we'll just have to all squeeze in. I just wanted to let you know. The guys at corporate are pleased with your results so far, Wendy. Very pleased."

Wendy smiled. "Good. Is that everything?"

Beau smiled too. "Yes, everything. I'll let you get back to your office now. I know you've got a stack of things to arrange today."

Wendy got to her feet and started towards the door. "I certainly have. It's going to be a long day."

"Oh, and I also sent word out to a few people that we're having a celebration in Paddy's tonight at eight."

"What?"

"I wanted to break the news about the office in a more casual environment to a few people. That way it won't seem such a surprise once it actually happens. Make sure you're there, Wendy."

"Sure. I'll be there."

* * *

The party was already in full swing by the time Wendy arrived later that evening. She squeezed herself onto a bench against the wall and pulled off her coat. It had been a long day. Beau pushed a beer over towards her.

"Here, drink this. It looks like you need it."

"I do," Wendy replied. "I've only just got caught up with everything. I had to finalize my report for Cindy and Ramitha. I told them it would be in their email by the time they arrived in San Diego." She took a swig from the bottle of beer and made a face. "What is this?" She looked at the label and put the bottle back down on the table. "I can't drink this. Get me a rum and coke will you?"

Beau laughed. "Sure."

"How's it going, Wendy?" Sam asked, taking a seat next to her.

"Crazy. I never realized it would be so much work being a director."

"Beau says we're getting more staff. Something about people moving from the East Cost office."

"So I understand. Just what I need. I don't have enough hours in the day as it is."

"I guess your sins are finally catching up with you, then."

"Thanks, Sam. I'll remember that when I'm snowed under. Maybe I'll reach out to you for help."

"Wish I could. Unfortunately it's not my specialty."

"Yeah, I'm on my own. I know that too." Wendy picked up the rum and coke that had been set down in front of her and took a sip. "That's better. Now I can start to relax a little."

Everyone went quiet as Beau started to bang on the table. "Sshhh. I just want to say a few words." He waited until they were all paying attention. "As you know I just wanted to invite you all here this evening to celebrate two things. And they're both to do with Wendy here." A few people cheered. "Firstly as I've already told a few of you, we're going to be getting some extra people in our office. Transfers from the East Coast office. Corporate is finally recognizing the good work you all do here." There was more cheering. "And secondly, and more importantly I might add, Wendy is getting a bigger department and more responsibility. She's going to be running a sort of think-tank within the company. And don't ask her what she's doing because she doesn't know." Beau waited for the laughs to die down. "No seriously, she can't tell you because she's not allowed to tell you. All her department's work is confidential and every member of her team has had to sign specific non-disclosures. So don't go asking her, okay? She won't tell you anything." He took a sip of his beer. "Anyway, enough boring news for tonight. Let's party." Beau turned to Sam. "Did we order food?"

"It's coming. Don't worry."

"Okay, good." Beau took another sip from his beer and leaned back in his chair. Sabrina was sat at the bar alongside Lucy and he let his eyes wander over the tall blonde for a few seconds. He watched as Lucy half-turned her head and caught his eyes for a moment. She smiled and he raised his beer to her. She smiled again and he watched her turn back to the conversation she was having with Sabrina. He took another sip of his beer and turned the bottle in his hands as he put it back on the table. She was very pretty. Surely it would be okay to date her for a while. He could be careful. He wouldn't let it happen to him again. Not like he did with Emily. He knew it was a mistake the moment she had persuaded him. Two years of a relationship ruined in one crazy moment of passion. He had buried her body. There was nothing else he could have done. Then he told all his friends she had just left him and returned back home. No, he wouldn't let that happen to Lucy. Not if he got the chance to date her. He would be extra careful with her. Just the occasional safe kiss. He knew how to do that now. Never any mushrooms either. And never any sex. There was never any going back once he gave into that desire. Beau gulped down the rest of his beer and got up from the table. He took a deep breath, sighed and went outside to get some fresh air.

37

"Busy?" Beau asked, pushing into Wendy's office late in the afternoon.

Wendy looked up from her desk and smiled. "Yeah, you could say that. I've still got two reports to get through before I can go home." She put her pen down. "What can I do for you?"

Beau pushed the office door shut behind him, walked over to Wendy's desk and sat down. "I just wanted to clear the air a little and to have a little chat."

Wendy closed the file that was open on her desk and looked up at Beau. "Go on."

"I was a little rude the other day in the office when we were discussing things. I came to apologize. I know it's a little late, but late is better than never."

"Go on."

"I get a little touchy about relationships. And that's another reason I wanted to talk to you, Wendy. I've been a member of the Anons for a few years now and I know just what it's like not being able to have a girlfriend; not being able to kiss people without the fear of killing them. You have absolutely no idea of the burden it places on you. But you will in time. I just wanted to talk a little about that."

Wendy picked up her pen and started rolling it through her fingers. "I guess I'd never really thought about that. But then again, I've never had a real boyfriend before so it's not something I would really miss, is it?"

Beau laughed. "It can't be that bad, Wendy. There has to have been some guy you've dated at some point."

"Oh yes, there were guys. But all they ever wanted was one thing. They didn't want a real relationship. And I wasn't prepared to be someone's notch on their bedpost." She smiled. "So it was quite appropriate that I had that guy in Vegas. It was like a few years of payback."

"I guess that's one way of looking at it." Beau leaned back in his chair and smiled again. "But seriously Wendy, I do want you to realize just what it's like being part of the Anons. You can never have a boyfriend. Never. I found that out to my costs before." He leaned forward again. "Can I tell you a story?"

"Sure."

"And this is something I never told you, just so we're clear." He paused and lowered his voice a little. "You probably heard that I had a girlfriend once and that she disappeared and went back home to her parents?"

"I've heard the story."

"Well, that's not quite true. Her name was Emily and I dated her for over two years before things got out of hand one night. I buried her body in a place that hopefully no one will ever find."

"What do you mean, *got out of hand?*"

"For two years I managed to just kiss her, not in a really passionate kind of way. And I managed not to actually have sex with her. Of course we did other things, but the point is, I stayed in control. Then one night she caught me in a weak moment and persuaded me to go the whole way with her. That was it. I killed her. Of course I didn't mean to and I regretted it more than I could ever regret anything. But I did kill her. There's no other way to say it. So when I say I'd be careful if I ever dated someone else. Someone like Lucy, then you have to believe me. I never want to go through that again."

"But how can you have a relationship with someone and not be fully committed? That's not fair on the other person either. No Beau, there's no way you can ever date anyone again."

"Okay Wendy, I hear you. For now we're going to have to disagree. When you've had the chance to be like me for a couple of years then maybe you'll change your mind. Look, I don't want to argue about it, I'm just giving you my side of the story."

Wendy got to her feet and wandered over to the window and looked out over the dark and almost empty parking lot. She turned to face Beau. "I feel very strongly about this Beau, and I'd appreciate it if while I feel like this you don't go against my wishes. Lucy is a friend of mine and if something ever happened to her I could never forgive you."

Beau relaxed in the chair a little and closed his eyes. "I hear you, Wendy." He put his hands behind his head and paused for a moment. "But at the end of the day, I'm going to do what I feel is the right thing to do. There's nothing you can say that will change my mind over this."

"Shit, Beau. Didn't you just hear what I said? I just said that she was my friend."

"Life is what it is, Wendy." Beau opened his eyes and smiled at Wendy.

"That's complete bullshit, and you know it is." She strode across the room and stood over Beau and continued shouting, almost spitting on him. "You have the freedom of choice. You don't have to even see her if you don't want to. Stop playing games."

Beau laughed. "I'm not playing games, Wendy. I'm just telling you not to get involved in my personal life. You don't understand. So until then, drop it."

"I don't believe it. You're an arrogant, small-minded, scumbag of a…"

Beau reached his arms up and placed them around Wendy's waist, pulling her towards him. She lost her balance and he turned her, pulling her onto his lap. Then he kissed her. Passionately. Wendy's arms reached around Beau and she could feel something probing at the edges of her mind. She pushed back. There was an explosion somewhere nearby and it came at her again. Stronger this time. She felt her body responding to Beau's embrace and for a moment she nearly let him into her mind. With a final push she shut the edges of her mind from him and broke free. Her lips ripped free of his and she staggered backwards, crashing onto the floor. For a moment she lay there dazed and confused.

* * *

Peter Ramsey closed his eyes and pushed back in his chair. He had read the memo from corporate three times just to make sure. "Crap!" He had a feeling something like this was going to happen. Ever since Beau had been promoted to Director, the writing had been on the wall. He should have done something about it then. Now it was too late. The memo said in very kind words that he had done a wonderful job for the company but that the direction was changing and that several offices were going to be consolidated. It didn't really need to say much more. Of course there was nothing explicit in it that said Beau would be taking over. It didn't need to. What it did say was that after giving twelve years of his life to Zygote Technologies, he was now surplus to requirements. The memo used words like severance package, full benefits and job placement, but it was the same thing. Kicked to the curb. "Crap!"

Peter took a kick at his desk and got to his feet. Maybe it was time to leave, but before he went he was going to give that piece of crap, Beau, a little of his wisdom. He had stored it all up inside for the past couple of months. Now it was time to let it out. He pushed his chair forcefully backwards and crossed to his office door. A few moments later he was walking down the corridor towards Beau's office. "Crap!" The office was empty. No doubt he had gone home already. Typical. The one day he wanted to give him a piece of his mind and he had already left. Spectacular! Further down the corridor there was a light coming from Wendy's office. He would go tell her instead. Actually, she may be a little sympathetic to him. Maybe she would even console him a little. He smiled. Until recently he had never realized just how attractive Wendy really was. Her new hairdo and wardrobe was getting her noticed everywhere she went. He walked down to Wendy's office and took a hold of the door handle, looking inside as he did so.

He couldn't believe what he saw. Wendy was sat on Beau's lap kissing him. Kissing him. No wonder she had got a promotion. She was having an affair with Beau. Crap! This was astonishing. Totally mind boggling. He took a sharp intake of breath and looked down at his hand. It was shaking. He let go of the door and lifted it up towards his face. Still it shook. Peter placed his other hand on it and tried to calm it, but it wouldn't stop shaking. His breath felt short. The door started to spin. He let go of his shaking hand and reached up to put it to his chest. His heart felt like it was going to explode. Nothing made sense. Something was inside him. His head was reliving experiences totally out of sequence. His mouth dropped open. He turned to one side and fell against the office wall. Then he lost his footing and slid down. Down and down. As his head hit the floor he blacked out.

* * *

"What the shit were you doing?" Wendy asked, struggling to regain her composure and think straight.

Beau had his head in his hands. "I don't know. I'm really sorry, Wendy. I really don't know what came over me. I just thought the best way to stop you shouting was to kiss you."

Wendy pulled herself to a sitting position. "You tried to get inside my head, Beau. I felt it. I had to push back with all my energy. You tried to kill me."

"I'm sorry. Really. This isn't what I was trying to do at all. I really don't know what came over me. Too many things happened at once. It was like that one time with Melody. Only different. My god you are strong, Wendy. Stronger than I imagined."

"Melody? Who's Melody?" Wendy rubbed her temples and took a few deep breaths.

"It doesn't matter. But you've got to believe me, I'm really sorry." Beau struggled to his feet. "Look, I'm just going to go home. We'll talk about this another time, when we're both calm and collected." Beau shuffled the few steps towards the door and pulled it open. He almost tripped over the lifeless body of Peter Ramsey as he went to leave. He turned back towards Wendy. "You'd better get over here. It's Peter. I think he's had a heart attack or something."

38

"Beau Tempest?" The police detective took a step closer to Beau after he opened the door to his apartment.

"Yes?" Just what he needed. Why were the police knocking on his door? Maybe it was about Peter.

"May we come in?" The detective waited for half an answer before stepping past Beau. The other detective followed.

Beau shut the door. "Take a seat. What can I do for you?"

"We just wanted to ask you a couple of questions, that's all. We thought maybe you could help us in a few things."

"Sure. Whatever I can do."

The first detective pulled out a photo from a file and placed it on the coffee table. "Do you know this woman?"

Beau's heart skipped a beat. "I don't think so. She looks kind of familiar, but I don't think so."

"Take another look. Take your time. We want to be sure."

Beau swallowed as carefully as he could and tried to keep his composure under control. "Like I said, she sort of looks familiar. I may have met her some time I guess. But I don't think I know her."

The second detective spoke. "Did you go to Dunkles nightclub on the evening of the fifth of April?"

"I don't remember," Beau answered. "I've been there once or twice during the past few months. Why?"

"This woman," the detective continued. "Do you remember meeting her there?"

Shit! The club must have had cameras either inside or outside. Or else somebody saw them together. "Let me take another look." Beau pulled the picture towards him a little more and studied it. "She looks a little like a woman I danced with there. I think, anyway. It's difficult to tell. It was dark in there and the blonde woman I danced with was wearing a lot of makeup."

The detective pulled the photo back again and picked it up. "So you might know her then?"

"I didn't say I knew her. I remember dancing with some blonde girl. I didn't get a name. We went outside and made out a little. Then I went home. That's if it's the same one."

"There were others?"

Beau smiled. "No, I didn't say there were others. I said if this was the same girl. That's all."

"You didn't go home with the woman then?"

"No. I didn't have my car. I was on foot that night. I don't go home with women if I don't have my car. I have to be able to get home again." Beau smiled at the detective. "If you know what I mean?"

The first detective allowed a smile to work at the edges of his mouth before he continued the questioning. "You didn't go home with her? Are you sure about that?"

"I just told you. Why? What is so important about this girl? Is she accusing me of something?"

"Should she be?"

"No. I was just asking what this is all about?"

"Don't you watch the news, sir?"

"Of course I do."

"And you don't remember?"

Beau paused. "Oh, the photo. The woman. The one that was murdered. My god, you don't think that was me, do you?"

"Like we said, we just wanted to ask you a few questions. The cameras at the nightclub showed you and her leaving together."

"Are you sure? I said we just made out a little. I didn't go home with her."

The detective smiled. "It showed you outside the nightclub. Yes, making out if you like."

The second detective got to his feet. "I think that's all we need to ask you, sir. Thanks for your time."

"No problem," Beau replied, getting to his feet and walking towards the door. "Glad I could help."

"Just one more thing," the first detective said as he reached the door. "Did you happen to take the woman's phone number?"

"Sorry, no. Like I said, we just made out a little and I went home. It wasn't something that was going anywhere."

"I see. Well thanks for your time. Have a good day."

Beau closed the door behind the two detectives and walked back to his couch and collapsed into it, heart still racing. He had never had a visit from the police before. He needed to be more careful in future. He waited a few minutes before getting up and pouring himself a whiskey. He almost dropped it as the noise of his ringing phone startled him. "Shit!" He put the glass down, licked his wet fingers and answered the phone. "Hello... Yes, that's me... That's right. Last night... I see... Certainly... No problem... I'll be there." Crap! Another matter to sort out. Peter Ramsey's brother wanted Beau to go over to the hospital. The family wasn't sure whether he was going to live or not and they wanted Beau to tell them a few things. It seemed Peter kept himself to himself mostly and his family didn't really know a lot about Peter's job.

Beau picked up his whiskey again and took a sip. Should he tell them about the memo Peter had just received from corporate? He'd been copied on it and knew Peter must have read it. What he was going to say, he didn't know. Perhaps it would be better if Peter didn't recover from his heart attack. There would be fewer questions that way. Still, the family had requested he go visit, so he'd better show some support. For now. Beau gulped back his whiskey and put the empty glass back down on the counter.

Beau pulled his Mercedes into the parking lot of the Queen's Arms a couple of hours later. He hadn't meant to spend as much time as he had at the hospital, but Peter's brother and sister had asked so many things about him. Peter had remained unconscious and the doctors had privately said they didn't expect him to live through the night. Beau had done his best to give them a little background to Peter's work at the office without giving any secrets away. He had even been asked to speak at the funeral service if there was one. He'd given them a non-committal answer and tried to remain positive for them. Now he needed a drink. Ordinarily he would have chosen Paddy's but tonight he wanted some peace and quiet and to not be interrupted. He was assured of that at the Queen's Arms. He got out of his car and locked it. The parking lot was fairly full and he hoped he didn't run into anyone that he knew.

Once inside he looked around for a quiet table but they all seemed to be full. Even the bar top was mostly occupied. At least he could get a seat there if he had to. He looked around the bar again and smiled. At a table in the corner with her back to him he recognized Lucy. He was sure it was her; he had studied her figure many times during the past few weeks.

"Hi there, Lucy isn't it?" he asked, crossing to her table.

Lucy looked up from a book. "Hi," she mumbled in reply. "Hello."

"Beau, Beau Tempest." He extended a hand. "I don't think we've been formally introduced."

Lucy smiled. "Not formally. We've just chatted a few times."

Beau laughed. "And now we're formally introduced, too." He let her hand go and looked around the restaurant. "I know it's really rude of me to ask, but do you think I could sit with you? The bar seems rather busy and there's not another free table."

"Sure." Lucy closed her book and motioned for Beau to sit.

"Thanks. I'll tell you what, let me buy you dinner. It's the least I can do." Beau squeezed onto a chair against the wall.

"I'm not hungry, but thanks."

"A drink?"

"You want me drunk again? I seem to remember that last time I met you I had to be taken home early."

Beau laughed. "Yes you did. I remember too."

"So, for now I'll turn down your drink request."

"Okay. You don't mind if I get one do you?"

Lucy laughed. "Good luck."

"So you come here often too then?"

Lucy laughed again. "Yes. I come here to escape from time to time. I just have to make sure I'm not too impatient to get a drink."

"I'm exactly the same. That's too funny."

"Can I get you something?" a server said, suddenly appearing at their table.

Beau laughed. "A Speckled Hen please. And some hot wings."

"You must have brought good luck today," Lucy said as the server disappeared again.

"That's not the usual server. It looks like normal service has been resumed."

Lucy took a sip from her cider. "If you want to do some work, I have my book." She picked it up to show Beau.

"No, I came here straight from the hospital actually. My boss is in critical condition. Heart attack. He's not expected to last past tonight."

"I'm sorry, that must be terrible."

"I never really liked him anyway."

Lucy laughed. "Don't say that. It's not kind."

"I know. He was okay. But he's a boss. You know what they're like?"

Lucy nodded. "I do. But my boss isn't too bad."

"Where do you work?"

"Nyble Storage. They're…"

"Yeah I know them. A cloud storage company. Got quite the following at the moment."

"They have?"

"Sorry. It's part of my job to know all the companies and what they do. But I'll try not to be the total work-head tonight."

Lucy looked at her watch. "It's okay. I've got to go anyway. I promised Sabrina I'd be home to watch a movie with her."

"Did I scare you away?"

"No seriously. It was already planned." She pulled ten dollars out of her purse. "Make sure the server gets this, will you?"

"Put it away," Beau said, reaching out towards Lucy's hand. I'll get it. It's the least I can do for stealing your table. Anyway, perhaps I'll let you buy me one another time."

Lucy pulled back her hand. "Okay. Thanks." She got to her feet. "See you again sometime."

"Wait," Beau called out. "You didn't give me your number."

Lucy turned her head back towards Beau. "If you can find out where I live then I'm sure you can find out my number. Call me!"

And before Beau could say anything else, she was gone.

39

Cars, driving, steep roads, paths that led nowhere in particular; these were all things going through Lucy's head as she slept. Her car had a mind of its own. It was taking her along freeways she had never driven before. Some of it was a lot like England. She smiled. There was the corner shop. What was that doing next to the highway? The car continued on. She didn't know just where the journey was taking her. After a while it turned off the freeway onto a smaller road that led up an impossibly steep hill. The car didn't have any trouble though, it continued on. Then they were in a forest and the shadows in the trees tried to eat the car. Still the car continued on. Suddenly it was over a cliff and gliding through the air. Lucy hung on. The car landed gracefully on the water. It was a lake and the car continued on once more. In the middle of the lake was an island. The car drove ashore and came to a stop. The doors opened.

Lucy got out and stood by the car. Then it turned into a house, a large house. She thought she could see the faces of Sabrina, Wendy, Ben and Beau at the windows. She opened the door and went inside. It was a large football stadium without a crowd. Lucy made her way to the half-way line and stood there, looking around. Suddenly she fell to the ground in pain and she put her hands to her temples. Her head was almost bursting apart with the pain. She screamed.

"Why are you here?" a voice from afar said, echoing around the empty stadium.

Lucy tried to look up but the sun was too bright and her head hurt too much. "Who are you?"

"I am the voice inside your head. A head that has been troubling over your migraines for far too long."

"What do you want with me?"

"I do not want anything. It is you that wants something. You want an answer."

"I do? I do not understand."

"I am the voice inside your head. You have been trying to figure out why you are getting all the migraines you have. Nothing about them makes sense to you. All I can tell you is that they are a warning. Listen to the migraines. Listen to what they have to say and where they take you."

Lucy shielded her eyes and tried to see who was speaking. "What do you mean?"

No one replied. There was silence again. The skies went dark and the football field turned into Lucy's bedroom. She could see herself asleep in her bed. She walked towards herself and reached out to touch the other sleeping Lucy. There was a flash of light and Lucy pressed her fingers hard against her temples again. "No," she screamed out.

* * *

Lucy rubbed her eyes and sat up with a start. Four-twenty-seven. She wiped the sweat from her brow. She remembered every detail of her dream. It was so clear. What did it mean? Her migraines were supposed to be a warning, but a warning to what? None of it was clear at all. And she was sure she'd seen the faces of her friends in the window of the house before it had turned into a football field. She lay back on her pillow and tried to calm herself. It wasn't doing any good. She could feel the edges of another migraine, a real migraine, starting to creep into her head. She tried again to relax. She breathed deeply and counted to a hundred. The migraine started to dissipate and she allowed herself to think a little more about the dream again. It just didn't make any sense though. None of it. Maybe it was just a dream. Nothing more. But why had it been so vivid? It was as if it was a message to her. Lucy closed her eyes and tried to work out what she should do. Four-thirty-one. She smiled. Of course.

The Pastor at church. That's what he was there for. He could probably explain it all for her. He would be able to tell if it was a vision or just something else. He must have had experience with this kind of thing before. Lucy turned on her bedside light and pulled a pad of paper from beside her bed. Then she wrote down everything she could remember about the dream. When she had finished, she turned off the light once more and tried to settle back down for another hour's sleep.

It was mid-morning by the time Lucy arrived at the church. Hopefully the Pastor would be inside and she could have a quick word with him. She got out of her car and walked across the parking lot and into the large church. Her eyes soon accustomed themselves to the dimly lit room and Lucy spotted the Pastor talking to a couple of older women near the altar. She slowly made her way towards him and waited a short distance away until he was free.

"Pastor, hello there. Excuse me."

The Pastor turned towards Lucy and smiled. "Good morning, young lady. What can I do for you?"

"Lucy. Lucy Weatherington. I come to your service every week. I was wondering whether I could discuss something with you?" She reached out her hand and the Pastor shook it firmly.

"Of course. Let's go and sit in my private room. I'm sure you want some privacy?"

Lucy smiled. "Thanks."

The Pastor led Lucy back behind the altar to a small room which he unlocked and the two of them went inside. He sat himself behind a paper covered desk. "I need to spend some time in here," he said, trying to make a little space. "Now, what can I do for you?"

Lucy sat herself down and told the Pastor all about her dream. "I was hoping you'd heard this kind of thing before and could help me."

The Pastor sat back in his chair and was silent for a moment or two. "I've had people come to me with strong dreams before. Even nightmares. Usually they are concerned with some event in the person's life. The brain has a way of dealing with things that we don't always understand." He sat up straight in his chair again before continuing. "You say you saw the faces of your friends before the house turned into a football field? This probably indicates you're worried about your friendship with them. Perhaps you believe the migraines are brought on because you can't always choose between your friends for certain things."

"I don't think so. One of my friends is dead. One is my best friend. One is someone I don't know too well and the other is a man who I may be dating soon." Lucy blushed.

"I see. And do any of these friends in particular make you feel like you are getting a migraine?"

"Not at all. I'm sure there's no connection between these people and my migraines. I think they were just my friends. On the football field I was all alone. They weren't there then. Do you think it could be some kind of warning? Something I should do?"

The Pastor laughed. "I don't think so, Lucy. You have been reading too many fiction books. Like I say, there's probably a totally rational explanation for it. Maybe God can help take your migraines away. Would you like me to pray for you?"

Lucy nodded. "Anything you can do to help, Pastor will be a blessing. I'd rather not have these migraines, believe me."

"Then let us pray. In the meantime, remember that dreams are just that. Dreams. They usually do not have any great significance." The Pastor bowed his head and led them both in prayer.

* * *

Lucy was deep in thought as she pulled out of the church parking lot and headed back home. The Pastor hadn't told her anything she had hoped for. But maybe he was right. After all, if every dream meant something then there would be a lot of things to process in life. She smiled. No, it was probably like he said. Her mind was probably just processing the events of the past few weeks. A lot had happened. She had met Ben and he had been murdered. She had gone to Vegas with Wendy and her best friend Sabrina. She had nearly been asked out by Beau on a date. And, of course, she had had several migraines. It was probably just her brain working through it all and trying to put some kind of order on it. And the car. Her car. She smiled. Yes, her faithful car had been central to it all. It was only the football field that didn't make any sense. She hadn't done anything recently that involved a football field. She tried to think if there was any connection, but there was none at all. Oh well. She wasn't going to worry about it. And the Pastor had said a personal prayer for her anyway, so maybe the migraines would go away. Or at least diminish. Lucy pulled into her apartment complex and found a parking space. She turned off the engine and sat back in her seat for a moment. Beau. She had almost forgotten about him during all this. Why hadn't he called yet? Was he finding it harder than she had imagined getting his number? She laughed to herself. "Calm down," she told herself. "You'll bring another migraine on!"

40

Lucy smiled as she walked across the street towards The Fish Plaice. Beau had finally called her this morning and suggested they have dinner at the local restaurant. It was only a three minute walk and she was happy to step into the cold April air and walk through the large parking lot that bordered the pubs, restaurants, cinema and various other establishments. She had had quite a boring day at work and the prospect of some good company for a few hours put a spring in her step. Sabrina had asked where she was going but she had decided not to say anything. At least not yet. The last thing she needed was a lecture about just what Beau was and wasn't. Well, from Sabrina's point of view anyway. She had decided she would make up her mind for herself.

Six-thirty-four. She let her scarf unfurl itself from her neck as she pulled open the door to the restaurant and stepped inside. Beau was seated on a bench to the right, waiting for her. "Hi. Hope I didn't keep you waiting too long."

Beau got to his feet and took the few steps to stand next to her. "Not at all. I've only just got here myself."

Beau and Lucy waited for the hostess and they were soon seated in a table at the back of the restaurant, up against a window. Lucy took off her coat and put it on the empty chair next to her.

"Very nice," Beau said, looking Lucy up and down as she took her seat.

Lucy blushed. "Thanks. It's always difficult knowing what to wear in this weather." She watched carefully as Beau took his seat across from her and smiled to herself. She had made the correct decision.

"Do you think we'll get any more snow?" Beau asked, trying to make some conversation.

"I hope not. I've already had one bad experience in it." Her face dropped as she remembered that had been when she first met Ben.

"You okay?"

"Yeah, I'm fine. Just some memories. Sorry."

Beau waited a moment before continuing. "I think we've seen the last of it. They say it's going to be a hot summer this year. Mind you, I'll believe that when I see it. Seattle isn't exactly Texas."

"You're from Texas?"

Beau laughed. "I guess I did give that away a little too easy, didn't I? Couldn't you tell from my accent?"

"What do I know about accents? I'm from England and to me most American accents sound the same. Well, if not the same then sort of similar. I can tell you a northern English accent from a London accent from a southern English accent, but Texas or New York or Seattle, not a clue." Lucy laughed.

"So anyway, I'm from Texas. Just outside Houston actually. Well, at least that's where I grew up. I didn't go to college in Texas though. I wanted to get away. Then my parents died while I was in college and so I've never been back. Not once. I'm an only child and there didn't seem any need. Now I'm here in Melrose, all I really miss are the hot summers sometimes. But the scenery more than makes up for it. The mountains are spectacular and the lakes are great. I'm looking forward to the summer again. It'll be..." Beau paused. "There I go again, taking up the whole conversation. Tell me a little about yourself."

Lucy smiled. "It's okay. I was enjoying the story." Lucy stopped as a server arrived and asked them what they wanted to drink. "I'll have a Bud please. In a bottle."

"Whiskey. Neat, no rocks" Beau replied. "With water on the side. Any single malt will do." He looked up at the server and paused while she wrote something down. "We're not quite ready to order anything to eat yet." Beau waited until the server was out of earshot before continuing. "Bud? Is that your drink of choice?"

Lucy smiled. "It depends. It seemed easier than looking through the whole list. Every bar has Budweiser in bottles."

"I guess." Beau took a quick glance through the menu. "Is there anything particular you want?"

"I thought I might have the pit roasted salmon. Salmon is one thing I can't get enough of up here."

"Good choice. I may have the same. Would you like an appetizer too?"

Lucy shook her head. "You can if you want. The salmon will be enough for me."

"That will do for me too then." Beau put the menu down and looked across at Lucy. "I was hoping you'd agree to go to dinner with me. Ever since I saw you the very first time in Paddy's I've been watching you. You're very attractive."

"Really? That's you best line?"

"What do you mean?"

"I remember seeing you in that nightclub, Dunkles. You were with some other girl then."

Beau blushed. "It didn't go anywhere. I was just dancing with her, that's all. Besides I had a lot of things on my mind that evening. I had just got promoted at the office and was letting off some steam."

"Is that what you call it? Well, just so you know, I'm not that kind of girl. If I agree to date you then there's no going off with other people. I'm an exclusive kind of person."

"So am I."

"Good. And just so you know, I'm a Christian kind of girl too. Church on Sundays."

"Oh."

"Is that a problem for you?"

"No. Not at all." Beau struggled to look relaxed about what he was hearing. "I like a girl that has good Christian morals."

"Budweiser?" the server said, putting Lucy's drink down in front of her. "And a single malt whiskey." She took a step back. "Did you decide on anything yet? Appetizers?"

"We're just going to have an entrée," Beau replied. "We're both going to have the pit roasted salmon."

"Fries, garlic smashed potatoes, baked potato?"

"Just vegetables for me," said Lucy.

Beau nodded.

"Thanks." The server made her way back towards the other side of the restaurant.

"You didn't have to have the same as me," Lucy said.

"It will do me good to eat properly for once. I eat too much fried and fast food. You never know, you might be a good influence on me."

"You never know," agreed Lucy. She took a sip of her beer and watched Beau as he drank a little whiskey. His black hair was perfectly styled and not a single hair was out of place. His charcoal roll-neck top matched his complexion well. She noticed he was wearing a gold band on the ring finger of his right hand. Maybe he had had a serious relationship before. Still, it didn't matter. Of course he had. He was the vice-president of a company. He was bound to have had lots of girlfriends before. Even Sabrina and Wendy had alluded to that.

"What are you thinking?" Beau said, snapping Lucy out of her thoughts.

"Nothing special. Just enjoying the evening."

"Good." Beau reached out a hand and brushed the fingers of her right hand that were resting on the table.

An electric shock went through Lucy's hand and up her arm. She instinctively pulled her hand back.

"Sorry."

"No, it was just a shock, that's all." She glanced down at her hand and smiled to herself. Maybe it was supposed to feel like electric when you met the right person. It certainly wasn't a bad feeling. Just a different one. She picked up her beer and took another sip. Oh no! There it was, on the edges of her head. She could feel it. She closed her eyes and tried to relax. Now was not a good time. Not a good time at all. "Just excuse me for a minute," she said, opening her eyes again and getting up from the table. "I'll be right back." Lucy put her napkin on the table, turned and hurried off towards the restroom. Inside she pulled open a door to one of the stalls and almost fell over as she took the two steps needed. She pushed the door closed behind her and leaned back against it. Her head was already starting to pound. "No, not now," she said out loud. "Not now." But it was no good. The early tell-tale signs of a migraine were impossible to ignore. There was nothing else for it; she was going to have to go home. She pressed her fingers to her temples and shut her eyes briefly. This hadn't gone at all as expected.

"I'm sorry Beau, but I'm going to have to leave you," she said, arriving back at their table a few minutes later, looking a very pale color. "I've got a migraine coming on and when I get them there's nothing I can do but go and find somewhere dark to sit it out. I'm going to have to cancel on you. Please forgive me. We can do this again another time."

Beau got to his feet. "You do look very pale. Are you sure you're alright? Can I walk you home?"

Lucy shook her head. "I'll be fine. Sorry." She picked up her coat and slipped it on. Then with a final wave she was gone.

Beau sat back down again and took a large swig of his whiskey.

"Two salmon?" the server said, arriving with the meals.

"Sorry Miss, but you're going to have to take one back. My friend was suddenly taken ill and had to leave."

The server put one of the plates down in front of Beau and just stood there with the other one in her hand. "What do you want me to do with this one then?"

"Really? I don't care. Give it to someone else, box it or eat it yourself. The lady isn't coming back."

The server turned her nose up at Beau and took the plate away. She hated first dates. So many of them never made it through the appetizers. She didn't have these two pegged for that though. The woman had seemed a cutie and he certainly looked attractive in a classic kind of way. Oh well.

The salmon would serve for her supper a little later. She returned to the kitchen area and boxed it up and put it to one side. A few minutes later she returned to his table. "Everything okay, Sir?"

Beau looked up from his meal. "Fine. I'll have another whiskey though. Thanks."

The server smiled to herself as she walked towards the bar. He seemed pretty mad about it all. Oh well, that's how it goes sometimes. She ordered him another whiskey and walked it back to his table.

"Thanks. I need this."
"She left you?"
"No like I said, she was taken ill."
The server smiled. "Anything else?"

Beau reached out his hand and touched the server's. "What time do you get off?"

A hot flush ran through the server. Was he really trying to pick her up? "Sorry?"

"What time do you get off? Would you like to go for a drink afterwards? My day has ended very unexpectedly."

The server laughed. "I'm sorry, Sir. But I need to get straight home after my shift." She turned to walk back to the kitchen but before she realized what was happening, he had gotten to his feet and was kissing her. On the lips. She stood there, a spectacle in front of the whole restaurant, as he kissed her. How dare he? And then she was kissing him back. It wasn't her plan. She was sure of that, but she couldn't stop herself. Flashes went through her head. Loud, bright flashes and then it was all over. He broke away from her and walked off into the distance. She steadied herself for a moment against the table and noticed the hundred dollar bill. At least he had paid. Then her legs gave way from under her and she collapsed to the floor.

41

By the time Beau reached his apartment he wasn't ready to just go inside. He pulled out his car key from his pocket and unlocked his Mercedes. He got in and headed off towards Bellevue and to nowhere in particular. Thirty-five minutes later Beau brought the car to a stop. He was parked in an unlit side street on the other side of the lake. He took the key out of the ignition and slumped back in his seat. Shit! The evening hadn't gone at all as expected. And he probably could never go to The Fish Plaice again. He hadn't meant to make an exhibition out of himself, things had just bubbled to the surface. He had so been looking forward to having a date with Lucy and now it was ruined. Damn these women! It was the kids that had saved the server. They had probably saved him too. Killing a server in front of a whole restaurant would have been a serious mistake. There would have been no going back from there. Yes, the kids had stopped him. As soon as he had seen them in her mind he had pulled back. Thank god for that. Beau slammed the steering wheel with his fist.

And now he was here, miles from home, with an angry mind and a longing in his belly. He had to do something about it. He looked around to make sure the street was deserted and then got out of his car. He pulled the hood of his coat up over his head and made his way towards the lake. He just hoped he wasn't too late. He rounded a corner, crossed the street and then disappeared into the trees that separated the road from the lake. He moved quietly between them, trying to see exactly where he was and what he was doing. It was dark here, but closer to the lake there were lights that illuminated the pathway. He leaned against a tree and waited.

It was about fifteen minutes later when he first heard the sound. The sound of someone jogging or running nearby. He took a step forward and tried to look along the path. He was in luck. A woman was jogging towards him, her hair bobbing in the evening air. Beau waited. As she passed him by he darted forward and placed a practiced hand around her mouth. He used the other to wrap around her waist and then used a leg to pull her off balance. He would only need a few seconds. Suddenly they were on the ground and he was grabbing at her arms with his free hand. He pulled her uncaringly over the pathway and back towards the safety of the trees. He rolled on top of her and released his hand just long enough to place his mouth over hers. She bit his lips and he punched her in the side. He daren't let go and so he pressed forward, trying to work his tongue into her mouth. He felt the touch of her teeth and realized she was slowly losing the battle against him. Within moments it was all over. A blinding flash of information shot through him and her mouth gave in to his. She returned his kiss. She wanted him. He let her arms go and she wrapped them around him and moaned softly, still underneath him. He lifted himself up and pulled roughly at her jogging pants until they were no longer an obstacle. Then he pushed himself back on top of her, into her. Her mind became one with his and she opened herself totally to him. He picked at the flesh of her mind and stole everything he wanted from her and then as they reached their frenzied peak, she collapsed underneath him and lay on the ground eyes wide open in disbelief. Lifeless.

Oh, Lucy. The name came so easily to his lips. Beau rolled off the dead woman and struggled to catch his breath. He closed his eyes and listened as the wind rustled the branches of the trees above him. Tears flowed as he promised to himself that no harm would ever come to Lucy.

A noise nearby woke Beau from his forced rest. Instinctively his eyes searched the area and he saw the man coming towards him, through the trees. Beau used all his energy to sit up; the man hadn't seen him, but something was bringing him his way. Beau took a deep breath and flexed his arms to see what strength had returned to him. He wasn't going to be able to run for a while. He scooted backwards and propped himself up against a tree to watch. When the man was less than ten feet away from Beau he stopped. He had seen the body. He was quickly on it and bending down over it. The man looked confused. What was once a human body was now most likely just a half-clothed hollow leather-like shell with bones protruding. No one was used to seeing such a thing. No one should see such a thing. Beau suddenly realized that this could be another mistake. He was going to have to do something about it. He closed his eyes briefly and sought out strength from deep inside himself. Then as silently as he could he sprang from his position and was on the man in a moment. He wrapped his arms around the man's neck and pulled him roughly to the ground. As they hit the bare hard winter grass, Beau adjusted his hold slightly and took a hold of the man's head. The element of surprise was still his. He twisted and there was a sudden snap. The man went limp in Beau's arms. Beau gently let the man fall to the ground and collapsed next to him. He pulled his phone from his pocket and dialed. "It's me. I need you. No questions. Just come." Then he gave directions and fell back to the ground. After regaining a little strength he got to his feet and dragged the man's body further into the cover of the trees. Then he sat down again and waited. And prayed. For the first time in a very long time Beau prayed.

"Over here," he half shouted, half whispered when he saw her walking towards him. "Wendy, over here."

Wendy turned towards Beau's voice and hurried towards him. "What the hell happened?" she asked, bending over him.

Beau nodded his head to his right. "Over there."

Wendy walked a further couple of steps and stood over the two bodies. "My god, Beau. What have you done? Who are they?"

Beau struggled to a sitting position. "The woman was a jogger and I don't know who the guy was. He was investigating. Maybe her husband. Who knows? Whatever, I had to kill him too. That's why I called you. I'm going to need your help to get rid of the bodies."

Wendy turned back towards Beau. "What?"

"We have to get rid of the bodies. I can't just leave them here. Goodness knows what kind of evidence is still on them." Beau wiped his brow. "And I'm still really weak. Did I tell you it gets worse each time? It takes longer and longer to recover. Remember that, Wendy."

"What do you want me to do?"

"Take the woman to the lake and put her in. She should float for a while before sinking somewhere. It's the guy I'm worried about. I never just killed someone like that before. What do we do with him?"

"Bury him?"

"You have a shovel?"

Wendy smiled. "I do in the car. I carry a lot of things with me you know." She took a hold of one of the man's arms. "Help me drag him into that undergrowth over there."

Beau got to his feet and stumbled towards Wendy and helped her drag the dead man into the undergrowth.

"I'll just get rid of the woman and then get my shovel. Sit tight."

Beau smiled. Sit tight. What else was he going to do? At this moment he didn't even have the energy to drive home. He hoped they could stay undetected for another half an hour. That was all he needed he was sure. Thirty more minutes.

* * *

Three-forty-eight. The second Almotriptan was starting to kick in at last. What had started as a mild migraine had become full on at some time before midnight. It had taken Lucy completely by surprise. Usually once the migraines were under control they never came back to life. But this one was different. This was like a new, second migraine.

Life was cruel. On the one night that she had finally got to be alone with Beau she had got a migraine. Why? It didn't make sense at all. Usually her migraines were like the last one, they came in the middle of the night. They never usually started when she was out in the evenings.

Lucy lay in bed and stared at the ceiling. It was difficult thinking straight. She was taking deep breaths and trying to take her mind off the pulsing throbbing pain as much as possible. If it hadn't been for the migraine then it would have been a good evening. Beau had some good stories to tell and he had a good sense of humor. He didn't seem as pushy as Wendy and Sabrina had made out either. No, she was sorry the two of them hadn't been able to complete their date. Next time. She smiled. She knew there would be a next time. And next time everything would go a lot better and they would be able to hold hands and kiss each other. She pulled a pillow from behind her head and clenched it tight across her chest. She remembered that touch of their fingers. It had been electrifying. Just like it was in the movies. She had never experienced it before and she definitely wanted to feel it again. She buried her head into her pillow and took in its fragrance. Then she closed her eyes and gently fell to sleep.

42

"Take a seat. All of you. Please take a seat as quickly as possible and let's get started. There's room at the back of the room to stand." Beau ushered everyone into the large conference room and waited for the last few stragglers to arrive. "Okay," he said, shutting the door behind him. He was moving a little slower this morning and looked like he hadn't slept in a while. He crossed over to the large conference table and stood at one end. "I have some bad news for you all, I'm afraid. Yesterday at about seven-thirty AM, Peter Ramsey passed away. For those of you that weren't aware, he had a massive heart attack a few of nights ago here in the office and he never recovered." Beau stopped talking and waited for the murmuring to die down. "I will let you all know about the funeral as soon as I find out." He took a few steps around the room. "Corporate have moved quickly to find a replacement and have named me as the new head of the office. I will be assuming the title of Senior Vice-President, North-Western Region. Any questions?"

The room remained quiet as Beau slowly paced it, looking for any tell-tale signs of unhappiness. When he had completed a full circuit of the room he returned and stood at the head of the table again. "I shall be recruiting for the position of Vice-President of Sales in the near future. Until then I will continue to cover for that role too. No doubt Wendy will be asked to step up for a while to help me take up some of the extra workload." He glanced over at Wendy and smiled.

"And I do want to take this opportunity of thanking Wendy for the great work she is already doing in this office. She has taken on her new role with dedication, over and above the cause. Thanks, Wendy." Beau waited while several people showed their appreciation for her. "Like I said, I will be recruiting for a new Sales VP and I will also be restructuring the office slightly too. I will be working with a few of you during the next few weeks to ask how we can become more efficient. No doubt there may be several other opportunities for promotion at that time."

Beau stepped back from the conference table and made his way to the door. "Okay, that's it. Back to work and look for the information about Peter's funeral. Thank you." He opened the door and quickly disappeared down the corridor towards his office.

"Wow, what was all that?" asked Tim, as several of them remained in the conference room after Beau had left.

"What do you mean?" asked Wendy.

"He looks like a man possessed. He's all purpose and no compassion today."

"He's had a lot thrown on his plate," replied Wendy. "How would you handle it all? He's now running the whole office. At twenty-three years of age. And he's had to help Peter's family fill in some gaps about Peter too."

"Even so Wendy, you've got to admit he does look rough. It looks like he hasn't slept for days. I just hope he's up for all this change and can manage the company successfully. Otherwise we're going to get another visit from the suits again."

Wendy got to her feet. "He'll be fine, I'm sure."

Tim smiled. "You would say that, wouldn't you? Are you changing too, Wendy? Are you becoming like Beau?"

Wendy turned to face Tim. "What is that supposed to mean?"

"I'd hate to see you lose your human side, Wendy. You're the one thing this office needs to keep its balance. You're the only one who can handle him and represent the rest of us."

Wendy smiled. "Don't worry, Tim. I haven't changed. But I've got a lot going on too at the moment. The last few weeks have been crazy. I had no idea what I was signing up for when I took over this new role. There are things I've discovered that I had no idea ever even existed."

"Like what?"

"Sorry, I can't tell you about that. It's confidential. At least until Zygote makes some decisions on it all." Wendy turned back towards the door. "Anyway, sorry but I need to get back to my office. There's a report I need to read from Cindy and Namitha. They're currently down in San Diego."

"We have an office in San Diego?"

"See you later, Tim. Bye." Wendy smiled to herself as she walked away. That would start a few rumors in the office for sure. Ultimately it would make it easier to introduce some of the technology they had down there. She shuddered involuntarily as she remembered reading the last report Cindy had sent. Wendy reached her office and went inside, closing the door behind her. That reminded her, she needed to make sure Cindy and Namitha got well taken care of on their return. They had been working extra hours in conditions that were not the most pleasant. She made a note on a piece of paper and pulled up her email. It was going to be another busy day.

* * *

Beau lounged in his office chair and tried to look busy. For the first time in as long as he could remember his heart wasn't in it. He had been close to making some very serious errors the night before and all because his date hadn't gone well. What had he been thinking? He couldn't continue like this. Somehow he had to find a balance. Some way to make it all work or else his life was going to be cut short, very short. Perhaps he should give up his pursuit of Lucy. He smiled. No, he couldn't do that. Lucy was the one thing that was keeping him sane. The thought of them together made him happy. One way or another he had to find a way to make it work between them.

Beau glanced down at his email. Nothing exciting except for the one that was marked private. He clicked on it and noticed it had a security icon. It was from the Anons. He opened the attachment and typed in the password he was asked for. A Word document appeared on his screen.

Beau,

Congratulations. I thought I would start with that. You have made it to the top of your office command in much less time than I would have imagined. Well done.

Alas, there are other matters to attend to. The meteoric rise you have made has been marked with many mistakes along the way. Things are going to have to change. Cleaning up after your carelessness of yesterday is not something we like to do on a regular basis. You are currently a little out of control and you are running a very high risk of discovery. If this should happen there is nothing we can do to protect you. Our very livelihood depends on our secrecy. You surely realize that.

During the next few weeks you are going to have to take a step back and re-evaluate how you are approaching things. Casual assignments with unsuspecting women are something you are going to have to seriously curtail. If you do not you are in great danger of never achieving your potential. Remember, our lives are long and the potential rewards are plentiful. I am sure you would want to live to experience them. Please use Wendy to help you maintain some kind of balance. The very reason there are two of you there in Zygote is for this purpose. Work out how you can co-exist and control your base urges. This is of the utmost importance.

Lastly, before I close out this letter to you, I want to impart a little knowledge that may be useful to you at some point in the future. We all have secrets and sometimes those secrets can be used for leverage. What I am about to tell you is one of those secrets. Do not take this information lightly and do not misjudge its usefulness.

Do you remember your recent trip to Las Vegas with Wendy? I am sure you do. And I am also sure you remember Wendy's initiation into the Anons. There is one piece of information that we did not impart to you that day. For good reason. However, that time has passed and now we would have you know. The man that Wendy used in Vegas was named Ben Hansen. You knew him simply as Ben. Yes that's right, the same Ben that you picked an argument with. We recognized he was somebody that you didn't like and wanted rid of. We provided that opportunity.

I am now also aware of just what is going through your mind right as you read this. Like we have said before, we do nothing that is not a part of the plan. Think very carefully about what you do in the future, Beau Tempest. You are not playing a game; you are using people's lives. Be careful that we do not use yours too.

Ted.

Beau sank back in his chair and resisted the urge to throw up. Ben? How could he have been a party to that? What would Lucy say if she had known that he was responsible for her boyfriend's death? Of course not directly, but definitely indirectly. And Wendy had been the one that had done it. No wonder they had kept that sight from him. He would have been able to recognize him. Shit! This was not at all a part of the plan. He put his hand to his mouth and bent doubled in his chair. A little bile made its way up from his stomach but he managed to swallow it back down. Shit! Maybe he should reconsider dating Lucy. The guilt of all this might prove too much. He could never make up for the fact that he was responsible for Ben's death. Beau wiped sweat from his brow and tried to sit properly in his chair again. His stomach was still turning over. The Anons were sending him a message. They were letting him know who was in charge; who were pulling the strings. Shit! He took a deep breath and got up from his chair. How dare they? How dare the Anons tell him how to run his life? No one threatened him like that. No, he was going to find a way to get to the top of this organization and make some changes. He may have a special talent, a nasty horrendous talent, but he wasn't going to let some secret organization dictate his life to him. That was overstepping the boundaries. He sat back down in his chair again and closed his Word document. Then he pushed himself back from his desk and let out a silent scream. "I will remember you, Ted. I hope you stay alert because you will never know when I will appear from the dark." Beau turned to one side and emptied the contents of his stomach into the waste can.

43

"Hi, it's Beau," he said into the telephone. It was early in the afternoon and he had been asked to join a conference call with the corporate offices of Zygote.

"Thanks for joining, Beau," a voice at the other end said. "Jim Martinez here. I also have Harry S Fornton and J.P. Clemmons here with me."

"Good afternoon," said Beau.

"I hope you've settled in okay," Jim continued. "I know the past couple of weeks have been a roller-coaster but hopefully things will start to sort themselves out now. Just remember, we're here to help you in whatever way we can." He paused. "Anyway, onto business. There have been some developments here that we want to bring you in the loop on. Peter was up to speed, but I know he wouldn't have said anything to you. Are you good to talk in private?"

"Not a problem. Go ahead."

There was a short delay on the phone before Jim continued. "The long and the short of it is that we've had a large investment of private capital made to us and we are going to start to get a little more aggressive with some of our projects. This means we are going to be buying one or two extra companies that you probably weren't aware of. Oh, and I needn't remind you that everything we discuss today is highly confidential and not to leave your office. Firstly we are looking to buy RamOne, the medical software company that specializes in experimental treatment technology. You should hear something about that in the next week or so. Then a little more longer-term, we're looking to get our hands on Nyble Storage. They're a cloud data storage company…"

"I'm a little familiar with them. They're based here in Seattle."

"Excellent. Then we may use that knowledge to help us transition, once we close the deal. Like I say, these are things that are currently in the works. There are a couple of other small companies we're looking at too, but they are a few months away from anything concrete. I've added you to one of our confidential distribution lists on email and you'll be receiving updates on all these things as they progress. We just wanted to give you a heads up."

"Thanks. I appreciate it."

There was a little mumbling in the background before Jim spoke again. "Yes, Harry just reminded me. We're going to have you come out here in the next couple of weeks. For the week. Just trying to get all the details together. We're going to have a think-tank session and we want your input. Any problems with that?"

"Not at all. I'd be delighted."

"Good, good. I'll let you know exactly when. In the meantime, take a read of the things we send you. Any questions?"

"I don't think so…"

"Good. Then we'll let you have some time back. Good luck and let us know if you need anything. Good day."

The phone went dead and Beau returned the handset to its cradle and sat back in his chair. Nyble Storage. That was the company where Lucy worked. That was going to be an interesting purchase. Maybe he could use their relationship to find out a little more about the place and the people. He smiled to himself and absentmindedly started doodling on his desk blotter. "Oh well," he said to himself a few minutes later. "I'd better get on with things. There's still so much to catch up on." He logged back into his computer and went over his task list to decide just which things he could get done before the end of the day.

* * *

"Is there something you forgot to tell me?" Sabrina asked, as Lucy walked through the door to their apartment.

Lucy took off her coat and put it down on the chair. "I don't think so. What do you mean?"

Sabrina pointed towards the kitchen counter.

Lucy smiled and walked into the kitchen. She opened the envelope that was lying next to the primroses, nicely arranged in a basket.

"Well?"

"What do you mean?" Lucy tucked the note back into the envelope and walked back into the living room. She picked up her coat and walked towards her bedroom.

"Stop! Right there. I think you've got some explaining to do."

"I do?"

"Don't play all coy with me, Lucy. I read the note. When did you go out with Beau?"

"A couple of nights ago." Lucy smiled. "Not that it's any of your business."

"Sabrina got to her feet. "It is my business. I thought we'd been over this, Lucy. Beau is not a good match for you. He's manipulative, domineering and downright deceitful."

"Actually he was the perfect gentleman."

"Part of his plan, I'm sure. Lucy, don't you get it? The guy is playing you."

Lucy pushed her bedroom door open and took a step inside.

"I'm serious, Lucy. Wendy and I both know what he's like."

Lucy took another step inside her room and turned her head back towards Sabrina. "Look Sabrina, I appreciate that you care about me, I really do. But it's my life and my decision to make. I went out for dinner with him the other night and didn't say anything for precisely this reason. I had a lovely time with Beau which was unfortunately cut short because I got a migraine. He sent me the flowers to wish me well. And for your information, I am going to see him again. I will continue to see him until he proves himself to be a jerk. But up until then I will give him the benefit of the doubt."

Lucy strode purposefully into her bedroom and pushed the door closed behind her. She threw her coat down on her bed and collapsed on top of it.

Lucy sunk her head into her pillow and cried. Why was everybody against her? This had been the one good thing to happen to her all day. Why wouldn't people just let her get on with her own life? This was exactly why she hadn't said anything to Sabrina in the first place. She looked up and turned her head as she heard her bedroom door creak open.

"Lucy? I'm sorry. I didn't mean to upset you." Sabrina walked over to the edge of Lucy's bed and sat down. She reached out an arm to touch her back. "Will you forgive me?"

Lucy half-smiled and rubbed an eye. "I know you mean well, Sabrina but you've got to let me run my own life. I'll find out soon enough if Beau is a jerk but, honestly, we had a good time. And right now I need someone who I can spend some quality time with." She reached out an arm to slap Sabrina. "Yes, I know you're here for me and you want to spend time with me, but that's not what I mean, and you know it. And besides, you need to get your own date. You can't live off my back all the time."

"Thanks. Glad to have a friend like you." Sabrina smiled. "You know it's just that I care?"

"Of course I do, but that doesn't make it any easier. And if you'd had the day I've had today, you would also be glad of some flowers. From anyone."

"What happened?"

Lucy pushed herself up and she got herself into a sitting position with her legs crossed on the bed. "I got called in by Human Resources today."

"You did? Why?"

"Why do you think? All that time off I've been having. Apparently there have been a couple of complaints by some of my co-workers. I can guess who they are."

"What did they say?"

"They gave me an official warning. They said that there was a strict company sick policy and that I needed to follow it. Going forward any days I take off have to be validated with a note from my doctor. They also asked if I was having any other problem that they should know about. Bloody cheek! I told them they should look at some of the other people in the office who sit around all day and do nothing. I told them I delivered on everything I was asked to do." She rubbed her nose with her wrist. "I don't think that was such a good idea in retrospect. They told me this was nothing to do with performance, it was about too many absences from the office. They also told me that the performance of others was not my concern unless I was their manager. I had to bite my lip to not actually respond to that statement."

Sabrina laughed. "Sounds like you really got into it today."

"I did. So the bottom line is that I'm now being treated like a five year-old school kid at the office. Ridiculous. You'd think they had better things to do with their time."

"I can see now why you're so happy about the flowers. I'm sorry. Can I get a hug?"

"Sure but no funny stuff, okay?" Lucy laughed and reached out her arms to Sabrina. Sabrina shuffled over on the bed and the two of them hugged each other for a moment.

"Want something to eat?" asked Sabrina, pulling away from Lucy and standing up by the side of the bed. "I'm sure it's my turn to cook."

"In that case I'd rather eat out."

"Thanks for the vote of confidence."

"Just joking, Sabrina. Your cooking is fine. You know that. But you know what? How about we go for a drink at Paddy's? It's been a long week already and I need to relax a little. Maybe some company and a martini will do the trick."

"Martinis? The men of Melrose had better watch out then. I've seen what you're like after a few drinks."

"I'm not planning on getting drunk, Sabrina. I just fancy a martini. Give me fifteen minutes and I'll be ready, okay?"

"Sure." Sabrina walked back out of Lucy's room, pulling her door shut behind her.

44

"Hi," said Wendy walking into Beau's office. "I need to chat to you about some of these reports that I've got back from Cindy and Namitha."

Beau looked up from his computer. "Thanks for knocking."

"If it wasn't important, do you think I'd be here?" She walked over to Beau's desk and pushed a folder across to him. "I've highlighted the important things."

Beau picked up the folder and thumbed through it, skimming the pages and making a few tutting noises as he did so. "I see. Certainly not quite what we expected. But along the same lines."

"What? These are along the same lines as you expected? You knew just what they were doing down there?"

"Mostly. Calm down, Wendy. This is just business. It's what we do."

"Well I wish I'd known before I sent my two people down there. They could at least have been prepared for what they were going to encounter."

"Like I said, there really wasn't much else we could have told them." He closed the folder again and pushed it back towards Wendy. "They're alright aren't they?"

"Do you really care, Beau? Do you really care how these two people are? Or are they expendable like those two people the other night?"

"That's not fair, Wendy. You know it's not. Those people the other night were completely different. They weren't our employees. They weren't even people we knew."

"They were still people. You seem to have a complete disregard for everyone nowadays, Beau. I really don't know what's becoming of you."

Beau laughed. "That's cheap Wendy, coming from you. Just remember who you are too. You've had your share of the action now as well. And you'll see, give it a year and I'll be having the same conversation with you."

Wendy got to her feet. "I don't think so. I'm going to make damn sure I control myself and just do those things that are necessary for me. I've already seen the crap you get yourself into."

"Sit down, Wendy. Let's talk about this rationally. I don't want to argue with you. We're supposed to be a team, remember?"

Wendy sat herself down and folded her arms. "I guess."

"Good. Now calm down." Beau placed his hands on his desk and interlocked his fingers. "I've also been giving this a lot of thought and I don't want to be going through life leaving a trail of devastation and destruction everywhere I go. So I'm going to change a little. I'm going to try and have a sensible relationship with someone. With Lucy actually, if you must know. I know I can control myself. I know I can be different."

Wendy jumped to her feet and took a couple of steps backwards. "What? Lucy? Are you completely crazy? After what we just said about friends and people we know. You can't date Lucy. I won't allow it."

"It's not your decision to make, Wendy."

"Really? Well maybe I'll tell her a few home truths about you. You know I can scare her off you enough if I really need to. No, I want you to drop it. I want you to promise that you won't date her."

"I'm not going to do that, Wendy. And do you know why?"

Wendy glared at Beau and stepped back towards his desk. "Why?"

"Because if you say anything to her then I will tell you and most likely the police about the man you killed."

Wendy laughed. "Idle threats, Beau. You know we're both in this together. I don't go down without you."

"But I do know something that you don't know. Something that will affect your decision, I'm sure."

"What?"

"I know the identity of the man you killed in Vegas."

Wendy crossed her arms. "So what?"

Beau smiled. "Yes, his name was Ben Hansen. Ring any bells?"

"Ben Hansen?" Wendy took a step backwards and turned visibly pale. "Ben Hansen?"

Beau nodded.

"As in Lucy's boyfriend?"

"The very same."

"You're messing with me."

Beau laughed. "Why would I lie? I have no reason to. In fact, until earlier today I didn't know who the person was either. Let's just say that someone from high up gave me the information." He leaned back in his chair and put his hands behind his head. "You see you and me, we're just the same. We both have dark secrets already. I'm sure that Ben was chosen for a reason. Probably exactly this. The Anons want you to know there's no getting out. We're both in this forever."

Wendy staggered back to the chair and slumped down in it.

"Are you sure? Ben? What do I say to Lucy? I killed her boyfriend. I'll never be able to look her in the face again."

A smirk washed across Beau's face. "Tough, isn't it? Now you know how I've felt sometimes. Being a part of the Anons isn't all about glory. Everything has its price. Your Director position cost you something very dear. And those poor staff members in San Diego have it easy compared to what you're going through right now. So do you want to complain to me about them again?"

Wendy shook her head.

"I didn't think so." Beau got up from his seat and walked around his desk to stand next to Wendy. He placed an arm around her shoulder. "Trust me, when I found out I felt sick too. In fact I was sick. Right there in the trash can. I know just what it's like to find out something like this. They used me too, Wendy. This was their way of warning me. And I'm going to be better prepared in future. I'm not going to let them interfere with my relationship with Lucy and I'm not going to mess it up either. I know I can control myself. I have to."

Wendy shrugged Beau's arm off her shoulder and looked up at him. "I don't understand you, Beau. How can you still say you're going to date Lucy after all this?"

"I'm not going to let them rule my life. I'm not going to allow myself to be their puppet. From now on I call my own shots. Yes I'll do a lot of the things I have to, but I'm going to stay my own person. I'm not going to be used for someone else's gain. If I don't look after myself, who will?"

Wendy thought for a moment and watched Beau as he walked back to his desk. "You're right, Beau. I don't want to let these people rule my life either. But I still don't know exactly what they want from me."

"Nor do I, but I intend to find out." He sat down again on his chair. "Do I have your support?"

Wendy half-smiled. "For now, Beau. For now. But just for the record, I'm still not okay about you dating Lucy. If anything ever happens to her, anything, then you had better be on your lookout for me. Because I promise you I will personally kill you if I have to. We may be Anons but we don't kill our friends or the friends of our friends."

Beau smiled. "That's fair. But just remember what you've said. I may have to remind you too one day."

Wendy picked up her folder and got to her feet again. "I need a drink. This day hasn't turned out at all what I expected."

"I was thinking the same actually. How about Paddy's a little later? Invite some of the others if you like."

"I'll see. Feelings in the office have changed, Beau. Not everyone is your biggest fan anymore."

"Yeah, I know. Oh well, it is what it is. I'll see you later."

"Yeah." Wendy turned around and walked from Beau's office back to hers. She threw the folder across the room and watched as the papers went everywhere. She slammed her door shut and leaned back against it. "Crap! Just what am I going to do now? Crap!"

Wendy walked over to her desk and sat down on her chair, not bothering to pick any of the scattered papers up on the way. She put her head in her arms and cried. How was she even going to face Sabrina now? She had betrayed both her friends with one moment of passion. And she had vowed to Sabrina to help keep Lucy away from Beau. How could she even keep that promise anymore? Beau was right; the price was expensive being an Anon. Very expensive. But there was no going back now; she had already paid her entry fee. Wendy sat up, wiped her eyes with a tissue and pulled a small mirror from her purse. She had to protect Lucy somehow. That was all she could do. She reapplied some mascara and a little blush to her cheeks. She was going to become Lucy's shadow. She had to find some way of getting closer to her. She smiled. Sabrina. Maybe she could suggest to Sabrina that the three of them rent an apartment together. That would save them all some money. She allowed herself a little laugh. If worse came to worst she could even date Sabrina. No, that probably wasn't a good idea. No dating. That was something else she had to make sure of. Like she had said to Beau, they had to protect their friends. Whatever the cost. She sat back in her chair and tried to think of ways she could help Lucy. It was going to be tough.

45

"Two martinis please," Sabrina said to the bartender at Paddy's. "I'll have vodka, two olives." She turned to Lucy. "And you?"

Lucy adjusted her stool and scooted up to the bar a little. "Gin please. And three olives."

"He's handsome, isn't he?" Sabrina whispered, once the bartender had left to make their drinks.

Lucy nodded. "Probably seeing several women already. I mean in that line of work you've got to meet a lot of people. I'm sure you get your pick of them."

"Maybe I need to work behind a bar then!"

"Maybe you do." Lucy brushed a few crumbs away from in front of her and took two coasters from the bar top.

"Cheers," Sabrina said, picking up her martini a minute or so later. "To a happy and stress free life."

"Cheers." Lucy took a sip of her drink and set it back down on the bar. "Are you going to be okay if I date Beau? Really?"

"I can't say I approve, Lucy. You know that. But it's your life and you're aware of just what his reputation is like. So I'm going to have to trust your judgment. Just don't come running to me in a month and say he is a pig! Actually I think I'd prefer that, to you continuing to date him."

Lucy squeezed Sabrina's arm. "Thanks. It means a lot to me. And I will be careful." She laughed. "Besides which I already told him I was a Christian kind of girl. I think that threw him off a little."

Sabrina laughed. "Good for you. Keep yourself pure for a while longer."

"I am, Sabrina. You know I am. I just wanted him to know up front that I'm not just going to jump into bed with him. It's going to…"

"Sshhh!"

"What?"

Sabrina leaned in close to Lucy and whispered. "Don't look now but he's just walked in the door. He's with Wendy."

"Really?"

"Yes. Stay calm. They're heading this way."

Beau put his arm around Lucy's shoulder and gave it a squeeze. "Do you mind if I sit next to you?"

A spark went through Lucy and she shivered and tried not to blush. "Hi there. Of course not." She took another sip of her martini as Beau sat down on the stool next to her and made himself comfortable. Wendy squeezed past them both and sat on the other side of Sabrina.

"Martinis? You must be feeling better tonight then?" Beau looked up at the bartender. "The usual, please."

"I'm feeling much better, thanks. And thank you for the flowers too. They were lovely. I like a man that buys flowers."

"I'll remember that. Special occasion, is it?"

"No, I just had a bad day at work that's all. It's a long story."

"I'm all ears."

"Did you know we would be down here tonight?" Sabrina asked Wendy.

"Not at all. If I had then I'm sure we wouldn't have come."

"So you don't think Beau planned this meeting?"

Wendy laughed. "Anything is possible with that man, but for once I think it's just a coincidence."

"You know they're dating, don't you?"

"I just found out. I can't say I'm happy about it. But I've done everything I can to stop them."

"Me too," said Sabrina. "So I guess we'll just have to let the inevitable happen."

"I'm going to watch them very carefully. I owe at least that much to Lucy."

"What do you mean?"

Wendy took a sip of her rum and coke before she replied. "I'd feel responsible if Beau hurt her in any way. That's all. I mean we both know what he's like."

Sabrina nodded. "But we can't be around twenty-four hours a day to watch them."

"Try me," laughed Wendy. "We can take alternate days."

"Cheers," Sabrina said, taking another sip of her martini. "It looks like we've both got our work cut out here."

"That's ridiculous," Beau said, after hearing Lucy's story. "Every absence you've taken has been legitimate."

"I know that, it just seems there's something else going on there. Like they're looking for excuses to fire people. Only last week two people got laid off and no one knew exactly why."

"Maybe the company is struggling with sales."

Lucy shrugged her shoulders. "If they were I would be the last to know."

Beau smiled. "I'm sure it'll turn out okay. You'll just have to keep your head down for a while. And who knows, if they are sold then maybe you'll get some nice new bosses."

"Yeah. We'll see about that. In my book there's no such thing as a nice boss."

Beau took a sip of his whiskey. "You know I'm a boss, don't you?"

"Of course. But I wasn't talking about you."

"So you know what kind of boss I am then?"

"That's not what I meant, and you know it. Stop trying to put words in my mouth."

"Well, I'm sure Sabrina and Wendy have both told you what I am like at work?"

"And what if they have?"

"Well, that may cloud your perception of me."

Lucy smiled. "I'm still here, aren't I?"

"You are, yes."

"Well then. Let's change the subject." Lucy let her fingers wander across the bar a little and placed one on top of Beau's. That electric shock hit her again and she quickly took it back.

"You okay?"

Lucy nodded. "Oh yes, I'm okay." Wow! That spark was still there. And so strong. She'd never experienced that before when she had touched a man. Maybe Beau was the right one for her after all. She turned her head towards him and smiled. "Tell me something about yourself. Something that no one else knows."

"You don't really want to know that," Beau replied. "There are some things that are meant to remain private."

"There must be something you can tell me?"

Beau took a drink of his water and sat back a little on his stool. "I don't think I've ever told anyone that I was a popular athlete in school."

"What did you do?"

"I played on the football team. Wide receiver for a complete year. Unfortunately I got injured. I've still got the scar. It effectively put an end to my career. Such a shame."

Lucy laughed. "You're telling me you could have been a star football player?"

"Maybe, who knows? It doesn't really matter now. Now I'm Beau Tempest, Senior Vice-President of the North-West Region for Zygote Technologies. It sounds so grand."

"Senior VP? I thought you were a Director or Vice-President?"

"Things move fast in our office, Lucy. A janitor one week and running the company the next. You'll have to keep up." He took a sip of his whiskey. "You okay?"

Lucy pressed a finger against her temple. "Yeah, just pushing back a little headache. I've been getting a lot of them recently. I'll be fine. Just give me a minute." She reached into her bag and pulled out a tablet. "At least I thought to carry them with me now." She picked up Beau's water and swallowed one down. "That's better. It'll soon go." She noticed him staring at her and she laughed. "You didn't mind, did you? I mean, if we're going to be dating we're going to be sharing more than each other's water from time to time."

Beau laughed. "No, you're right I guess. I just wasn't expecting it." He watched her as she put the glass back down again. "So we are going to date then?"

"I told you that before, didn't I?"

"I just thought after the other night when you left me in the restaurant that maybe you'd changed your mind."

"Not at all. I told you, I was feeling ill. That's all." Lucy reached out her hand and placed it on Beau's. That electric shock ran through her again and she let the feeling wash over her. She interlocked his fingers with his. "Is that alright?"

Beau tried not to lean in and kiss her. The temptation was already there. He took back his hand and used it to pick up his drink. He was going to have to control himself. "Of course. It's more than I could have hoped for." He took another sip from his drink and kept it rested in his hand. "So, tell me a little more about yourself." He laughed. "Tell me one of your secrets. That's only fair."

Lucy pulled her hand back and pressed another finger to her temple. A few more minutes and the pain should be gone. She could see this one through. "I suppose it is. I just wish I had something exciting to tell you."

"There must be something?"

Lucy tried to think back through her childhood but there was nothing special that came to mind. "I've got nothing."

"But you owe me."

"Then I'll have to owe you. Maybe I'll think of something another time. In the meantime you'll have to make do with a forfeit." Lucy leaned towards him and kissed him on the cheek. Another electric shock went through her. She almost fainted and she put her hands to her head.

"You sure you're okay?"

Lucy shook her head. "I don't know. I think maybe my migraine is getting the better of me." She looked up at Beau. "You're going to think I'm trying to stay away from you deliberately."

"Not at all. I'm sure you're not making it up. I just wish I could do something for you."

Lucy picked up her purse and took out a twenty dollar bill. She put it on the bar. "You can. You can walk me home if you don't mind."

"Are you sure?"

Lucy nodded. "Yes. I'd like that very much. I just need to get home and get some rest." She picked up her coat and slid off her stool and started walking towards the door. She glanced over her shoulder and smiled as she saw Beau following close behind her.

When she was safely outside she put on her coat and waited for Beau to catch up. He slipped an arm around her and they walked through the parking lot towards Lucy's apartment. Lucy smiled and leaned into Beau's shoulder. Even though her head was full of shooting pain, she didn't care. It was good to be in the arms of a man. A nice, caring man.

"You okay?" Beau asked as they walked. He saw the smile on Lucy's face and leaned his head in towards her too. As they walked he breathed in the smell of her perfume. It smelt so good and she felt so alive to him. Better than he had imagined. He pulled her a little nearer to him and enjoyed her closeness. He was glad he had made the right decision. It would be nice to have a real girlfriend again. Someone to hold at nights. Someone to explore the wonders of life with. Someone to keep close. Someone to kiss. Yes, kiss. He wanted to kiss her. To feel her breath on his. He knew she wouldn't mind. She had said the same thing. She wanted to be his girlfriend. His girlfriend. And all boyfriends and girlfriends kissed. It was only natural. He stopped walking and turned to face her. Just one kiss. That was all he wanted.

46

"I'm glad you're still there," Sabrina said. I don't think I'd want to work there if it was just Beau."

"Thanks. Although sometimes I don't know why I am still there. You know I ended up at Zygote completely by mistake don't you?"

"No. What happened?"

"I was actually supposed to join Microsoft as a contractor. I had an offer and everything. But there was a mix up with the company I was working for and somehow they gave me the wrong information. Someone else got sent to work at Microsoft and I got sent to work at Zygote. I thought it was a little odd when I first got there. Nothing looked like Microsoft at all and by the time I called the office they just told me to stay there. It seems Microsoft really liked the other woman that went there instead of me and so I was stuck at Zygote. Thankfully after my three month contract was over, Zygote offered me a job. I don't know what I would have done if they hadn't."

"That's funny. Even funnier that you've been there ever since."

"Another round ladies?" the bartender stopped in front of Wendy.

"You know it," she replied, looking along the bar. "Where are Lucy and Beau?"

"What?" Sabrina looked behind her. "When did they leave? I didn't see them go."

Wendy turned back to the barman. "Did you see when our friends left?"

"About five minutes ago. They were walking arm in arm in the parking lot the last time I saw them."

"Crap!" said Wendy, getting to her feet. "I've got to get after them.

"Just let them be, Wendy. There's nothing we can do now."

"No, you don't understand. They can't be together. Not like that. They can't."

"What are you talking about?" Sabrina pulled on Wendy's jacket as she tried to leave.

"I haven't got time to explain now, Sabrina. Seriously." Wendy brushed Sabrina's arm away and rushed out of the bar.

"Wendy?"

Wendy ran through Paddy's door and out into the parking lot. Crap! Where had they gone? She looked around. Beau's car was still there. Good. Lucy's apartment. They must be headed there. She slipped off her heels and gripped them in her hands. Then she ran barefoot across the parking lot trying to ignore the pain as she ran. Then she saw them. Beau was standing in front of Lucy, his finger under her chin, slowly moving her face up towards his. She had to stop them. She had made a promise and she wasn't going to break it now. "Lucy! Beau!" She screamed as loud as she could. And again. Beau's head turned briefly as he heard his name. "Beau. Stop. Please!"

She slowed as she saw him drop his hand back down to his side and take a step backwards. Breathless she finally reached their side. "Hi."

Lucy looked at Wendy with confusion. "Wendy?"

Wendy took a hold of Beau's arm and gave it a tug. "Did you forget?"

Beau looked at Wendy, a little confused.

"It's your round. We're waiting for you."

"I was just taking Lucy home."

"I saw." Wendy turned to Lucy. "You okay?"

"No. My head is hurting like it's never hurt before. It feels like someone has been walking inside it. I feel terrible. I just need to lie down."

A thousand thoughts went through Wendy's head and she slapped Beau hard across the face. "You stupid idiot! I thought we had an agreement. What the crap do you think you're doing, kissing her?"

Beau rubbed his red face and turned again towards Wendy. "I was just taking her home. She has a migraine. A migraine. I didn't kiss her."

"No you didn't kiss me," said Lucy. "Don't I get a goodnight kiss?"

Wendy took a hold of Lucy's arm, slipped her heels back on and started to walk away. She turned her head back towards Beau. "Get back inside the bar. I'll be back in a few minutes. And for god's sake just get another drink will you?"

"What's happening?" asked Lucy. "Why won't Beau kiss me?"

"Let's get you home. It seems you need to get some rest as it is. Perhaps it was too much excitement."

Lucy put a hand to her head and grimaced. "Something, definitely. I've never felt like this before. Certainly not after I've taken one of my tablets. This is going to be a really bad migraine. I can tell."

"Just get some rest. You'll feel better in the morning I'm sure."

"Tell me, Wendy. What's wrong with Beau? It was like he wanted to kiss me and yet he wouldn't. Like he was scared to. He just stood there. Has he been hurt before? Is that it? He must have told you."

"Not tonight, Lucy. Another night. Let's just get you home." She pulled Lucy along with her as she walked and a couple of minutes later she was helping Lucy into her bedroom. "You going to be okay?"

"I'll be fine. I've taken another tablet and I'll soon be asleep I'm sure. I just need rest and darkness now. Thanks for bringing me home, Wendy." Lucy climbed into bed and got under the covers. "And say goodnight to Beau for me, will you?"

"Sure." Wendy pulled Lucy's door to and let herself out of the apartment. Just how often was she going to have to do this? This was never going to work on a long term basis. Sooner or later Beau would kill Lucy unless she could do something to break them up permanently. Crap! This wasn't at all what she wanted from her life.

* * *

Three-forty-seven. Beau looked at his watch as he rounded the corner to Lucy's apartment building. Ever since he had returned home all he had done was to toss and turn. He knew he wasn't going to be able to sleep until he had seen her. He should be at home, not out on the streets, but there was something about her, something special. She was different than the rest of them. He knew that. Perhaps she was his destiny after all. He could only hope. Beau leaned against the apartment building and watched his cold breath curl away from him by the light of a nearby lamp. He should turn around and go back home. But he couldn't. No, he was decided.

Beau ducked into the shadows as a battered car drove slowly by. After it had passed he climbed the stairs to Lucy's apartment and walked the small landing that separated the row of three apartments. How was he going to get in? Should he ring the bell? It was nearly four o'clock in the morning! He smiled. A window was open a crack. He could see it behind the protective screen. It should be easy enough. His hands worked to remove the screen from the window and within a few minutes he was inside. He closed the window silently behind him and stood still, allowing his eyes to become accustomed to the darkness.

He could almost smell her scent in the air. He licked his lips in anticipation. Just one kiss. She would understand. Beau carefully made his way across the living room towards a slightly open door and took a look inside. He saw and smelled the primroses. He had got it correct the first time. Thank goodness it hadn't been too difficult. Entering the wrong bedroom would be a huge mistake at this juncture. Beau took a step inside the bedroom and closed the door quietly behind him. In the quietness he could hear her almost silent breathing from across the room. He bent over and took in the aroma of the flowers, those flowers he had picked out himself and sent to her. A piece of paper fluttered unnoticed from the dresser and fell to the floor. Beau took off his coat and laid it carefully down on the chair next to the dresser. He stopped as he heard a quiet moan and saw her half-turn in her sleep. Then she was silent again.

Should he cross to her and kiss her, or should he just go to her? Should he wake her and talk? Or should he just sit on her bed and watch her? His heart beat faster as he let the thought of her wash through him. He wanted her. Just once. Just one kiss. He would be controlled. He wouldn't harm her. He couldn't. Not Lucy. No, not Lucy. Beau pulled off his sweater, then his shirt and finally his shoes and pants. She would understand. She wouldn't scream. Just one kiss and she would be his after all.

Almost naked, Beau crossed the room and lifted the covers of the bed. He swallowed hard as he slipped in behind her, letting the covers drop back down over him. He could smell her now, that sweet perfume he had been thinking about all evening. His hand caressed the ends of her hair and he inched himself closer to her. He stopped as she almost awoke, but then inched a little closer still as her breathing dropped back into rhythm. Now he was next to her, touching the contours of her body, breathing in her aroma and imagining that first kiss. He let his hand brush her arm and she rolled over a little and let out a small sigh. Beau's hand moved across her chest and he lifted his face above hers. One kiss.

No, not like this. What had he done? He could feel the surprise within her as he kissed her. Even as she responded to him, he knew it was a mistake. Her eyes opened wide and stared up at him. Why me, was what she was thinking. Why me? There was no going back now though, Beau knew that. He kissed her harder and relaxed a little as she kissed him back. Her arms embraced his body even as her eyes darted back and forth, questioning.

Crap! This wasn't how it was supposed to be. But it was too soon to stop now. No, he had to kiss her a little longer. He needed to leave her unconscious. He would have to judge that moment carefully, to leave her unsure with scattered memories. But he mustn't kill her. He knew that would be wrong. Just a few more seconds. He took a little more of her and inwardly smiled as she willingly gave. Then he let her drop back onto the bed and he rolled over, off the bed and onto the floor. The room was spinning and Beau took several deep breaths to steady himself. He wanted to throw up, but knew that would leave too much evidence. Instead he fought back the lump in his throat and tried to sit upright. The room was still spinning but he had to leave, to get out of there as fast as possible. He crawled across the room, pulled his clothes from the chair and disjointedly put them back on. Then he pulled himself up using the dresser as a help and struggled to his feet. "Such a waste," he muttered, looking at her one last time before he opened the bedroom door and staggered back across the living room. "Just one kiss. That was all I wanted." Beau half stumbled, half fell out of the apartment as he closed the door behind him and made his way back across Melrose towards the sanctuary of his home.

* * *

Cars, driving, steep roads, paths that led nowhere in particular; these were all things going through Lucy's head as she slept. Her car had a mind of its own. It was taking her along freeways she had never driven before. Some of it was a lot like England. She smiled. There was the corner shop. What was that doing next to the highway? The car continued on. She didn't know just where the journey was taking her. After a while it turned off the freeway onto a smaller road that led up an impossibly steep hill. The car didn't have any trouble though, it continued on. Then they were in a forest and the shadows in the trees tried to eat the car. Still the car continued on. Suddenly it was over a cliff and gliding through the air. Lucy hung on. The car landed gracefully on the water. It was a lake and the car continued on once more. In the middle of the lake was an island. The car drove ashore and came to a stop. The doors opened.

Lucy got out and stood by the car. Then it turned into a house, a large house. She definitely could see the faces of Sabrina, Wendy, Ben and Beau at the windows. She opened the door and went inside. It was a large football stadium without a crowd. Lucy made her way to the half-way line and stood there, looking around. Suddenly she fell to the ground in pain and she put her hands to her temples. Her head was almost bursting apart with the pain. She screamed.

"Why are you here?" a voice from afar said, echoing around the empty stadium.

Lucy tried to look up but the sun was too bright and her head hurt too much. "Who are you?"

"You know who I am. You have been here once before. Concentrate. Everything you need has been provided to you. You have all you need."

Two-fifty. Lucy sat bolt upright in her bed, dripping in sweat. Her migraine had gone. Beau. Where was Beau? Then she remembered. The pub. Football. He had once played football. The dream was about Beau. The migraines were warnings. There was something her head was trying to tell her. She wiped her face and tried to remember every detail of the dream. She had everything she needed. But for what? Her car. Of course. A journey. She was taking a journey. All she needed to know was where this journey was taking her and just what Beau had to do with it? Beau. Yes, he was the reason for everything. She was sure of that now, she just didn't know why yet.

Lucy forced herself from her bed and got dressed. She pulled a small travel case from out of her wardrobe and hastily filled it with clothes and items from the bathroom. She needed to get away for a while. Just a few days at least. They would all understand, even Sabrina. Sabrina! She had to leave her a note of some sort. Lucy found a piece of paper and jotted down a few sentences telling her not to worry, that she was going to take a few days off and that she would contact her again very soon. Then she took Beau's primroses from the kitchen and carefully placed them in Sabrina's room, along with the note. With a last look around the apartment, Lucy pulled her bedroom door to, took her travel bag and slipped outside into the cold night air. She involuntarily shivered as she descended the stairs towards where her car was parked.

With a final look in her mirror, Lucy pulled out of her parking spot and drove past her building. She briefly spotted a man ducking into the shadows as she passed. She checked her windows and exited the complex onto the road and headed towards I-520. She knew she would miss Beau, but she needed some space just to work things through in her mind. She smiled as her thoughts were briefly interrupted by the radio playing all night love songs, and then her mind wandered back to him once more. Oh Beau! Why was he so irresistible? She so just wanted to kiss him. Once would be enough. Once would surely be enough for any woman.

THE END

- - -

Follow my blog online at: http://pauldorset.blogspot.com
Follow me on Twitter: @jcx27

Coming Soon:

Unicorns (Melrose Part Two)

Made in the USA
Lexington, KY
22 October 2011